THE·MYSTERY·WRITERS of AMERICA·ANTHOLOGY

Beastly Tales

Acknowledgments

Grateful acknowledgment is made by Mystery Writers of America and WYNWOOD Press for permission to include the following:

"Spring Fever" by Dorothy Salisbury Davis. Copyright © 1952 by Dorothy Salisbury Davis. Copyright © renewed 1980 by Dorothy Salisbury Davis. First published in *Ellery Queen's Mystery Magazine*.

"Dwindle, Peak and Pine" by Joyce Harrington. Copyright © 1989 by Joyce Harrington.

"A Cat Too Small for His Whiskers" by Lilian Jackson Braun. Copyright © 1988 by Lilian Jackson Braun. Reprinted by permission of the author.

"The White Death" by Justin Scott. Copyright © 1989 by Justin Scott.

"A Visitor to Mombasa" by James Holding. Copyright © 1974 by H.S.D. Publications. First published in *Alfred Hitchcock's Mystery Magazine*. Reprinted by permission of the author and Scott Meredith, the author's agent, 845 Third Ave., New York, NY 10022.

"A Good Story" by Donald E. Westlake. Copyright © 1984 by Donald E. Westlake. Originally appeared in *Playboy* Magazine.

Contents

Introduction

by SARA PARETSKY

Our earliest stories show how closely humans see their lives intertwined with those of other animals. Circe changed Odysseus's ravening band to swine; Artemis turned herself into a hind when men came too close to her; carnal knowledge came to Eden in the form of a serpent.

Beyond that, animals seem to have magical qualities men and women long to possess: the wisdom—or wiliness—of the serpent; the bravery of a tiger; the steadfastness of a dog. The ancients would drink the blood of animals they wished to emulate so that they could take on their spirits as totems.

Many animals in stories speak—from the ants and rams who aided Psyche to the lion and other beasts in C. S. Lewis's Narnia chronicles. And, unlike humans, when they speak, they utter pure truth. Perhaps, in addition to longing for bravery or loyalty or other animal qualities, humans also believe they will receive from these honest dogs or cats or ants the perfect understanding they can't get from other people.

Whatever the reason, stories in which animals play a major role are as popular today as they were three thousand years ago. Witness the spectacular reception given *Watership Down* or the perennial reprinting of *Wind in the Willows*.

So it shouldn't come as a surprise to find that mystery writers, too, feel an affinity to animals and have drawers full of stories about them. Still, when the Mystery Writers of America put out a call for an anthology with an animal theme, I didn't have any great expectations of a response.

I was stunned when the manuscripts began rolling in. Stories about dogs, about cats, monkeys, horses, hamsters, leopards, pythons—think of an animal and I can now tell you at least two mystery writers who've made it central to a story.

It was my privilege, as well as my misfortune, to help Joyce Harrington edit this collection. My privilege lay in the chance to read so many unusual stories by so many good writers. In fact, I felt quite greedy as I saw names I didn't know and realized my editing work was introducing me to a whole new list of writers.

My misfortune was having to pick and choose among these good stories. That's never an easy task. I don't know why anyone would willingly undertake it. When the writing is good, the story beguiling, and you can use only fifteen, it's a hideous job. Now that I've done it once, I hope I never have to do it again.

Most of the ways humans view animals are represented in this collection. We see them as prey, as companions, as sentient creatures conversing in their own world, as almost supernatural adjuncts to human life.

In "A Visitor to Mombasa," James Holding gives us the classic African hunter with a leopard as prey, and a chilling twist at the end. Another hunted animal, the buffalo, provides a far different kind of hunter—and heroism—in Clark Howard's "Plateau."

The good dog, idealized companion of all our childhoods, provides a moving and unusual rescue for the heroine of Margaret Maron's "On Windy Ridge." And

Justin Scott, in "The White Death," tells us what all these dogs are really thinking, with one of the most engaging detectives I've encountered in years: a cat.

Hope Raymond's "Neighbors" sent a chill down my spine; the lady in the case has some unusual ones who come to her rescue in a tale that might have originated in the twilight zone. And if you're reading these late at night, save Donald E. Westlake's "A Good Story" for the morning.

When we picked these stories, we wanted to show a range of different animals, viewed in all the many ways storytelling has treated them. We also wanted to give you a sampling of some of the many different forms of the mystery short story, from thriller to detective story to Gothic horror, not forgetting the spy and the adventure story.

Dorothy Salisbury Davis is, perhaps, the greatest living writer of the mystery short story. Her prizewinning "Spring Fever," included here, defies categorization but examines human longing and despair with a poignance you will not easily forget.

Another story beyond categories is "Stork Trek," by Ed Wellen and Josh Pachter. This brooding tale shows us that we cannot escape our fate, even though we travel to the other side of the earth to avert it.

In a lighter vein is Isaac Asimov's "The Lost Dog," a rational exercise in the happy mode of the classical detective, as is Edward Hoch's "Problem of the Hunting Lodge." Joyce Harrington brings a marvelous new hard-boiled detective to life in "Dwindle, Peak and Pine." In fact, she gives us three detectives who are definitely not your run-of-the-mill gumshoes. I recommend Harrington or Asimov *after* Davis if you need a peaceful rest, or just want to go to dinner with a smile on your face.

Lilian Jackson Braun and Gahan Wilson both make use

of the mystery's Gothic origins with their touches of the supernatural—Braun with her lovely, light-hearted look at the lives of the rich in "A Cat Too Small for His Whiskers," Wilson in a somber, almost heavy, vein with "A Gift of the Gods" (another story not to be read before bedtime).

Joan Richter provides a classic kind of thriller with "Intruder in the Maize," another story dealing with Europeans in Africa. Richter's story covers a great deal of ground and leaves us with some compelling insights into what terrible things can go wrong when we abuse the trust of others, and willfully fail to understand their values.

Dick Stodghill has another kind of suspense story, the good man brought unwillingly into a life of evil and deceit. In "Best Evidence," a tenderhearted woman's love for her hamster provides her husband with the clue to a dastardly crime.

If you never cheered Charlotte's clever defense of Wilbur, never wept over Black Beauty's harsh fate as a drayhorse, shared Rat's exuberance messing about in a boat, or Toad's embarrassment caught speeding in a motor car, you should quietly close this volume now and turn to the financial pages. There neither poetry nor allegory will try to divert you from the stern business of living.

But if Bambi or Old Yeller touched your heart, I know you will share my pleasure in these stories. As you read them, I hope you'll remember, too, the many animals we've driven from the planet—the black rhinoceros, the Siberian tiger, leopards, a host of others. I hope reading these tales—man-told from the voice of animals—will make you want to save others now facing extinction. As you read this, the high Mexican plateau where Monarch butterflies go to breed is being denuded of trees. In another few years, we will have no more of these beautiful companions of the spring. Already, dozens of species of North American songbirds have disappeared. When they get to their winter homes in the Amazon, they find no place to nest and nothing to eat.

If this anthology does nothing else, I hope it will remind you that we share this planet as stewards with a myriad of other creatures. And, perhaps, none of our murders is more brutal than those we perpetrate against these more defenseless species.

DOROTHY SALISBURY DAVIS

Spring Fever

Sarah Shepherd watched her husband come down the stairs. He set his suitcase at the front door, checked his watch with the hall clock, and examined beneath his chin in the mirror. There was one spot he sometimes missed in shaving. He stepped back and examined himself full length, frowning a little. He was getting paunchy and not liking it. That critical of himself, how much more critical of her he might be. But he said nothing either in criticism or compliment, and she remembered, uncomfortably, doing all sorts of stunts to attract his eye: coy things—more becoming a girl than a woman of fifty-five. She did not feel her twelve years over Gerald . . . most of the time. Scarcely aware of the movement, she traced the shape of her stomach with her fingertips.

Gerald brought his sample spice kit into the living room and opened it. The aroma would linger for some time after he was gone. "There's enough wood, dear, if it gets cold tonight," he said. "And I wish you wouldn't haul things from the village. That's what delivery trucks are for . . ." He numbered his solicitudes as he did the bottles in the sample case, and with the same noncommittal attention.

As he took the case from the table, she got up and went to the door with him. On the porch he hesitated a moment, flexing his shoulders and breathing deeply. "On a morning like this I almost wish I drove a car."

"You could learn, Gerald. You could reach your accounts in half the time, and—"

"No, dear. I'm quite content with my paper in the bus, and in a town a car's a nuisance." He stooped and brushed her cheek with his lips. "Hello there!" he called out as he straightened up.

Her eyes followed the direction in which he had called. Their only close neighbor, a vegetable and flower grower, was following a plow behind his horse, his head as high as the horse's was low, the morning wind catching his thatch of gray hair and pointing it like a shock of wheat.

"That old boy has the life," Gerald said. "When I'm his age that's for me."

"He's not so old," she said.

"No. I guess he's not at that," he said. "Well, dear, I must be off. Till tomorrow night, take care of yourself."

His step down the road was almost jaunty. It was strange that he could not abide an automobile. But not having one was rather in the pattern. A car would be a tangible link between his life away and theirs at home. Climbing into it of an evening, she would have a feeling of his travels. The dust would rub off on her. As it was, the most she had of him away was the lingering pungency of a sample spice kit.

When he was out of sight she began her household chores—the breakfast dishes, beds, dusting. She had brought altogether too many things from the city. Her mother had left seventy years' accumulation in the old house, and now it was impossible to lay a book on the table without first moving a figurine, a vase, a piece of delft. Really the place was a clutter of bric-a-brac. Small wonder Gerald had changed toward her. It was not marriage that had changed him—it was this house, and herself settling in it like an old buddha with a bowl of incense in his lap.

A queer thing that this should occur to her only now, she thought. But it was not the first time. She was only now finding a word for it. Nor had Gerald always been this remote. Separating a memory of a particular moment in their early days, she caught his eyes searching hers—not numbering her years, as she might think were he to do it now, but measuring his own worth in her esteem.

She lined up several ornaments that might be put away, or better, sold to a junkman. But from the lineup she drew out pieces of which she had grown especially fond. They had become like children to her, as Gerald made children of the books with which he spent his evenings home. Making a basket of her apron she swept the whole tableful of trinkets into it.

Without a downward glance, she hurried them to the ash-box in the backyard. Shed of them, she felt a good deal lighter, and with the May wind in her face and the sun gentle, like an arm across her shoulders, she felt very nearly capersome. Across the fence the jonquils were in bloom, and the tulips nodding like fat little boys. Mr. Joyce had unhitched the horse. He saw her then.

"Fine day this morning," he called. He gave the horse a slap on the rump that sent him into the pasture, and came to the fence.

"I'm admiring the flowers," she said.

"Lazy year for them. Two weeks late they are."

"Is that a fact?" Of course it's a fact, she thought. A silly remark, and another after it: "I've never seen them lovelier, though. What comes out next?"

"Snaps, I guess this year. Late roses, too. The iris don't sell much, so I'm letting 'em come or stay as they like."

"That should bring them out."

"Now isn't that the truth? You can coax and tickle all

year and not get a bloom for thanks. Turn your back on
'em and they run you down."

Like love, she thought, and caught her tongue. But a
splash of color took to her cheeks.

"Say, you're looking nice, Mrs. Shepherd, if you don't
mind my saying it."

"Thank you. A touch of spring, I suppose."

"Don't it just send your blood racing? How would you
like an armful of these?"

"I'd be very pleased, Mr. Joyce. But I'd like to pay you
for them."

"Indeed not. I won't sell half of them—they come in a
heap."

She watched his expert hand nip the blooms. He was
already tanned, and he stooped and rose with a fine grace.
In all the years he had lived next to them he had never
been in the house, nor they in his except the day of his
wife's funeral. He hadn't grieved much, she commented
to Gerald at the time. And little wonder. The woman was
pinched and whining, and there wasn't a sunny day she
didn't expect a drizzle before nightfall. Now that Sarah
thought of it, Joyce looked younger than he did when
Mrs. Joyce was still alive.

"There. For goodness' sakes, Mr. Joyce. That's plenty."

"I'd give you the field of them this morning," he said,
piling her arms with the flowers.

"I've got half of it now."

"And what a picture you are with them."

"Well, I must hurry them into water," she said. "Thank
you."

She hastened toward the house, flying like a young flirt
from her first conquest, and aware of the pleased eye
following her. The whole morning glowed in the company she kept with the flowers. She snapped off the radio:
no tears for Miss Julia today. At noon she heard Mr.

Joyce's wagon roll out of the yard as he started to his highway stand. She watched at the window. He looked up and lifted his hat.

At odd moments during the day, she thought of him. He had given her a fine sense of herself and she was grateful. She began to wish that Gerald was returning that night. Take your time, Sarah, she told herself. You don't put away old habits and the years like bric-a-brac. She had softened up, no doubt of it. Not a fat woman, maybe, but plump. Plump. She repeated the word aloud. It had the sound of a potato falling into a tub of water.

But the afternoon sun was warm and the old laziness came over her. Only when Mr. Joyce came home, his voice in a song ahead of him, did she pull herself up. She hurried a chicken out of the refrigerator and then called to him from the porch.

"Mr. Joyce, would you like to have supper with me? Gerald won't be home, and I do hate cooking for just myself."

"Oh, that'd be grand. I've nothing in the house but a shank of ham that a dog wouldn't bark for. What can I bring?"

"Just come along when you're ready."

Sarah, she told herself, setting the table, you're an old bat trying your wings in daylight. A half hour later she glanced out the window in time to see Mr. Joyce skipping over the fence like a stiff-legged colt. He was dressed in his Sunday suit and brandishing a bottle as he cleared the barbed wire. Sarah choked down a lump of apprehension. For all that she planned a little fun for herself, she was not up to galloping through the house with an old Don Juan on her heels. Mr. Joyce, however, was a well-mannered guest. The bottle was May wine. He drank sparingly and was lavish in his praise of the dinner.

"You've no idea the way I envy you folks. Mrs. Shep-

herd. Your husband especially. How can he bear the time
he spends away?"

He bears it all too well, she thought. "It's his work. He's
a salesman. He sells spices."

Mr. Joyce showed a fine set of teeth in his smile—his
own teeth, she marveled, tracing her bridgework with the
tip of her tongue while he spoke. "Then he's got sugar
and spice and everything nice, as they say."

What a one he must have been with the girls, she
thought, and to marry a quince as he had. It was done in
a hurry no doubt, and maybe at the end of a big stick.

"It must be very lonesome for you since Mrs. Joyce
passed away," she said, more lugubriously than she
intended. After all, the woman was gone three years.

"No more than when she was with me." His voice
matched hers in seriousness. "It's·a hard thing to say of
the dead, but if she hasn't improved her disposition
since, we're all in for a damp eternity." He stuffed the
bowl of his pipe. "Do you mind?"

"No, I like the smell of tobacco around the house."

"Does your husband smoke?"

"Yes," she said in some surprise at the question.

"He didn't look the kind to follow a pipe," he said,
pulling noisily at his. "No, dear lady," he added when the
smoke was shooting from it, "you're blessed in not
knowing the plague of a silent house."

It occurred to her then that he was exploring the
situation. She would give him small satisfaction. "Yes. I
count that among my blessings."

There was a kind of amusement in his eyes. You're as
lonesome as me, old girl, they seemed to say, and their
frankness bade her to add: "But I do wish Gerald was
home more of the time."

"Ah, well, he's at the age when most men look to a last

trot around the paddock," he said, squinting at her through the smoke.

"Gerald is only forty-three," she said, loosing the words before she knew it.

"There's some take it at forty, and others among us leaping after it from the rocking chair."

The conversation had taken a turn she certainly had not intended, and she found herself threshing around in it. Beating a fire with a feather duster. "There's the moon," she said, charging to the window as though to wave to an old friend.

"Aye," he said, "there's the moon. Are you up to a trot in it?"

"What did you say, Mr. Joyce?"

"I'd better say what I was thinking first. If I hitch Micky to the old rig, would you take a turn with me on the Mill Pond Road?"

She saw his reflection in the window, a smug, daring little grin on his face. In sixteen years of settling she had forgotten her way with men. But it was something you never really forgot. Like riding a bicycle, you picked it up again after a few turns. "I would," she said.

The horse ahead of the rig was a different animal from the one on the plow that morning. Mr. Joyce had no more than thrown the reins over his rump than he took a turn that almost tumbled Sarah into the sun frames. But Mr. Joyce leaped to the seat and pulled Micky up on his hind legs with one hand and Sarah down to her cushion with the other, and they were off in the wake of the moon . . .

The sun was full in her face when Sarah awoke the next morning. As usual, she looked to see if Gerald were in his bed by way of acclimating herself to the day and its routine. With the first turn of her body she decided that a gallop in a rusty-springed rig was not the way to assert a stay of youth. She lay a few moments thinking about it and then got up to an aching sense of folly. It remained with her through the day, giving way at times to a nostalgia for her bric-a-brac. She had never realized how much of her life was spent in the care of it.

By the time Gerald came home she was almost the person he had left the day before. She had held out against the ornaments, however. Only the flowers decorated the living room. It was not until supper was over and Gerald had settled with his book that he commented.

"Sarah, what happened to the old Chinese philosopher?"

"I put him away. Didn't you notice? I took all the clutter out of here."

He looked about him vacantly as though trying to recall some of it. "So you did. I'll miss that old boy. He gave me something to think about."

"What?"

"Oh, I don't know. Confucius says . . . that sort of thing."

"He wasn't a philosopher at all," she said, having no notion what he was. "He was a farmer."

"Was he? Well, there's a small difference." He opened the book.

"Aren't the flowers nice, Gerald?"

"Beautiful."

"Mr. Joyce gave them to me, fresh out of his garden."

"That's nice."

"Must you read every night, Gerald? I'm here all day with no one to talk to, and when you get home you stick your nose into a book . . ." When the words were half out she regretted them. "I didn't tell you, Gerald. I had Mr. Joyce to dinner last night."

"That was very decent of you, dear. The old gentleman must find it lonesome."

"I don't think so. It was a relief to him when his wife died."

Gerald looked up. "Did he say that?"

"Not in so many words, but practically."

"He must be a strange sort. What did she die of?"

"I don't remember. A heart condition, I think."

"Interesting." He returned to his book.

"After dinner he took me for a ride in the horse and buggy. All the way to Cos Corner and back."

"Ha!" was his only comment.

"Gerald, you're getting fat."

He looked up. "I don't think so. I'm about my usual weight. A couple of pounds maybe."

"Then you're carrying it in your stomach. I noticed you've cut the elastic out of your shorts."

"These new fabrics," he said testily.

"They're preshrunken," she said. "It's your stomach. And haven't you noticed how you pull at your collar all the time?"

"I meant to mention that, Sarah. You put too much starch in them."

"I ran out of starch last week and forgot to order it. You can take a size fifteen and a half now."

"Good Lord, Sarah, you're going to tell me next I should wear a horse collar." He let the book slide closed between his thighs. "I get home only three or four nights a week. I'm tired. I wish you wouldn't aggravate me, dear."

She went to his chair and sat on the arm of it. "Did you know that I was beginning to wonder if you'd respond to the poke of a hat pin?"

He looked directly up at her for the first time in what had seemed like years. His eyes fell away. "I've been working very hard, dear."

"I don't care what you've been doing, Gerald. I'm just glad to find out that you're still human."

He slid his arm around her and tightened it.

"Aren't spring flowers lovely?" she said.

"Yes," he said, "and so is spring."

She leaned across him and took a flower from the vase. She lingered there a moment. He touched his hand to her. "And you're lovely, too."

This is simple, she thought, getting upright again. If the rabbit had sat on a thistle, he'd have won the race.

"The three most beautiful things in the world," Gerald said thoughtfully, "a white bird flying, a field of wheat, and a woman's body."

"Is that your own, Gerald?"

"I don't know. I think it is."

"It's been a long time since you wrote any poetry. You did nice things once."

"That's how I got you," he said quietly.

"And I got you with an old house. I remember the day my mother's will was probated. The truth, Gerald— wasn't it then you made up your mind?"

He didn't speak for a moment, and then it was a continuance of some thought of his own, a subtle twist of association. "Do you remember the piece I wrote on the house?"

"I read it the other day. I often read them again."

"Do you, Sarah? And never a mention of it."

It was almost all the reading she did anymore. His devotion to books had turned her from them. "Remember how you used to let me read them to you, Gerald? You thought that I was the only one besides yourself who could do them justice."

"I remember."

"Or was that flattery?"

He smiled. "It was courtship, I'm afraid. No one ever

thinks anybody else can do his poetry justice. But Sarah, do you know—I'd listen tonight if you'd read some of them. Just for old times' sake."

For old times' sake, she thought, getting the folder from the cabinet and settling opposite him. He was slouched in his chair, pulling at his pipe, his eyes half closed. Long ago this same contemplativeness in him had softened the first shock of the difference in their ages.

"I've always liked this one best—The Morning of My Days."

"Well you might," he murmured. "It was written for you."

She read one piece after another, wondering now and then what pictures he was conjuring up of the moment he had written them. He would suck on his pipe at times. The sound was like a baby pulling at an empty bottle. She was reading them well, she thought, giving them a mellow vibrance, an old love's tenderness. Surely there was a moment coming when he would rise from the chair and come to her. Still he sat, his eyes almost closed, the pipe now in hand on the chair's arm. A huskiness crept into her voice, so rarely used to this length anymore, and she thought of the nightingale's singing, the thorn against its breast. A slit of pain in her own throat pressed her to greater effort, for the poems were almost done.

She stopped abruptly, a phrase unfinished, at a noise in the room. The pipe had clattered to the floor, Gerald's hand still cupped in its shape, but his chin now on his breast. Laying the folder aside, she went over and picked up the pipe with a rather empty regret, as she would pick up a bird that had fallen dead at her feet.

Gerald's departure in the morning was in the tradition of all their days, even to the kiss upon her cheek and the words, "Till tomorrow evening, dear, take care."

Take care, she thought, going indoors. Take care of what? For what? Heat a boiler of water to cook an egg? She hurried her chores and dressed. When she saw Mr. Joyce hitch the wagon of flowers, she locked the door and waited boldly at the road for him.

"May I have a lift to the highway?" she called out, as he reined up beside her.

"You may have a lift to the world's end, Mrs. Shepherd. Give me your hand." He gave the horse its rein when she was beside him. "I see your old fella's taken himself off again. I daresay it gave him a laugh, our ride in the moonlight."

"It was a giddy business," she said.

"Did you enjoy yourself?"

"I did. But I paid for it afterwards." Her hand went to her back.

"I let out a squeal now and then bending over, myself. But I counted it cheap for the pleasure we had. I'll take you into the village. I've to buy a length of hose anyway. Or do you think you'll be taken for a fool riding in on a wagon?"

"It won't be the first time," she said. "My life's full of foolishness."

"It's a wise fool who laughs at his own folly. We've that in common, you and me. Where'll we take our supper tonight?"

He was sharp as mustard.

"You're welcome to come over," she said.

He nodded. "I'll fetch us a steak, and we'll give Micky his heels again after."

Sarah got off at the post office and stayed in the building until Joyce was out of sight—Joyce and the gapers who had stopped to see her get out of the wagon. Getting in was one thing, getting out another. A bumble-bee after a violet. It was time for this trip. She walked to the doctor's office and waited her turn among the villagers.

"I thought I'd come in for a check-up, Dr. Philips," she said at his desk. "And maybe you'd give me a diet."

"A diet?" He took off his glasses and measured her with the naked eye.

"I'm getting a little fat," she said. "They say it's a strain on the heart at my age."

"Your heart could do for a woman of twenty," he said, "but we'll have a listen."

"I'm not worried about my heart, Doctor, you understand. I just feel that I'd like to lose a few pounds."

"Uh-huh," he said. "Open your dress." He got his stethoscope.

Diet, apparently, was the rarest of his prescriptions. Given as a last resort. She should have gone into town for this, not to a country physician who measured a woman by the children she bore. "The woman next door to us died of a heart condition," she said, as though that should explain her visit.

"Who's that?" he asked, putting away the instrument.

"Mrs. Joyce. Some years ago."

"She had a heart to worry about. Living for years on stimulants. Yours is as sound as a bullet. Let's have your arm."

She pushed up her sleeve as he prepared the apparatus for measuring her blood pressure. That, she felt, was rising out of all proportion. She was ashamed of herself before this man, and angry at herself for it, and at him for no reason more than that he was being patient with her. "We're planning insurance," she lied. "I wanted our own doctor's opinion first."

"You'll have no trouble getting it, Mrs. Shepherd. And no need of a diet." He grinned and removed the apparatus. "Go easy on potatoes and bread, and on the sweets. You'll outlive your husband by twenty years. How is he, by the way?"

"Fine. Just fine, Doctor, thank you."

What a nice show you're making of yourself these days, Sarah, she thought, outdoors again. Well, come in or go out, old girl, and slam the door behind you . . .

Micky took to his heels that night. He had had a day of ease, and new shoes were stinging his hooves by nightfall. The skipping of Joyce with each snap of the harness teased him, the giggling from the rig adding a prickle. After the wagon, the rig was no more than a fly on his tail. He took the full reins when they slapped on his flanks and charged out from the laughter behind him. It rose to a shriek the faster he galloped and tickled his ears like something alive that slithered from them down his neck and his belly and into his loins. Faster and faster he plunged, the sparks from his shoes like ocean spray. He fought a jerk of the reins, the saw of the bit in his mouth a fierce pleasure. He took turns at his own fancy and only in sight of his own yard again did he yield in the fight, choking on the spume that lathered his tongue.

"By the holy, the night a horse beats me, I'll lie down in my grave," Joyce cried. "Get up now, you buzzard. You're not turning in till you go to the highway and back. Are you all right, Sarah?"

Am I all right, she thought. When in years had she known a wild ecstasy like this? From the first leap of the horse she had burst the girdle of fear and shame. If the wheels had spun out from beneath them, she would have rolled into the ditch contented.

"I've never been better," she said.

He leaned close to her to see her, for the moon had just risen. The wind had stung the tears to her eyes, but they were laughing. "By the Horn Spoon," he said, "you liked it!" He let the horse have his own way into the drive after all. He jumped down from the rig and held his hand up to her. "What a beautiful thing to be hanging in the back of the closet all these years."

"If that's a compliment," she said, "it's got a nasty bite."

"Aye. But it's my way of saying you're a beautiful woman."

"Will you come over for a cup of coffee?"

"I will. I'll put up the horse and be over."

The kettle had just come to the boil when he arrived. "Maybe you'd rather have tea, Mr. Joyce?"

"Coffee or tea, so long as it's not water. And I'd like you to call me Frank. They christened me Francis but I got free of it early."

"And you know mine, I noticed," she said.

"It slipped out in the excitement. There isn't a woman I know who wouldn't've collapsed in a ride like that."

"It was wonderful." She poured the water into the coffee pot.

"There's nothing like getting behind a horse," he said, "unless it's getting astride him. I wouldn't trade Micky for a Mack truck."

"I used to ride when I was younger," she said.

"How did you pick up the man you got, if you don't mind my asking?"

And you the old woman, she thought; where did you get her? "I worked for a publishing house and he brought in some poetry."

"Ah, that's it." He nodded. "And he thought with a place like this he could pour it out like water from a spout."

"Gerald and I were in love," she said, irked that he should define so bluntly her own thoughts on the matter.

"Don't I remember it? In them days you didn't pull the blinds. It used to put me in a fine state."

"Do you take cream in your coffee? I've forgotten."

"Aye, thank you, and plenty of sugar."

"You haven't missed much," she said.

"There's things you see through a window you'd miss sitting down in the living room. I'll wager you've wondered about the old lady and me?"

"A little. She wasn't so old, was she, Mr. Joyce?" Frank, she thought. Too frank.

"That one was old in her crib. But she came with a greenhouse. I worked for her father."

Sarah poured the coffee, "You're a cold-blooded old rogue," she said.

He grinned. "No. Cool-headed I am, and warm-blooded. When I was young, I made out it was the likes of poetry. She sang like a bird on a convent wall. But when I caged her she turned into an old crow."

"That's a terrible thing to say, Mr. Joyce."

The humor left his face for an instant. "It's a terribler thing to live with. It'd put a man off his nut. You don't have a bit of cake in the house, Sarah, to go with this?"

"How about muffins and jam?"

"That'll go fine." He smiled again. "Where does your old fella spend the night in his travels?"

"In the hotel in whatever town he happens to be in."

"That's a lonesome sort of life for a married man," he said.

She pulled a chair to the cupboard and climbed up to get a jar of preserves. He made no move to help her although she still could not reach the jar. She looked down at him. "You could give me a hand."

"Try it again. You almost had it that time." He grinned, almost gleeful at her discomfort.

She bounced down in one step. "Get it yourself if you want it. I'm satisfied with a cup of coffee."

He pounded his fist on the table, getting up. "You're right, Sarah. Never fetch a man anything he can fetch himself. Which bottle is it?"

"The strawberry."

He hopped up and down, nimble as a goat. "But then maybe he doesn't travel alone?"

"What?"

"I was suggesting your man might have an outside interest. Salesmen have the great temptation, you know."

"That's rather impertinent, Mr. Joyce."

"You're right, Sarah, it is. My tongue's been home so long it doesn't know how to behave in company. This is a fine cup of coffee."

She sipped hers without speaking. It was time she faced that question, she thought. She had been hedging around it for a long time, and last night with Gerald should have forced it upon her. "And if he does have an outside interest," she said, lifting her chin, "what of it?"

"Ah, Sarah, you're a wise woman, and worth waiting the acquaintance of. You like me a little now, don't you?"

"A little."

"Well," he said, getting up, "I'll take that to keep me warm for the night."

And what have I got to keep me warm, she thought. "Thank you for the ride, Frank. It was thrilling."

"Was it?" he said, coming near her. He lifted her chin with his forefinger. "We've many a night like this ahead, Sarah, if you say the word." And then when she left her chin on his finger, he bent down and kissed her, taking himself to the door after it with a skip and a jump. He paused there and looked back at her. "Will I stay or go?"

"You'd better go," she choked out, wanting to be angry but finding no anger in herself at all.

*   *   *

All the next day Sarah tried to anchor herself from her peculiar flights of fancy. She had no feeling for the man, she told herself. It was a fine state a woman reached when a kiss from a stranger could do that to her. It was the ride made you giddy, she said aloud. You were thinking of Gerald. You were thinking of . . . the Lord knows what. She worked upstairs until she heard the wagon go by. She would get some perspective when Gerald came home. It seemed as though he'd been gone a long time.

The day was close and damp, and the flies clung to the screens. There was a dull stillness in the atmosphere. By late afternoon the clouds rolled heavier, mulling about one another like dough in a pan. While she was peeling potatoes for supper, Frank drove in. He unhitched the horse but left him in the harness, and set about immediately building frames along the rows of flowers. He was expecting a storm. She looked at the clock. It was almost time for Gerald.

She went out on the front porch and watched for the bus. There was a haze in the sweep of land between her and the highway, and the traffic through it seemed to float thickly, slowly. The bus glided toward the intersection and past it without stopping. She felt a sudden anger. Her whole day had been strung up to this peak. Since he had not called, it meant merely that he had missed the bus. The next one was in two hours. She crossed the yard to the fence. You're starting up again, Sarah, she warned herself, and took no heed of the warning.

Frank looked up from his work. "You'd better fasten the house," he said. "There's a fine blow coming."

"Frank, if you're in a hurry, I'll give you something to eat."

"That'd be a great kindness. I may have to go back to the stand at a gallop."

He was at the kitchen table, shoveling in the food
without a word, when the heavy sky lightened. He went
to the window. "By the glory, it may blow over." He
looked around at her. "Your old boy missed the bus, did
he?"

"He must have."

Frank looked out again. "I do like a good blow. Even if
it impoverished me, there's nothing in the world like a
storm."

An automobile horn sounded on the road. It occurred
to Sarah that on a couple of occasions Gerald had received
a ride from the city. The car passed, but watching its dust
she was left with a feeling of suspended urgency. Joyce
was chatting now. He had tilted back in the chair and for
the first time since she had known him, he was rambling
on about weather, vegetables, and the price of eggs. She
found it more disconcerting than his bursts of intimate
comment, and she hung from one sentence to the next
waiting for the end of it. Finally she passed in back of his
chair and touched her fingers briefly to his neck.

"You need a haircut, Frank."

He sat bolt upright. "I never notice it till I have to
scratch. Could I have a drop more coffee?"

She filled his cup, aware of his eyes on her. "Last night
was something I'll never forget—that ride," she said.

"And something else last night, do you remember
that?"

"Yes."

"Would you give me another now to match it if I was to
ask?"

"No."

"What if I took it without asking?"

"I don't think I'd like it, Frank."

He pushed away from the table, slopping the coffee into
the saucer. "Then what are you tempting me for?"

"You've a funny notion of temptation," she flared up, knowing the anger was against herself.

Joyce spread his dirt-grimed fingers on the table. "Sarah, do you know what you want?"

The tears were gathering. She fought them back. "Yes, I know what I want!" she cried.

Joyce shook his head. "He's got you by the heart, hasn't he, Sarah?"

"My heart's my own!" She flung her head up.

Joyce slapped his hand on the table. "Ho! Look at the spark of the woman! That'd scorch a man if there was a stick in him for kindling." He moistened his lips and in spite of herself Sarah took a step backwards. "I'll not chase you, Sarah. Never fear that. My chasing days are over. I'll neither chase nor run, but I'll stand my ground for what's coming to me." He jerked his head toward the window. "That was only a lull in the wind. There's a big blow coming now for certain."

She watched the first drops of rain splash on the glass. "Gerald's going to get drenched in it."

"Maybe it'll drown him," Joyce said, grinning from the door. "Thanks for the supper."

Let it come on hail, thunder, and lightning. Blow the roof from the house and tumble the chimney. I'd go out from it then and never turn back. When an old man can laugh at your trying to cuckold a husband, and the husband asking it, begging it, shame on you. She went through the house clamping the locks on the windows. More pleasure putting the broom through them.

An early darkness folded into the storm, and the walls of rain bleared the highway lights. There was an ugly yellow tinge to the water from the dust swirled into it. The wind sluiced down the chimney spitting bits of soot on the living room floor. She spread newspapers to catch it. A sudden blow, it would soon be spent. She went to the hall clock. The bus was due in ten minutes. What matter? A quick supper, a good book, and a long sleep. The wily old imp was right. A prophet needing a haircut.

The lights flickered off for a moment, then on again. Let them go out, Sarah. What's left for you, you can see by candlelight. She went to the basement and brought up the kerosene lamp and then got a flashlight from the pantry. As she returned to the living room, a fresh gust of wind sent the newspapers out of the grate like scud. The lights flickered again. A sound drew her to the hall. She thought the wind might be muffling the ring of the telephone. When she got there, the clock was striking. The bus was now twenty minutes late. There was something about the look of the phone that convinced her the line was dead. It was unnerving to find it in order. Imagination, she murmured. Everything was going perverse to her expectations. And then, annoyed with herself, she grew angry with Gerald again. This was insult. Insult on top of indifference.

She followed a thumping noise upstairs. It was on the outside of the house. She turned off the light and pressed her face against the window. A giant maple tree was rocking and churning, one branch thudding against the house. There was not even a blur of light from the highway now. Blacked out. While she watched, a pinpoint of light shaped before her. It grew larger, weaving a little. A flashlight, she thought, and wondered if Gerald had one. Then she recognized the motion: a lantern on a wagon. Frank was returning.

When she touched the light switch there was no response. Groping her way to the hall she saw that all the lights were out now. Step by step she made her way downstairs. A dankness had washed in through the chimney, stale and sickening. She lit the lamp and carried it to the kitchen. From the window there, she saw

Frank's lantern bobbing as he led the horse into the barn.
She could not see man or horse, only the fading of the
light until it disappeared inside. When it reappeared she
lifted her kerosene lamp, a greeting to him. This time he
came around the fence. She held the door against the
wind.

"I've no time now, Sarah. I've work to do," he shouted.
"He didn't come, did he?"

"No!"

"Is the phone working?"

She nodded that it was and waved him close to her.
"Did the bus come through?"

"It's come and gone. Close the door or you'll have the
house in a shambles." He waved his lantern and was
gone.

She put the pot roast she had prepared for Gerald in the
refrigerator and set the perishables close to the freezing
unit. She wound the clock and put away the dishes.
Anything to keep busy. She washed the kitchen floor that
had been washed only the day before. The lantern across
the way swung on a hook at the barn, sometimes moving
toward the ground and back as Joyce examined the frames
he was reinforcing.

Finally she returned to the living room. She sat for a
long time in Gerald's chair, watching the pattern of smoke
in the lamp chimney. Not even a dog or cat to keep her
company. Not even a laughing piece of delft to look out at
her from the mantelpiece; only the cold-eyed forebears,
whom she could not remember, staring down at her from
the gilt frames, their eyes fixed upon her, the last and the
least of them who would leave after her—nothing.

It was not to be endured. She lunged out of the chair. In
the hall she climbed to the first landing where she could
see Joyce's yard. He was through work now, the lantern
hanging from the porch although the house was darkened.

It was the only light anywhere, and swayed in the wind like a will-o'-the-wisp.

She bounded down the stairs and caught up her raincoat. Taking the flashlight she went out into the storm. She made her way around the fence, sometimes leaning into the wind, sometimes resting against it. Joyce met her in his driveway. He had been waiting, she thought, testing his nerves against her own, expecting her. Without a word, he caught her hand and led her to his back steps and into the house. "I've an oil lamp," he said then. "Hold your light there till I fix it."

She watched his wet face in the half-light. His mouth was lined with malicious humor, and his eyes as he squinted at the first flame of the wick were fierce, as fierce as the storm, and as strange to her. When the light flared up, she followed its reaches over the dirty wall, the faded calendar, the gaping cupboards, the electric cord hanging from a naked bulb over the sink to the back door. There were dishes stacked on the table where they no doubt stood from one meal to the next. The curtains were stiff with dirt, three years of it. Only then did she take a full glimpse of the folly that had brought her here.

"I just ran over for a minute, Frank . . ."

"A minute or the night, sit there, Sarah, and let me get out of these clothes."

She took the chair he motioned her into, and watched him fling his coat into the corner. Nor could she take her eyes from him as he sat down and removed his boots and socks. Each motion fascinated her separately, fascinated and revolted her. He wiped between his toes with the socks. He went barefoot toward the front of the house. In the doorway he paused, becoming a giant in the weird light.

"Put us up a pot of coffee, dear woman. The makings are there on the stove."

"I must go home. Gerald—"

"To hell with Gerald," he interrupted. "He's snug for the night, wherever he is. Maybe he won't come back to you at all. It's happened before, you know, men vanishing from women they don't know the worth of."

Alone, she sat stiff and erect at the table. He was just talking, poisoning her mind against Gerald. How should she get out of here? Run like a frightened doe and never face him again? No, Sarah. Stay for the bitter coffee. Scald the giddiness out of you once and for all. But on top of the resolve came the wish that Gerald might somehow appear at the door and take her home. Dear, gentle Gerald.

She got up and went to the sink to draw the water for coffee. A row of medicine bottles stood on the window-sill, crusted with dust. Household remedies. She leaned close and examined a faded label: "Mrs. Joyce—Take immediately upon need."

She turned from the window. A rocker stood in the corner of the room. In the old days the sick woman had sat in it on the back porch, rocking, and speaking to no one. The stale sickness of her was still about the house, Sarah thought. What did she know of people like this?

He was threshing around upstairs like a penned bull. His muddy boots lay where he had taken them off, a pool of water gathering about them. Again she looked at the windowsill. No May wine there. Suddenly she remembered Dr. Philips' words: "Lived on stimulants for years." She could almost see the sour woman, even to her gasping for breath . . . "Take immediately."

Fix the coffee, Sarah. What kind of teasing is this? Teasing the dead from her grave before you. Teasing. Something in the thought disturbed her further . . . an association: Joyce watching her reach for the preserves last night, grinning at her. "Try it again, Sarah. You almost had it that time." And she could still hear him asking, "Which bottle?" Not which jar, but which bottle.

She grabbed the kettle and filled it. Stop it, Sarah. It's the storm, the waiting, too much waiting . . . your time of life. She drew herself up against his coming, hearing his quick steps on the stairs.

"Will you give us a bit of iodine there from the window, Sarah? I've scratched myself on those blamed frames."

She selected the bottle carefully with her eyes, so that her trembling hand might not betray her.

"Dab it on here," he said, holding a white cuff away from his wrist.

The palm of his hand was moist as she bent over it and she could smell the earth and the horse from it. Familiar. Everything about him had become familiar, too familiar. She felt his breath on her neck, and the hissing sound of it was the only sound in the room. She smeared the iodine on the cut and pulled away. His lips tightened across his teeth in a grin.

"A kiss would make a tickle of the pain," he said.

Sarah thrust the iodine bottle from her and grabbed the flashlight. "I'm going home."

His jaw sagged as he stared at her. "Then what did you come for?"

"Because I was lonesome. I was foolish . . ." Fear choked off her voice. A little trickle of saliva dribbled from the corner of his mouth.

"No! You came to torture me!"

She forced one foot toward the door and the other after it. His voice rose in laughter as she lumbered away from him. "Good Lord, Sarah. Where's the magnificent woman who rode to the winds with me last night?"

She lunged into the electric cord in her retreat, searing her cheek on it. Joyce caught it and wrenched it from the wall, it's splayed end springing along the floor like a whip. "And me thinking the greatest kindness would be if he never came home!"

The doorknob slipped in her sweaty hand. She dried it frantically. He's crazy, she thought. Mad-crazy.

"You're a lump, Sarah," he shouted. "And Mr. Joyce is a joker. A joker and a dunce. He always was and he will be till the day they hang him!"

The door yielded and she plunged down the steps and into the yard. In her wild haste she hurled herself against the rig and spun away from it as though it were something alive. She sucked in her breath to keep from screaming. She tore her coat on the fence hurtling past it, leaving a swatch of it on the wire. Take a deep breath, she told herself as she stumbled up the steps. Don't faint. Don't fall. The door swung from her grasp, the wind clamoring through the house. She forced it closed, the glass plate tingling, and bolted it. She thrust the flashlight on the table and caught up the phone. She clicked it wildly.

Finally it was the operator who broke through. "I have a call for you from Mr. Gerald Shepherd. Will you hold on, please?"

Sarah could hear only her own sobbing breath in the hollow of the mouthpiece. She tried to settle her mind by pinning her eyes on the stairway. But the spokes of the staircase seemed to be shivering dizzily in the circle of light, like the plucked strings of a harp. Even the sound of them was vibrant in her head, whirring over the rasp of her breath. Then came the pounding footfalls and Joyce's fists on the door. Vainly she signaled the operator. And somewhere in the tumult of her mind she grasped at the thought that if she unlocked the door, Joyce would come in and sit down. They might even light the fire. There was plenty of wood in the basement. But she could not speak. And it was too late.

Joyce's fist crashed through the glass and drew the bolt.

With the door's opening the wind whipped her coat over her head; with its closing, her coat fell limp, it's little pressure about her knees seeming to buckle them.

"I'm sorry," came the operator's voice, "the call was canceled ten minutes ago."

She let the phone clatter onto the table and waited, her back still to the door. Ten minutes was not very long ago, she reasoned in sudden desolate calmness. She measured each of Joyce's footfalls toward her, knowing they marked all of time that was left to her. And somehow, she felt, she wanted very little more of it.

For only an instant she saw the loop he had made of the electric cord, and the white cuffs over the strong, gnarled hands. She closed her eyes and lifted her head high, expecting that in that way the end would come more quickly . . .

JOYCE HARRINGTON

Dwindle, Peak and Pine

Max Dwindle held a flaming safety match to the charred end of his three-day-old cigar and created a noisome stench. Safe in his fetid cloud, he beheld the weeping girl slumped despairingly in a chair across the room. "Loretta, dollink, don't cry. Could be Lower East Side love potions don't work on goyim from Sheboygan. Anyway, you're better off without him, a shmendrick like that. Why don't you feed the rat?"

"I fed him already," the girl wailed. "Darn rat eats more than a mule, and he's twice as thick-headed. Don't know why we couldn't have something cute for a familiar. Back home, I had a skunk, and I didn't have to keep running out to get pizza for him. He foraged for hisself. He was the prettiest little thing. Got any Kleenex, Max?" She snuffled loudly and dashed the tears from her eyes with her fingertips.

Max sighed and shuffled to the tall metal cabinet against one wall. He swung open its double doors and pondered its contents. The top shelf was stacked with cigar boxes; the next two shelves were given over to candy bars, chewing gum, cough drops, breath mints, miniature sewing kits, and a box of outdated lottery tickets. The bottom shelf was stuffed with magazines. The news in the newsweeklies was all six months old.

The cabinet contained the remnants of Max Dwindle's life. Until six months ago, he had been the contented proprietor of a news-candy-tobacco kiosk in the lobby of a Park Avenue South office building. For over forty years, he had supplied the trivial daily needs of a constantly shifting clientele. For the pretty young secretaries who came and went like a summer's day, there were Juicy Fruit and spare pantyhose. For the paunched and balding operators of marginal businesses, there were White Owl cigars and single dose packets of Alka-Seltzer. And for the young hot-shots in their three-piece suits, there were racing forms and girlie magazines to be folded into the sedate disguising pages of *The Wall Street Journal*. For all his customers, Max Dwindle had a cheery grumble, and for those who had proven discreet and loyal, he provided potions and curses and spells, and an occasional glimpse into a cloudy future. Max Dwindle was a kindly old warlock.

But six months ago, Max had been turfed out and the building had come down. He could have put a curse on the wrecking crew, causing them to lose fingers or toes as they demolished the site of his past contentment. But he was too dispirited to work up a good curse. Instead, he packed up the remainder of his stock, stored it with a friend in the Transit Authority who had access to an empty shop in the Fourteenth Street subway station, and whiled away his empty days sitting on a bench in Union Square Park. There he had met Loretta Peak and Peter Pine, teenaged country witch and ex-advertising clairvoyant respectively.

"How about some Life Savers?" he asked the girl as he located one of the few remaining pocket packs of Kleenex.

Loretta cried a lot. "Wintogreen? Tropical Fruit? Make you feel better."

"Don't mind if I do." Loretta ate up almost as many rolls of Life Savers as she used up packs of Kleenex. "Got any butterscotch left?"

She lurched to her large bare feet and angled her way to the cabinet to peer over Max's head.

"Nope," said Max. "You ate 'em all."

"Hot damn!" said Loretta. "So I did." She plucked a roll of Tropical Fruit off the shelf, opened the pack of Kleenex, blew her nose, and settled back into the lumpy leather armchair they had rescued from the street a few nights before.

"So where's that Peter the Nogoodnik?" asked Max. "Why isn't he back yet? You think maybe the police picked him up?"

"Don't worry, Max." Loretta sucked happily on a circle of tangerine candy. "It takes time to stick up the whole BMT subway. I should have gone along to help him."

From a carton beside her chair, she took a sheet of paper on which the printer's ink was barely dry. "Dwindle, Peak and Pine," she read. "Psychic Detectives. Missing persons found. Lost objects located. Ectoplasmic surveillance. Milk curdled While-U-Wait. Other services upon request. Reasonable rates." On the bottom of the poster was their address on the east side of Union Square, and a telephone number.

"So who's worrying?" said Max. "Never in all my forty years of business did I ever have to advertise. Everybody knew Max Dwindle and what he could do." He stubbed his cigar out carefully and laid it aside for future reference. "Now," he ranted on, "I'm in business with an underage witch from the sticks and a clairvoyant dropout from Madison Avenue. 'Advertise,' he says. Do you know what kind of crazies ride the BMT? Race-track

bums, that's who. Low-grade Mafia bums. Bigmouth
yentas from Brooklyn. Voodoo crazies from the Bronx. I
ain't killing no chickens, no matter who comes knocking
on that door."

There was a soft knock on the door.

"Go away!" roared Max. "We ain't open for business
yet."

"Come in," cried Loretta, swallowing her Life Saver.
She flew to the door, levitating slightly in her excitement,
and swung it open. "Welcome to the headquarters of
Dwindle, Peak and Pine. I'm Loretta Peak. This is Max
Dwindle. Mr. Pine is out doing market research. How may
we help you?" Loretta had once worked as a temporary
receptionist at the very advertising agency from which
Peter Pine had dropped out.

A black-veiled figure languished in the doorway. From
beneath the smoky layers of nylon a throaty contralto
murmured. "Help. Oh, help."

With a fluttering of black draperies, the wispy figure
staggered into the room and into Loretta's sturdy country
arms. Max shook his head and reignited his loathsome
cigar.

"Come on in, honey." Loretta guided the drooping
woman to the lumpy armchair and let her fall gracefully
onto its protruding springs. The woman murmured in
surprise and shifted delicately until she was comfortable.
"Now, honey, what's the trouble?" Loretta pursued. "I
can dry up a cow at fifty paces, and Max here can tell you
if your firstborn will be a boy or a girl."

The woman unwound her veils and removed her broad-
brimmed black hat, revealing unnaturally glossy black
hair falling straight to her shoulders, huge and flashing
black eyes set in a face that was all cheekbones, heavily
pancaked white skin, and voluptuously shaped scarlet
lips. "My firstborn was my lastborn and he's away at

veterinary college. He may know a few cows, but that's not what I'm here about. I saw your ad in the subway. My name is Tatiana Petrovna Smith."

"It knew it! I knew it!" Max broke in. "A BMT crazy. The last of the Romanoffs, I betcha! A Russian princess from Sheepshead Bay. Out! Get rid of her!"

The woman stared at Max in amazement. "Wonderful!" she breathed. "You're absolutely right. Now I know I've come to the right place. My son, the vet, does not care for his royal heritage. He wants to be plain John Smith, American. So, in effect, I am the last of my line. And it's true I live in Sheepshead Bay, a nice little cottage with attached garage. The Winter Palace, it's not. But what with the servant situation these days, I don't think I could manage a full-scale palace. You don't know of a good reliable daily woman, do you?"

Max gnawed his cigar and grated through the flecks of tobacco that clung to his teeth, "You came here to find a maid? You take me, Max Dwindle, for a supplier of scrubladies? Out! Out!" Max's entire five-foot collection of rotundities quivered with indignation; every gray hair on his head was alive with shock. He hauled open the door and gestured imperiously with his cigar. "Leave, lady, before I give you a case of terminal dandruff."

Her hand flew to her glossy black tresses and she smiled winningly. "It's a wig," she said. "Very realistic, don't you think? No," she went on, "I didn't come here for a cleaning lady. Although I could use one. If I live." She lowered her voice to a hoarse whisper and beckoned Max and Loretta closer. "Someone is trying to kill me."

Max closed the door. "Ssh," he shushed. "Not so loud. There could be bad influences out in the hall. In here is safe. In here, we have the pentagram." He pointed to the white lines painted on the floor forming a five-pointed star which encompassed most of the room. While Loretta

perched protectively on the arm of the lumpy chair, Max
installed himself importantly behind the desk which
filled up one point of the star. "Now, lady, who is trying
to kill you, and why, and how?"

Tatiana Petrovna Smith shrugged. "The who of it is
why I'm here. I don't know who. The why could be
anything. It depends on the who. The how is easy.
Whoever-it-is is trying to scare me to death." She sighed
and placed a slender white hand tipped with scarlet
fingernails on her bosom. "I have a weak heart."

Loretta clucked sympathetically and offered her roll of
Life Savers. Tatiana Petrovna took one and popped it
delicately between her lips. "If I had a clear mountain
pool," said Loretta, "I could scry out who your enemy is.
I used to do it all the time back home. It doesn't work so
good with city tap water. Too much chlorine, I guess. The
pictures are all fuzzy."

"Enemies, hah!" huffed the noble Tatiana. "I guess I
know who my enemies are. Every one of those alley cats
at the Wednesday mah-jongg would love to see me
rubbed out. They're all jealous."

"What about Mr. Smith?" asked Max.

"Who?"

"Mr. Smith. Your husband. Most murders are done by
relatives or close friends. This I read in the newspapers."

"Oh, him." Tatiana waved her hand dismissively,
flashing a large stone. "Poor dear Alexei. He died two
years ago. Fell off a golf cart in Miami and broke his neck.
I am inconsolable. As you see, I am still in mourning."
She adjusted the folds of her rustling black skirt the better
to display skinny ankles and scrawny calves shimmering
in black nylon.

"It suits you just fine," said Loretta.

"Thank you," said Tatiana.

"Alexei," mused Max. "Your husband was also a Russian aristocrat?"

Tatiana trilled with laughter. "Not Alexei, oh, no. But can you imagine *me* married to an Albert? I made him change his name before the wedding. It would have been twenty-five years tomorrow." She grew suddenly serious. "And that's the thing that's frightening me to death. I have received messages. In the middle of the night, the telephone will ring. I listen. First, there is just noise, a howling sound, inhuman, like fingernails on the blackboard only worse. 'Hello,' I say, 'who's there?' Then the voice, far away and tinny, like an old phonograph record. 'Tati?' it says, 'Tati, this is Al. I will see you soon. We will celebrate our anniversary together.' Well, if it's Alexei, where is he telephoning from? He's the only one who ever called me Tati. But I don't think it's Alexei. I think it's some nut trying to scare me. I went to the police but they told me to take it up with the phone company. And *they* told me to get an unlisted number."

"Wowee!" said Loretta. "I never heard tell of the spirits using the telephone before. But whyever not? Wouldn't it be great if we could just dial a number to raise the dead instead of all that hocus-pocus we have to do?" She bounced up and down excitedly on the arm of the chair, causing Tatiana Petrovna to wince. "Did you get his number, honey?"

"No. He always hangs up before I can say anything."

The telephone on the scarred oak desk jangled, and Max snatched up the receiver. "Yah?" he said. "Max Dwindle speaking." He listened for a moment, frowning, and then dropped his cigar in favor of a stubby pencil, nodded gravely and began making notes. After a few scribbles, he said, "Hokay, I'll have her call you back," and hung up the phone.

He turned to stare at Tatiana Petrovna. "You tell anybody you was coming here?" he demanded.

She shook her head. "I didn't even know myself until I got on the subway and saw your ad. I was on my way to Bloomingdale's. I figured if there was a chance I might kick off tomorrow, I wanted a new dress to do it in. New underwear, too." She smiled up at Loretta. "You know how it is, dear."

Loretta slid her bare feet into a pair of outsize yellow work shoes and brushed ineffectually at the paint stains on her ragged jeans. " 'Deed I do," she said.

Max blinked at the scrap of paper in his hand and then scowled at the woman in the chair. "I got here a telephone number. This guy on the phone says he's Al Smith and he wants you to lay off the heat—it's hot enough already where he is—and call him back. He'll tell you where to meet him tomorrow."

Tatiana Petrovna shrieked and fell back in the chair. Her already white face paled even more and she seemed to stop breathing. Loretta leaped to her feet and shrank away from the stricken woman.

"Max!" she cried. "Do something! Her aura is flickering! You know I can't stand dead bodies!"

Max trundled around the desk and approached Tatiana Petrovna with a glint in his eye. "Mouth-to-mouth," he muttered and bent over the arm of the chair. Behind him, the door opened.

"There must be a better way," said Peter Pine, drooping in the doorway. "I have ranged from Coney Island to the wilds of the Bronx and back again. I have been hustled, mugged, and graffitied." He turned and exhibited with some chagrin an illegible spray paint smear on the back of his toffee-colored, pinch-waisted leather jacket. "I have been set upon by ravening packs of schoolgirls and I have been interminably lectured by an Aesthetic Realist out of the West Fourth Street station. What's going on here?''

He eyed the prostrate form of Tatiana Petrovna and Max arrested in the act of engulfing her lips with his. Peter pressed his fingertips to his temples and cried, "Don't tell me! I got it! She's our first client and Max's famous Manischewitz love potion has backfired again."

"Wrong!" cried Loretta. "Well, half wrong anyway. She is our first client, Tatiana Petrovna Smith, but she's not swooning with passion. She's being scared to death."

Peter Pine strode into the room, slamming the door behind him. "Stand back," he ordered. "Let a real professional handle this. I'll soon have this poor woman in top form." He quickly arranged himself in the lotus position at Tatiana Petrovna's feet and began a loud muttering hum. Before he had chanted his mantra through twice, the unconscious woman fluttered her eyelashes and groaned.

"Foo!" she said, turning her face away from Max's hovering lips, "your breath smells of horrible old cigars. It's disgusting. Just like poor dear Alexei. I could never forgive him for that."

Max trudged back to his desk and dropped sulkily into his creaking chair. "Hokay, lady," he muttered. "I was only trying to help. You don't have to be insulting. You want this phone number or not?"

Tatiana Petrovna looked as if she might have a relapse. "I don't know," she quavered. She glanced at Peter Pine, still contorted on the floor and emitting his rumbling hum. "Who's this idiot and what's he doing?" she demanded.

Peter's eyes flapped open. "Madam," he announced, "Peter Pine, at your service. I have the answer to your problem. We'll all go to your place and hold a séance. Someone is trying to kill you. The spirits will tell us who it is."

"Oh, Peter!" cried Loretta, helping him to unwind his long legs from the lotus position. "We *know* that. It's so exciting! We have a telephone number to the spirit world!" She hauled him to his feet. "We don't have to hold séances anymore. We can just call them up. Isn't that right, Max?"

"Could be, could be." Max unwrapped a fresh cigar, but before lighting it, surreptitiously slipped a breath mint into his mouth. "Guy said if the line was busy to try again. Said he was calling from a phone booth in the fifth circle and there were lots of poor saps there trying to make contact." He turned to Tatiana Petrovna. "What do you think, lady? We charge fifty dollars a day plus expenses, like long distance phone calls."

Tatiana Petrovna drew a dainty black-bordered hankie from her handbag and patted her mascara. "I can't believe that poor dear Alexei would want to kill me."

"I can," muttered Max.

"Fifty dollars is a lot for staying alive just one day. But if I'm dead tomorrow, I don't have to pay. And if I live through the day, I'm safe. How much does it cost to call that place?"

Max shrugged. "Want me to ask the phone company?"

Peter Pine sat on the edge of Max's desk. "Mind if I take a look at that phone number?"

Max handed him the slip of paper and Peter studied it quietly, glancing from time to time at the face of the telephone dial.

"I still think I ought to get a new dress," said Tatiana Petrovna. "Just in case. Something bright and cheerful. Would you like to come along?" she asked Loretta.

"Sure thing. That'd be real nice."

"Madam," said Peter Pine, after scribbling a few calculations on the slip of paper. "Your birthday is in late summer. August or September. Correct?"

"Oh, right," she simpered. "August twenty-ninth. But I'm not telling which year."

"I make it 1935, but that doesn't matter. You're a Virgo. So far so good. The spirit who is trying to contact you was in life a Capricorn, and he's trying to warn you against a Scorpio. Or maybe it's the other way around. It's hard to tell from reading a phone number. But I think we're on the right track. You know any Scorpios or Capricorns?"

Tatiana Petrovna frowned. "Heavens! I don't know. I never paid any attention to that astrology stuff. I had a scarf once with all those funny signs on it, but I lost it. Isn't Capricorn a goat? That must be Alexei. He was an old goat, always chasing the young girls."

"When was his birthday?" asked Max.

"January third."

"Well, there you are," said Peter Pine. "Two out of three. Now all we have to do is figure out who the Scorpio is and what he's up to. I think you should dial that number."

"Wait a minute, boy genius," said Max, retrieving the slip of paper. "How do you figure all that from a telephone number? I'm looking at it and all I see is numbers plus now a lot of scribbles."

"Simple," said Peter Pine, "for anyone who knows the Tarot. Look at the area code—686. Change the numbers into a set of corresponding letters from the phone dial and you get the combination NUN. You can get other combinations, of course, but that's the only one that makes any sense. It's the name of the fourteenth letter of the Hebrew alphabet. You ought to know that, Max."

"Yah. I flunked Hebrew school."

"Anyway," Peter went on, "NUN correlates to the Tarot Key of Death which, in turn, falls under the Zodiac sign of Scorpio. Same with the rest of the telephone number. The first part—963—translates to YOD, the Hermit Key in

Virgo, while the last part—2946—spells out AYIN and
turns up the Devil card under Capricorn. It's easy when
you know how."

"Oh, Peter, you're wonderful," sighed Loretta. She
smiled at Tatiana Petrovna. "Don't you think he's wonderful?"

Tatiana Petrovna gripped the arms of the chair. "You
mean that really is Alexei calling? I won't talk to him. I
refuse absolutely to call that number."

From under Max's desk, a scrabbling sound was heard,
accompanied by a shrill squealing. "Oh, dear," said
Loretta. "Ralph's having nightmares again. It's all that
pizza he eats." She dropped to her knees and reached
under the desk, murmuring tender consolations. "Come
on out, baby. It's all right. It's only a dream. Loretta won't
let anyone hurt you." She drew forth a sleek gray bundle
with a thin, twitching tail and quivering translucent ears.

Tatiana Petrovna swallowed a shriek. "That's a rat,
isn't it?" she demanded. "A dirty, filthy, disgusting New
York City rat! You people are weird!"

"You were expecting maybe Dorothy and the Wizard of
Oz?" asked Max, grinning around his fresh cigar.

Cradled in Loretta's arms, Ralph the Rat regarded
Tatiana Petrovna balefully. He stretched his neck, encir-
cled by a leather collar studded with red stones, and
bared his teeth at her.

"Now you've hurt his feelings," said Loretta. "He's
very sensitive and not a bit dirty." She stroked Ralph's
head until he closed his eyes and nuzzled into the crook
of her arm.

"Well, I'm sorry I'm sure," said Tatiana Petrovna, "but
I don't quite see how a rat can help me."

Ralph's tail twitched, Loretta muttered a few twangy
words, and small toads began dropping out of the air and
showering the chair in which Tatiana Petrovna cowered.

"Stop it! Stop it!" she cried, batting toads out of her wig.

"That's always been one of my best spells," said Loretta proudly. "The Rain of Toads. Don't get to use it too often. Ralph's an awful good worker when it comes to toads." She waved her hand and the toads disappeared. "Didn't mean to scare you."

"Toads are all very well," said Peter Pine, "but they don't solve this lady's problem. She has received a death threat and our mission is to protect her and find out who is behind it."

Tatiana Petrovna nodded approvingly and readjusted her skirt to reveal knees that may once have been dimpled.

"I take it," Peter went on, "that you do not wish to be reunited with your beloved departed husband just yet."

"B-r-r-r," said Tatiana. "Maybe on some other anniversary, like the fiftieth or the one-hundredth."

"And you do not want to talk to the caller who left this phone number, whoever he may be?"

Tatiana shook her head. "To be perfectly honest, I couldn't care less about getting in touch with poor dear Alexei. I'm going to marry again next month, if I live, and I don't want to encourage him to keep calling me up. He was always very jealous."

"Nevertheless, we might learn something by calling this number. May I suggest, madam, that as your representative I place the call and try to ascertain the intentions of this restless shade?"

Tatiana shrugged. "No harm in that, I guess. Just so long as I don't have to talk to him or, God forbid, see him. I think I'd die if Alexei's ghost started hanging around."

"Very well." Peter Pine strode to the telephone and began dialing the number. The others settled down to eavesdrop on the conversation, Tatiana with a long white hand shading her eyes. Loretta hunkered down on the floor in the center of the pentagram with Ralph snoozing in her arms. Max Dwindle puffed away at his cigar and scowled reflectively into its swirling cloud of smoke.

Peter Pine, with the receiver pressed to his ear, listened to the distant and yet more distant clicking of relays. When at last the ringing signal sounded, he raised his hand and the eavesdroppers leaned toward him. The phone at the other end was answered on the second ring.

A voice, faint and hollow, said, "Tell her to meet me at the zoo in Prospect Park at noon tomorrow. I mean her no harm, but if she fails to keep this appointment, she will be in terrible danger."

"The zoo in Prospect Park," Peter repeated. "What kind of danger? Can you tell me anything else? How will she recognize you? In what shape will you materialize?"

But Peter's questions went unanswered. The receiver at the other end was replaced and the line went dead.

"The zoo!" cried Tatiana Petrovna. "Tomorrow! But I can't! It's Wednesday. He must know that. What about my mah-jongg?"

"Maybe you ought to skip it just this once," said Loretta.

"Hush," said Peter. "I'll try to get him back."

Peter dialed the number again and again, but each time the line was busy. "Well," he said finally, "I guess we all go to the zoo tomorrow."

"I haven't been to the zoo in years," said Tatiana Petrovna, "not since my Johnny was a little boy. He always loved animals." She smiled tenderly. "In fact, that's where I met poor dear Alexei. In the elephant house. I was teaching kindergarten in those days and had the whole class with me. Alexei bought peanuts for everyone, including the elephants. How sweet of him to remember."

"In that case," said Peter, "we'll meet at the elephant house. Twelve o'clock sharp. Agreed?"

Tatiana Petrovna arose from the lumpy armchair with a sigh of relief. "I'll be there," she said, "but I never heard of a ghost appearing in broad daylight. Don't they usually sneak up on you at midnight?"

"Time means nothing on the other side," said Peter. "The spirits use whatever avenues present themselves. If the zoo has strong associations for your husband, it will probably be easier for him to appear there than anywhere else."

"Well, then," said Tatiana, "I'm off to Bloomingdale's. I think a pair of Ralph Lauren slacks and a blazer would be just right for visiting the zoo. Are you coming?" She paused at the door and glanced back at Loretta, who was still sitting in the middle of the pentagram.

"Sure thing," said Loretta. She lay herself down, feet pointing south, head pointing north, crossed her arms upon her breast and closed her eyes. Ralph the Rat, disturbed from his nap, waddled away to his customary hiding place under the desk.

"Let's go," said Tatiana impatiently.

Loretta raised her head from the floor and opened her eyes. "I'm going," she said. "I was almost gone. You run along, honey, and I'll meet you there. Just watch for a kind of shimmer in the air over your head. That'll be me. It's a real kick to travel by astral body. No hassle, and it saves carfare." She resumed her trance position and said no more. A faint haze issued from her slightly open mouth and disappeared through the ceiling.

"Better hurry," said Max. "She'll get there before you do. If she gets bored, she might start shoplifting."

Tatiana stared at the supine girl. "What about tomorrow?" she asked. "I don't want to get to the zoo with nothing but astral bodies for company."

"Don't worry," said Peter. "We'll all be there. In the flesh. In the meantime, keep to a vegetarian diet and watch out for a tall blond man in a brown suit."

"What? What does that mean?"

"Beats me. It came to me in a flash. I just relay the messages." Peter picked up a stack of advertising flyers. "Come on. I'll take you to the subway. I want to cover the Lexington Avenue line before the rush hour starts."

The next day, Wednesday, was bright and clear, a perfect day for visiting the zoo. Dwindle, Peak and Pine arrived at Prospect Park in the heart of Brooklyn at fifteen minutes before the hour of noon. The elephants stood stolidly about their barred enclosure, moodily munching clumps of hay. Grave children with ice-cream-smeared faces stared at the beasts until their mothers called them away to see the funny monkeys or the playful seals in the pool at the center of the zoo.

The three psychic detectives sat on a shaded bench across from the elephant yard. Loretta yawned.

"Guess I stayed out too late last night, but I thought I ought to keep an eye on her until she went to bed."

"Anything happen?" asked Max. "Any more phone calls?"

"Nope. Not a peep. Her boyfriend came over for dinner and they watched television until he left. She sure looks different without her wig."

"Is he a tall blond man in a brown suit?" asked Peter.

"Heck, no. He's not much taller than Max and he's practically bald-headed. Wore a plaid jacket that like to give me a headache if I'd been there in person."

"What did they have for dinner?"

"She didn't eat much of anything. Too nervous, I guess. Looked like rabbit food to me. Come to think of it, I'm starving. Haven't had anything to eat since lunch yesterday."

"So far, so good," said Peter.

"So far, no good," said Max, staring morosely at the dial of a large gold watch he had pulled from the watch pocket of his ancient suit. "She's late. It's five after twelve."

"Hey," said Loretta. "That's funny. Look at those elephants."

The five or six elephants in the enclosure had gathered at the far end and settled onto their knees, heads together and tiny eyes closed. They looked like cumbrous gray football players in a huddle. As the three watched, one beast rose from the huddle and lumbered over to the iron fence nearest to them. He waved his trunk at them through the bars and said, "Psst. Come closer."

Loretta, in her excitement, transported instantly across the paved path to the elephant's side.

"Careful," muttered Max, following more sedately, with Peter slouching languidly along beside him.

"Who are you?" Loretta asked eagerly.

"I am he whom you seek," replied the elephant. "Got any peanuts?"

"I'll get some," cried Loretta and disappeared in her high-flown fashion.

"A bit flighty, isn't she?" remarked the elephant. "Where's my darling, my beloved, my bride of twenty-five years? Where's my Tati?"

Max Dwindle shrugged. "She's late. She must be coming by subway. Anything could happen."

"Ah, yes," the elephant sighed. "I used to think that waiting for the D train was sheer hell. But just imagine a subway platform crowded from edge to edge with poor damned souls waiting for a train that never comes. Why, it was only last week they put in the phone booth, one single phone booth for the entire fifth circle. Even Mr. Bell himself is allowed only a few seconds of use."

"Here you are!" cried Loretta, drifting in for a perfect two-point landing. She held out a white paper sack brimming with goobers. The elephant grasped them with his trunk and stuffed them, sack and all, into his mouth. He munched happily for a few moments, his eyes glazing in ecstasy.

"You're a good girl," he said, swallowing the last of the tidbit. "I'll recommend you to the boss."

"The boss?" breathed Loretta.

"You know, the guy with the pitchfork. He's turned into a lazy slob over the centuries and he won't appear for just anybody. I'll put in a good word for you."

"Thanks," said Loretta dubiously. "I'm not sure I—"

But the elephant trumpeted loudly and flapped his ears. "Here she comes!" he bellowed. "I knew she wouldn't stand me up! Isn't she beautiful?"

Dwindle, Peak and Pine turned to stare up the path. Prancing into view was a dainty figure got up in magenta slacks, bright green velvet jacket, and rhinestone-rimmed sunglasses. The whole ensemble was topped off by a feathery mass of copper-colored curls gleaming in the sun. In one hand, Tatiana Petrovna Smith carried a Bloomingdale's shopping bag.

She hurried up to the group at the elephant enclosure, breathless and apologetic.

"Sorry I'm late," she chattered, "but just as I was leaving, the United Parcel man arrived with a package. It was marked perishable, so I thought I'd better open it right away, and you'll never guess what was in it."

"Tati," murmured the elephant, but she ignored him and plunged a hand into the shopping bag. It came out holding triumphantly aloft a one-pound jar of caviar.

"Caviar!" she exulted. "The real Beluga! Isn't that wonderful? I would have taken it to the Wednesday mah-jongg and shown those cats a thing or two, but since

I was coming here instead, I thought we could have a picnic. I boiled some eggs and there's Melba toast in the bag. Caviar! I can't wait any longer."

She twisted the lid off the jar and reached into the bag for a spoon.

"Tati!" cried the elephant. "Don't eat it!"

"Alexei? Is that you?" Tatiana Petrovna looked around the park, ignoring the elephant who gazed at her pleadingly. "Where are you hiding? And why shouldn't I eat the caviar? You know how I love it." She dipped the spoon daintily into the jar.

"Tati!" the elephant bawled."Listen to me! It's poisoned! Take one bite and you're dead!"

"Nonsense," said Tatiana, finally realizing the source of poor dear Alexei's voice. "Why should I listen to an elephant? Who would poison a whole pound of caviar? It would be sacrilegious." She lifted the spoon to her mouth.

The elephant's trunk whipped out between the bars, dashing the spoon from her hand. Then it grasped the jar and withdrew to safety behind the bars.

"Alexei!" Tatiana pouted. "Give that back instantly! And what are you doing in that ridiculous disguise? Come out and face me like a man, and tell me what this is all about."

For a moment, it seemed that the elephant would return the jar to her outstretched hand. He glanced at her angry frown and her impatiently tapping foot, and his trunk uncurled the slightest bit in her direction. But then he sighed and shook his massive head.

"No, my dear," he murmured. "I don't think Hell is ready for you yet." The trunk, still holding the opened jar, rose in a gallant salute, and then dipped toward the elephant's mouth. The jar disappeared within. The elephant swallowed, shivered, shuddered, and belched.

Then with a sigh, it sank to its knees. "Farewell, Tati.
May you live forever." Alexei's voice was faint and
growing fainter. The elephant toppled over onto its side,
sending tremors through the ground beneath their feet.
Across the enclosure, the other elephants stirred uneasily.

"Al!" cried Max Dwindle. "Don't leave! You gotta tell
us who sent the caviar."

There was only a faint murmur of breeze that lifted the
hay in the enclosure and then was gone.

"The United Parcel man," Peter Pine demanded of
Tatiana "was he a tall blond man in a brown suit?"

"Well, they all wear brown uniforms, don't they?" said
she. "He was taller than I am, but I don't know about his
hair. He didn't take his cap off. He had a dirty yellow
moustache."

"You see!" said Peter, gloating. "I was right."

"Oh, Peter, you're wonderful!" exclaimed Loretta. "But
who bought the caviar and poisoned it?"

"We'll never know," lamented Max, "unless we can get
Al back."

"Don't try," said Tatiana. "I've had enough communing
with spirits. What if he comes back as an alligator next
time?"

"Mother! Mother!"

Hurried footsteps pit-patted along the paved pathway,
and an agitated young man scurried up to them and
enfolded Tatiana in a bear hug.

"Oh, thank God you're all right! When I found out I left
school immediately and took the train and went straight
from the station to your Wednesday mah-jongg. I was sure
you'd take it there and I'd find a dozen poisoned tile
pushers. But they were alive and well, and told me you'd
come here. It was Mary Ann, my fiancée, but it's my fault
for telling her so much about you, your habits, and your
royal lineage and the money I would inherit one day. She

couldn't wait. As soon as we graduate next month, she wants us to get married and set up a joint practice, Smith and Smith, Veterinary Clinic. She's very ambitious. But last night, she got a little tipsy. We were celebrating her birthday and she told me what she had done. So I got on the train right away, and here I am to save you. Where's the caviar? We'll need it for evidence. There'll be finger-prints on the jar."

"Oh, Johnny," sighed Tatiana. "After all I told you about girls. And now your father is dead."

"He's been dead for two years."

"Again," said Tatiana, gesturing sadly at the fallen elephant.

"What's wrong with that poor pachyderm?" the young man demanded.

"I just told you. He's dead. He ate the caviar."

"Oh, my God!" cried the young man. "There was enough cyanide in it to kill an elephant!"

"Exactly," said Max. "And how come you know so much? Did your girlfriend tell you? Or did you put it there yourself?"

"When's your birthday?" Peter queried. "If your girl-friend's was yesterday, that makes her a Gemini and we're looking for a Scorpio."

"His birthday is November fourth," said his mother. "I'll never forget. It was such a difficult birth. And he was such a greedy baby."

"Aha!" said Peter. "We've got him! The Scorpio."

"Oho!" said Max, "a rotten kid."

"Still greedy," said Loretta, "after all these years."

"Hey! Wait a minute," said plain John Smith. "You've got it all wrong. I came to save her. What kind of son would do in his dear little mother just to get married and start a veterinary practice? Who are you guys anyway?"

"Dwindle, Peak and Pine," said Max, "and we'll show you who we are. Take him up, Loretta."

"Hoo boy!" shouted Loretta, grasping the young man about his slightly pudgy waist and quickly levitating above the tops of the surrounding trees. "Ready to 'fess up?"

The young man howled, "Put me down! Put me down!"

"Right now?" asked Loretta, loosening the grip of her sturdy country arms.

The young man screeched, and from the other side of the zoo the monkeys answered in unison.

"I did it! I did it!" the young man chittered, sounding more simian than the monkey chorus. "Now can we get down?"

Loretta settled gently down and deposited the limp young man on the bench under the tree. "Shame on you," she said. "After all your mother's done for you, sending you to vet school and all."

Plain John Smith hung his head in mortification. "I know, I know," he said. "I am ashamed. That poor elephant died because of me. But I'll make it up to him. I'll become a veterinary missionary. I'll go live alone in the African veldt and minister to his fellows in the wild until I have removed the stain of pachydermicide from my conscience. Farewell, Mother. I'll be back in about ten or twenty years." The young man slunk away, followed by the mournful bellowing of the remaining elephants, who now gathered around their defunct companion.

Tatiana Petrovna Smith shook her head. "That kid always was an oddball. Well, how about some hard-boiled eggs? At least we know they're not poisoned."

"Don't mind if I do," said Loretta. "I'm starving."

LILIAN JACKSON BRAUN

A Cat Too Small for His Whiskers

C ompared to other country estates in the vicinity, Hopplewood Farm was not extensive. There was just enough acreage to accommodate the needs of Mr. and Mrs. Hopple and their three children—an eight-bedroom house and six-car garage; swimming pool, tennis court, and putting green; a stable with adjoining corral, fenced with half a mile of split rail; a meadow just large enough for Mr. Hopple to land his small plane; and, of course, the necessary servants' quarters, greenhouse, and hangar.

The house was an old stone mill with a giant waterwheel that no longer turned. Its present owners had remodeled the building at great cost and furnished it with American antiques dating back two centuries or more. Twice it had been featured in architectural magazines.

The Hopples, whose ancestors had been early settlers in America, were good-hearted, wholesome people with simple tastes and a love of family and nature. They enjoyed picnics in the meadow and camping trips in their forty-foot recreation vehicle, and they surrounded themselves with animals. Besides the four top Arab mares and the hackney pony, there were registered hunting dogs in a kennel behind the greenhouse, a hutch of Angora rabbits, some Polish chickens that laid odd-colored eggs,

and—in the house—four exotic cats that the family called
the Gang.

Also, for one brief period there was a cat too small for
his whiskers.

The Gang included a pair of chocolate-point Siamese, a
tortoiseshell Persian, and a red Abyssinian. Their pedi-
grees were impressive, and they seemed to know it. They
never soiled their feet by going out-of-doors but were
quite happy in a spacious suite furnished with plush
carpet, cushioned perches, an upholstered ladder, secret
hideaways, and four sleeping baskets. Sunny windows
overlooked the waterwheel, in which birds now made
their nests, and for good weather there was a screened
balcony. Four commodes in the bathroom were inscribed
with their names.

When the cat who was too small for his whiskers came
into the picture, it was early June, and only one of the
Hopple children was living at home. Donald, a little boy
of six with large wondering eyes, was chauffeured daily
to a private school in the next county. John was attending
a military academy in Ohio, and Mary was enrolled in a
girls' school in Virginia. Donald. John. Mary. The Hopples liked plain, honest names rooted in tradition.

On their youngest child they lavished affection and
attention as well as playthings intended to shape his
interests. He had his own computer and telescope and
video library, his child-size guitar and golf clubs, his little
NASA space suit. To the great concern of his father, none
of these appealed to Donald in the least. His chief joy was
romping with the assorted cats in the stable and telling
them bedtime stories.

The subject was discussed one Friday evening in early
June. Mr. Hopple had just flown in from Chicago, following a ten-day business trip to the Orient. In his London-
tailored worsted, his custom-made wing tips, and his

realistic toupee, he looked every inch the successful entrepreneur. The Jeep was waiting for him in the meadow, and his wife greeted him happily and affectionately, while his son jumped up and down with excitement and asked to carry his briefcase.

Then, while little Donald showered and dressed for dinner, his parents enjoyed their Quiet Hour in the master suite. Mr. Hopple, wearing a silk dressing gown, opened an enormous Dutch cupboard said to have belonged to Peter Stuyvesant and now outfitted as a bar. "Will you have the usual, sweetheart?" he asked.

"Don't you think the occasion calls for champagne, darling?" his wife replied. "I'm so happy to see you safely home. There's a bottle of D.P. chilling in the refrigerator."

Her husband poured the champagne and proposed a sentimental toast to his lovely wife. Mrs. Hopple had been a national beauty queen twenty years before and still looked the part, whether wearing a Paris original to a charity ball or designer jeans around the farm.

"First tell me about the small fry," Mr. Hopple said. "They've been on my mind all week." The Hopples never called their children "kids."

"Good news from John," said his wife, looking radiant. "He's won two more honors in math and has made the golf team. He wants to attend a math camp this summer, but first he'd like to bring five schoolmates home for a week of fishing and shooting."

"Good boy! He has a well-balanced perspective. Is he interested in girls as yet?"

"I don't think so, dear. He's only ten, you know. Mary is having her first date this weekend, and it's with an ambassador's son—"

"From which country?" Mr. Hopple cut in quickly.

"Something South American, I believe. By the way, she's won all kinds of equestrian ribbons this spring, and she wants our permission to play polo. Her grades are excellent. She's beginning to talk about Harvard—and business administration."

"Good girl! Someday it will be Hopple & Daughter, Inc. And how is Donald progressing?"

Mrs. Hopple glowed with pleasure. "His teacher says he's three years ahead of his age group in reading, and he has a vivid imagination. We may have a writer in the family, dear. Donald is always making up little stories."

Mr. Hopple shook his head regretfully. "I had hoped for something better than that for Donald. How much time does he spend with his computer and his telescope?"

"None at all, I'm afraid, but I don't press him. He's such a bright, conscientious child, and so good! Cats are his chief interest right now. The calico in the stable had a litter last month, you remember, and Donald acts like a doting godfather. Sometimes I think that he may be headed for veterinary medicine."

"I hardly relish the prospect of introducing 'my son the horse doctor.' I'd rather have a writer in the family." Mr. Hopple poured champagne again. "And how is the household running, dear?"

"The week was rather eventful, darling. I've made a list. First, it appears there was a power outage Wednesday night; all the electric clocks were forty-seven minutes slow on Thursday morning. There was no storm to account for it. I wish there had been. We need rain badly. Ever since the outage, television reception has been poor. The repairman checked all our receivers and can find nothing wrong. The staff is quite upset. The houseman blames it on secret nuclear testing."

"And how is the staff otherwise?" The Hopples never referred to "servants."

"There are several developments. Both maids have announced that they're pregnant. . . . I've had to dismiss the stableboy because of his bad language. . . . And the cook is demanding more fringe benefits."

"Give her whatever she asks," Mr. Hopple said. "We don't want to lose Suzette. I trust the gardeners are well and happy."

Mrs. Hopple referred to her list. "Mr. Bunsen's arthritis is somewhat worse. We should hire another helper for him."

"Hire two. He's a loyal employee," her husband said. "Is the new houseman satisfactory?"

"I have only one complaint. When he drives Donald to school he alarms the boy with nonsense about Russian plots and visitors from outer space and poisons in our food."

"I'll speak to the man immediately. Were you able to replace the stableboy?"

"Happily, yes. The school principal sent me a senior who speaks decently. He's well mannered and has just won a statewide science competition. He may have a good influence on our son, dear. Today Donald wore his NASA suit for the first time."

"That's promising. What's the boy's name?"

"Bobbie Wynkopp. He lives in the little house beyond our south gate."

"Remind me to inquire, dear, if he's noticed any trespassers in the south meadow. I saw evidence of a bonfire when I came in for a landing this afternoon. I don't object to picnickers, but I don't want them to start grass fires in this dry weather."

A melodious bell rang, and the Hopples finished dressing and went downstairs to dinner.

Donald appeared at the table in his little white Italian silk suit, basking in his parents' approval and waiting eagerly for the conversation to be directed his way. After the maid had served the leeks vinaigrette, Mr. Hopple

said: "Well, young man, have you had any adventures
this week?"

"Yes, sir," the boy said, his large eyes sparkling. "I saw
a weird cat in the stable." Elevated on two cushions, he
attacked the leeks proficiently with his junior-size knife
and fork, crafted to match the family's heirloom sterling.
"I don't know where he came from. He's got long whiskers." Donald held up both hands to indicate roughly
eighteen inches.

"That sounds like a fish story to me," said Mr. Hopple
with a broad wink.

Donald smiled at his father's badinage. "It's true. He's
too little to have such long whiskers. He's weird."

His mother said gently: "Young cats have long whiskers
and large ears, darling. Then they grow up to match
them."

Donald shook his head. "He's not a kitten, Mother. He
acts grown-up. Sometimes his whiskers are long, and
sometimes they're short. He's weird. I call him Whiskers."

"Imagine that!" his father said, striving to maintain a
serious mien. "Retractile whiskers!"

Donald explained: "They get long when he's looking
for something. He sticks his nose in everything. He's
nosy."

"The word we use, darling, is *inquisitive*," his mother
said quietly.

"His whiskers light up in the dark," the boy went on with
a sense of importance as his confidence grew. "When he's
in a dark corner they're green like our computer screens.
And his ears go round and round." Donald twirled his
finger to suggest a spinning top. "That's how he flies. He
goes straight up like a helicopter."

A swift glance passed between the adults. "This Mr.
Whiskers is a clever fellow," said Mr. Hopple. "What
color is he?"

Donald thought for a moment. "Sometimes he's blue. Most of the time's he's green. I saw him turn purple yesterday. That's because he was mad."

"Angry, darling," his mother murmured. "And what does the new stableboy think of Whiskers?"

"Bobbie couldn't see him. Whiskers doesn't like big people. When he sees grown-ups he disappears. Whoof! Like that!"

Mrs. Hopple rang the bell for the next course. "And what kind of voice does this wonderful little animal have, dear? Does he scold like the Siamese or meow like the other cats?"

Donald considered his reply while he properly chewed and swallowed the last mouthful of leek. Then he erupted into a loud babel of sounds: "AWK AWK ngngngngng hhh-hhhhhhhhhhhh beep-beep-beep beep beep-beep AWK."

The maid's eyes expressed alarm as she entered the dining room to remove the plates, and she was still regarding Donald with suspicion when she served the next course.

At that moment the boy shouted: "There he is! There's Whiskers!" He pointed to the window, but by the time the adults had turned their heads to look, Whiskers had disappeared.

The main course was the kind of simple provincial dish the Hopples approved: a medley of white beans, lamb, pork ribs, homemade sausages, herbs, and a little potted pheasant. Their cook, imported from the French wine country, would have nothing to do with microwave ovens or food processors, so they had built a primitive kitchen with a walk-in fireplace to keep Suzette happy. The cassoulet that was now served had been simmering in the brick oven all day. With it came a change of subject matter, and the meal ended without further reference to Whiskers.

After dinner Donald performed his regular chore of feeding the Gang—taking their dinner tray upstairs in the glass-enclosed elevator, rinsing their antique silver drinking bowl (attributed to Paul Revere), and filling it with bottled water. Meanwhile his parents were served their coffee in the library.

"You were right about the boy," Mr. Hopple remarked. "His imagination runs away with him."

His wife said: "Donald's story is probably an elaboration on an actual occurrence. No doubt the cat is a stray, perhaps the runt of a litter, unwanted, and thrown out of a passing car."

"You have an explanation for everything, sweetheart. And you are so efficient. Did you make any plans for the weekend?"

"No, darling. I knew you'd be coping with jet lag. But I invited the gardener's grandchildren to have lunch with Donald. They're his own age, and he needs to meet town children occasionally."

On Saturdays the Hopples usually breakfasted in festive style in the conservatory, but both maids were suffering from morning sickness the next day, so the family trooped into the kitchen. There they sat at an ancient wooden table from a French monastery, under a canopy of copper pots and drying herbs, while Suzette cooked an omelette in a long-handled copper skillet over an open fire.

After breakfast Donald said: "Mother, can I take some of the Gang's catfood to the kittens in the stable?"

"*May I*, darling," she corrected softly. "Yes, you may, but ask yourself if it's advisable to spoil them. After all, they're only barn cats."

"Two of the kittens are very smart, Mother. They're as smart as the Siamese."

"All right, Donald. I value your opinion." After he had scampered away, Mrs. Hopple said to her husband: "See?

The Whiskers story was only a fantasy. He's forgotten about it already. . . . By the way, don't forget to ask Bobbie about the bonfire, dear."

Her husband thanked her for the reminder and went to buzz the stable on the intercom. "Good morning, Bobbie. This is Hopple speaking. We haven't met as yet, but I've heard good reports of you."

"Thank you, sir."

"Since you live near the south gate, I'm wondering if you've observed any trespassing in the meadow. Someone had a bonfire there, and that's bad business."

"No, sir. Never saw anything like that," the new stableboy said, "but I've been away for three days at a science conference, you know."

"If you notice any unauthorized activity, please telephone us immediately—any hour of the day or evening."

"Sure thing," said Bobbie.

"One more question: Have you seen any . . . *unusual* cats in the stable or on the grounds?"

"Only a bunch of kittens and an old mother cat."

"No strange-looking stray with long whiskers?"

There was a pause, and then the young man said: "No, I only heard some funny noises—like a duck quacking, and then some kind of electronic beep. I couldn't figure where it came from."

"Thank you, Bobbie. Keep up the good work."

Mr. Hopple flicked off the intercom and said to his wife: "Donald is making those ridiculous noises in the stable. How long should we allow this to go on before consulting the doctor?"

"Darling, he's just playing games. He'll grow out of it soon. It's common for young children to invent imaginary friends and have conversations with them."

"I can assure you that *I* never did," said her husband, and he went to his study, asking not to be disturbed.

Before noon the houseman took the Mercedes into town to pick up the Bunsen twins, a boy and a girl. Mrs. Hopple welcomed them warmly and gave them a picnic basket in which the cook had packed food enough for twelve children. "Wear your beeper, Donald darling," she reminded him. "I'll let you know when it's time to bring your guests back."

Donald drove the twins to the meadow in the pony cart. Having observed his father in social situations, he played the role of host nicely, and the picnic went smoothly. No one fell down. No one picked a fight. No one got sick.

When Mrs. Hopple beeped her son, he drove his guests back to the house with brief detours to the dog kennel, rabbit hutch, chicken coop, and horse stable.

"Did you have a nice time?" Mrs. Hopple asked the excited twins.

"I ate four chocolate things," said the boy.

"My mother told me to say thank you," said the girl.

"I saw a snake," the boy said.

"We saw Whiskers," the girl said.

"He's green!"

"No, he's blue with green whiskers."

"His eyes light up."

"Sparks come out of his whiskers."

"He can fly."

"Really?" said Donald's mother. "Did he say anything to you?"

The twins looked at each other. Then the boy quacked like a duck, and the girl said: "Beep beep beep!"

Mrs. Hopple thought: Donald has coached them! Still, the mention of sparks made her uneasy. Living so far from town, the Hopples had an understandable fear of fire. She left the house hurriedly and rode a moped to the stable.

Bobbie was in the corral, exercising the horses. Donald was unhitching the pony. The barn cats were in evidence, but there was no sign of a creature with red-hot whiskers. Her usual buoyant spirit returned, and she laughed at herself for being gullible.

On the way back to the house she overtook the head gardener, laboring arthritically up the hill, carrying a basket of tulips and daffodils. She rebuked him kindly. "Mr. Bunsen, why didn't you send the flowers up with one of the boys?"

"Gotta keep movin'," he said, "or the old joints turn to ce-ment."

"Mr. Hopple is arranging to hire some more help for you."

"Well, 'twon't do no good. Nobody wants to do any work these days."

"By the way, you have two delightful grandchildren, Mr. Bunsen. It was a pleasure to have them visit us."

"They watch too much TV," he complained. . . . "Look; it that grass turnin' brown. No rain for ten days! . . . Somethin' else, too. Some kind of critter's been gettin' in the greenhouse. Eats the buds off the geraniums. And now the tractor's broke. Don't know what happened. Just conked out this afternoon."

"You must call the mechanic early Monday morning," Mrs. Hopple said encouragingly. "Ask for priority service."

"Well, 'twon't make no difference. They come when they feel like it."

The gardener's grouchy outlook had no effect on Mrs. Hopple, who was always cheerful. Mentally reciting a few lines of Wordsworth, she carried the flowers into the potting shed, a room entirely lined with ceramic tile. There she was selecting vases from a collection of fifty or more when a commotion in the nearby kitchen sent her hurrying to investigate.

Suzette was standing in the fireplace—which was now

cold and swept clean—and she was banging pots and
pans and screaming up the chimney. From the cook's
raving—three parts English and two parts French—it
appeared that a *diable* up on the *toit* was trying to get
down the *cheminée* into the *cuisine*.

Mrs. Hopple commended the cook on her bravery in
driving a devil off the roof but assured her that the
chimney was securely screened and nothing could possibly enter the kitchen by that route, whether a raccoon or
squirrel or field mouse or devil.

Back in the potting shed she found a silver champagne
bucket for the red tulips and was choosing something for
the daffodils, when the buzzing intercom interrupted.

"Tractor's okay, Miz Hopple," said the gardener.
"Started up again all by itself. But there's some glass
busted out in the greenhouse."

She thanked Mr. Bunsen and went back to her flowers,
smiling at the man's perverse habit of tempering good
news with a bit of bad. As she was arranging daffodils in
a copper jug, Donald burst into the potting shed. "I
couldn't find you, Mother," he said in great distress. "The
rabbits are gone! I think somebody stole them!"

"No, dear," she replied calmly. "I think you'll find
them in the greenhouse, gorging on geranium buds. Now,
how would you like strawberries Chantilly tonight?" It
was the family's favorite dessert, and Donald jumped up
and down and gave his mother a hug.

Later, she said to Suzette, speaking the cook's special
language: "I'll drive to the *ferme* and pick up the *fraises*
and the *crème*." Mrs. Hopple liked an excuse to breeze
around the country roads in the Ferrari convertible with
the top down. Today she would drive to the strawberry
farm for freshly picked fruit and to the dairy farm for
heavy cream.

First she ran upstairs to find a scarf for her hair. As she

passed the door of the Gang's suite, she heard Donald making his ridiculous noises and the cats replying with yowling and mewing. She put her hand on the doorknob, then decided not to embarrass her son by intruding.

When she returned a moment later, silk-scarved and cashmere-sweatered, Donald was leaving the suite, looking pleased with himself.

"Are you having fun, darling?" she asked.

"Whiskers was in there," he replied. "He was climbing around the waterwheel, and he looked in the window. I let him in. He likes our cats a lot."

"He likes them *very much*, darling. I hope you closed the window again. We don't want the Gang to get out, do we?"

Blithely Mrs. Hopple went to the garage and slipped into the seat of the Ferrari. She pressed a button to lift the garage door and turned the key in the ignition. Nothing happened. There was not even a cough from the motor and not even a shudder from the big door. She persevered. She used sheer willpower. Nothing happened.

The houseman had not returned with the Mercedes after taking the twins home, but there were three other cars. She climbed into the Rolls; it would not start. The Caddy was equally dead. So was the Jeep.

Something, she thought, is mysteriously wrong. The houseman would blame it on the KGB or acid rain.

Resolutely she marched back to the house and confronted her husband in his study, where he was locked in with computer, briefcase, and dictating machine. He listened to her incredible story, sighed, then went to inspect the situation, while Mrs. Hopple did a few deep-breathing exercises to restore her equanimity.

"Nothing wrong," he said when he returned. "The cars start, and the doors open. I think you need a change of scene, sweetheart. We'll go out to dinner tonight. Wear your new Saint Laurent, and we'll go to the club. Suzette can give the boy his dinner."

"We can't, darling. We're having strawberries Chantilly, and I promised Donald."

So the Hopples stayed home and enjoyed an old-fashioned family evening. Dinner was served on the terrace, followed by croquet on the lawn and corn-popping over hot coals in the outdoor fireplace. Donald made no mention of Whiskers, and his parents made no inquiries.

Early Sunday morning, when the June sunrise and chattering birds were trying to rouse everyone at an abnormal hour, the telephone rang at Hopplewood Farm.

Mr. Hopple rose sleepily on an elbow and squinted at the digital clock radio. "Four-thirty! Who would call at this ungodly hour?"

Mrs. Hopple sat up in bed. "It's five twenty-five by the old clock on the mantel. There's been another power failure."

Her husband cleared his throat and picked up the receiver. "Yes?"

"Hi, Mr. Hopple. This is Bobbie Wynkopp. Sorry to call so early, but you told me—if I saw anything . . ."

"Yes, Bobbie. What is it?"

"That place in the meadow that was burned—how big was it?"

"Hmm . . . as well as I could estimate from the air . . . it was . . . about ten feet in diameter. A circular patch."

"Well, there's another one just like it."

"What! Did you see any trespassing?" Mr. Hopple was fully awake now.

There was a pause. "Mr. Hopple, you're not gonna believe this, but last night I woke up because my room was all lit up. I sleep in the attic, on the side near the meadow, you know. It was kind of a green light. I looked out the window. . . . You're not gonna believe this, Mr. Hopple."

"Go ahead, Bobbie—please."

"Well, there was this aircraft coming down. Not like your kind of plane, Mr. Hopple. It was round, like a Frisbee. It came straight down—very slow, very quiet, you know. And it gave off a lot of light."

"If you're suggesting a flying saucer, Bobbie, I say you've been dreaming—or hallucinating."

"I was wide awake, sir. I swear! And I don't smoke. Ask anyone."

"Go on, Bobbie."

"The funny thing was . . . it was so *small!* Too small to carry a crew, you know, unless they happened to be like ten inches high. It landed, and there was some kind of activity around it. I couldn't see exactly. There was a fog rising over the meadow. So I ran downstairs to get my dad's binoculars. They were hard to find in the dark. The lights wouldn't go on. We were blacked out, you know. . . . Are you still there, Mr. Hopple?"

"I'm listening. What about your parents? Did they see the aircraft?"

"No, but I wish they had. Then I wouldn't sound like some kind of crazy. My mother works nights at the hospital, and when Dad goes to bed, he flakes right out."

"What did you see with the binoculars?"

"I was too late. They were taking off. The thing rose straight up—very slow, you know. And when it got up there . . . ZIP! It disappeared. No kidding, I couldn't sleep after that. When it got halfway daylight I went out to the meadow and had a look. The thing scorched a circle, about ten feet across. You can see for yourself. Maybe you should have it tested for radioactivity or something. Maybe I shouldn't have gone near it, you know."

"Thank you, Bobbie. That's an extremely interesting

account. We'll discuss it further, after I've made some inquiries. Meanwhile, I'd consider it classified information if I were you."

"Classified! Don't worry, Mr. Hopple."

"Was that the stableboy?" his wife asked. "Is anything wrong?. . . *Darling, is anything wrong?*"

Mr. Hopple had walked to the south window and was gazing in the direction of the meadow—a study in preoccupation. "I beg your pardon. What did you say? That boy told me a wild story. . . . Ten-foot diameter! He's right; that's remarkably small."

There was a loud thump as a six-year-old threw himself against the bedroom door and hurtled into the room.

"Darling," his mother reminded him, "we always knock before entering."

"They're gone! They're gone!" he shouted in a childish treble. "I wanted to say good morning, and they're not there!"

"*Who's* not there, darling?"

"The Gang! They got out the window and climbed down the waterwheel!"

"Donald! Did you leave the window open?"

"No, Mother. The window's *broke*. Broken," he added, catching his mother's eye. "The glass is kind of . . . *melted!* I think Whiskers did it. He kidnapped them!"

She shooed him out of the bedroom. "Go and get dressed, dear. We'll find the Gang. We'll organize a search party."

Mrs. Hopple slipped into a peignoir and left the suite. When she returned, a moment later, her husband was still staring into space at the south window. "Donald's right," she said. "The glass has actually been *melted*. How very strange!"

Still Mr. Hopple stared, as if in a trance.

"Dearest, are you all right? Did you hear what Donald said?"

Her husband stirred himself and walked away from the window. He said: "You can organize a search party if you wish, but you'll never find the Gang. They're not coming back. Neither is Whiskers."

He was right. They never came back. The two smartest kittens in the stable also disappeared that night, according to Donald, but the rabbits were found in the greenhouse, having the time of their lives.

Life at Hopplewood Farm is quite ordinary now. Garage doors open. Cars start. Television reception is perfect. Only during severe electrical storms does the power fail. No one lets the rabbits out of the hutch. The tractor is entirely reliable. Nothing tries to sneak down the chimney. Window glass never melts.

And little Donald, who may suspect more than he's telling, discusses planets and asteroids at the dinner table and spends hours peering through his telescope when his parents think he's asleep.

JUSTIN SCOTT

The White Death

The cat had little use for dogs, but he liked action.
Comings and goings around the farm beat the long nothing times in between. So when the new dogs arrived in
big red, white, and blue Air France crates peppered with
air holes, the cat was on hand for the opening.

The humans were excited. They'd been tearing their
hair since the coyotes got into the sheep. There weren't
even supposed to be coyotes in Connecticut, but suddenly
there were, big, mean, and hungry. They were averaging a
lamb a night and twice they'd taken a ewe. The humans
called them a vicious pack. They cat knew better. He had
done a little prowling himself and had observed, carefully, that they were not a pack, but a family—three
nearly grown male pups and a mother and father, who
seemed quite devoted to each other. Whether they were
vicious involved subtleties that did not interest the cat.
But the fact was, the coyotes regarded anything they
could catch and overpower as dinner, which was why the
humans had sent away for three dogs specially trained in
France to protect sheep.

The cat expected standard poodles, for his only experience with French dogs was his old housemate Roger, an
enormous poodle who was so old that his teeth were
falling out; the cat often found them in odd corners, worn
smooth like pebbles in the stream.

Instead, out of the Air France crates came three monsters as unlike old Roger as hawks from a chicken. White as clouds, big as lawn tractors and armed with teeth you had to see to believe, they glowered about suspiciously. Attaining another perspective atop the pickup truck, the cat named the newcomers White Death One, Two, and Three to keep track of them. Even the humans were awed until, apparently satisfied no coyotes were lurking, White Death One, Two, and Three wagged their extravagant tails. Then there was a bit of applause and checking names and showing them their beds in the barn and throwing sticks and Frisbees. The cat went indoors for a nap.

With the White Death roaming the farm, that night not a sheep was killed. And when the neighbor's dog was discovered dead in the morning, the humans said the coyote pack had attacked him instead. Family, thought the cat, they're not a pack, they're a family, mother, father, three big pups. A vicious pack, the humans said, the poor dog didn't have a chance.

The cat failed to understand the tragedy. The poor dog in question was a vicious brute who had taken pleasure in annihilating rabbits, chipmunks, and cats. Things had worked out rather nicely, in fact.

The following morning, the sheep were fine and another neighbor's dog had been killed. The coyotes, the humans said, were getting desperate. One of these days they would run into the wrong dog. There was even talk of lending out the White Death. The cat went for a look at the body.

Another miscreant sent to a well-deserved grave. Curiously, though, the coyotes hadn't eaten him, just torn out his throat as neatly as if the vet had done it with his knife. "What are you looking at?" yelled a human with a shovel, obviously put out at losing his dog.

Nothing, the cat mumbled to himself and walked away.

Things were quiet for the next few nights, sheep zero, dogs zero, coyotes zero. The coyotes had gone, the humans said, which was not true. They were quiet, mulling things over. The cat could smell them and had come upon one of their kills, some dumb possum they'd caught in the open. Accordingly, he maintained cautious habits, paying particular attention to the wind direction, avoiding open spaces and, when he had to cross them, first plotting escape routes which, with coyotes, meant trees. There was no point in seeking cover they could dig up. It was trees or nothing.

Meanwhile, the White Death formed a routine of sleeping most of the day in the barn, waking occasionally to frolic with the children, doze in the sun, and eat. The cat felt their eyes on him at odd moments and made a habit of staying out of their way. Nonetheless, he had a nasty scare, thanks to the human mother who was as fast as a snake sometimes. She scooped him off the warm hood of the pickup and started one of her amusing (to her) waltzes around the yard with him in her arms, right up to the White Death, singing which of them would like the next dance, dangling him like a morsel of fresh liver. When the cat went rigid, she laughed and hugged him and said, "They won't hurt you, cat, they are very well trained. Aren't you?" she asked, and all three White Death looked up with complexity in their beady black eyes.

The humans were discussing another dead dog with a neighbor who drove up in a station wagon. Throat torn out again, the cat discovered when he went to check. A big golden retriever, dog enough to feed a whole coyote family. But his body was unmarked except, the cat noticed on closer inspection, for a crushed leg. The dog had put up a fight, all right.

It started to rain and the cat headed home, thinking

things over, and regretting his curiosity. He had come a
long way and he was getting wet. He broke into a smooth
miles-eating gait and took a shortcut across a broad
hayfield. He had known that dog, hadn't cared for him
one way or another, just a dog too fat to chase cats.

Protracted thinking was not his strong suit. His mind
ran more toward quick decisions, quickly forgotten. He
got so tangled in his thinking that he practically broke a
leg falling over a startled chipmunk. Calculating the
hours until dinner, he thought what the hell and started
after a snack. The chipmunk had a head start and dove
into a hole. Digging him out in the rain sounded muddy.
He was just turning away, when he sensed a rush from
behind.

Dumb, he thought, pressing flat instinctively in the wet
grass, *you deserve to die*. The coyote, thank the moon,
flew over him like a golden express train. And die he
would have, had it been the father coyote instead of a
clumsy pup. Leaping twelve feet, the cat hit the grass
running, searching frantically for a tree, which experience
told him tended to be scarce in hayfields. *Dumb, dumb,
dumb*. The coyote was after him, yapping, covering
ground fast, calling his relations. Ahead was a stone wall
and beyond the wall another empty hayfield. He leaped
onto the wall and ran along it. The coyote practically
howled for joy at how slow he went, and gathered his
skinny legs for a killing jump. The cat located the hole he
was hoping for and dove into a little cave among the big
stones. He crouched inside, catching his breath, lowering
his heartbeat, while the coyote family gathered, raging
with frustration.

Other than being alive, the cat was not pleased. Rain-
water was dripping on his back. The moon alone knew
how long it would take a family of starving coyotes to get
bored, for starving they were, all skin and bones and

teeth. He hated sleeping wet. Outside the coyotes paced. Inside, the cat heard a hiss and tracked the sound through the dark until he saw a snake coiled in a corner. He had had just about enough. Spreading his foreclaws and baring his teeth, he snarled, "Screw off, scurf head!"

The snake blinked and slithered away, disappearing into a crack like a tongue between teeth.

When he got home that night, the human mother scooped him up and nearly crushed the life out of him, crying, "Thank God! I thought the coyotes got you. They killed two more dogs. I thought they'd got you, too. Poor baby, you're wet! Are you hungry?"

The cat allowed he was and the human mother heaped so much chicken in his dish that old Roger the poodle moseyed out to see what he would leave. "Don't even think about it," said the cat and Roger said, "Okay," and lay down to watch him eat, which made the very good chicken taste even more delicious.

Roger lay there, his milky eyes aglow with misguided hope, his ancient stomach rumbling, his failing ears pricking feebly at the sounds of the night.

"Coyotes," the cat explained. "Four miles."

"Right," Roger lied. "I thought so."

The cat ate some more. Roger's ears flailed about.

"Great-barred owl."

"I know."

Pan-Am's New York-to-Boston shuttle flew over, five minutes late, and the cat said, "Pickup truck on the wooden bridge."

"Right."

The cat sighed. "Listen, Roger, do me a favor."

"What?"

"Don't go out at night."

"Why not?"

"Just don't go out at night."

"I only go for a little walk. You know that. Oh, you think the coyotes will take a shot at me? Forget it. I don't go far. Besides, we've got the Great Pyrenees protecting us."

"Yeah."

The cat did not have a great memory. Most days started off new for him and he often delighted in discoveries like blue sky, white clouds, trees, even the taste of food. He got through the serious parts of life by instinct: his body knew to duck a flying coyote, which actually worked faster than thinking about it. But he possessed certain core memories in addition to instinct—four memories to be exact. One had to do with the smell of the human mother, which sometimes made his knees go weak. The other three all involved Roger. He had slept on Roger's huge dome of a head when he was a kitten, warm in its woolly fuzz. Roger would lie there, without moving for hours in front of the fire while the cat slept. Then, one day when he was grown and rarely noticed Roger, a fast and nasty little terrier caught him in the open and it looked bad until with a bone-chilling bay Roger came galloping from the house, a Roger he had never seen before, with long teeth and murder in his eye. As far as he knew, the terrier was still running. The third memory was vintage Roger. Some wit from New York visiting the humans had remarked that if his miniature poodle could jump over a sofa, perhaps a big standard like Roger could clear the garage. To the cat's astonishment, Roger had tried, twice, which was why the cat said, "Roger, let's just stay in, tonight. Okay?"

"Okay. But just tonight. I need my exercise."

The cat sat up with him until Roger fell asleep and the humans locked the door. It took a while and he got a later start then he had hoped, but it couldn't be helped. He slipped out, using an upstairs bathroom window instead of his cat door, in case the killer was watching.

He observed the farm from the gutter, his back to the house lights, until his eyes had adjusted fully to the dark. The sheep were grazing. He could hear their chopping at the grass. The White Death had set up their usual perimeter, one between the house and the sheep, two pacing the rim of the outer field. Every fifteen minutes or so one conferred with the other two and sometimes they exchanged positions. Once, they seemed to lay a trap, two falling back to the house, the third hiding among the sheep, white and woolly as they, tempting the coyotes to try something. The coyotes weren't buying it. The cat heard them on the wind, five miles off, at least. After two hours, the White Death changed tactics, huddling for a strategy conference before sending one of their number off into the dark.

The cat, whose hearing was superb when he remembered to listen to it, overheard their strategy and started out after the Great Pyrenees. It was White Death Two, whose rangy silhouette the cat recognized flitting through the trees.

He found it tough keeping up, at first. The big dog was putting distance between himself and the farm and the cat had to run flat out at a pace he thought he couldn't hold more than two miles. He hung in for three before the beast slowed to sniff the wind. The cat climbed gratefully onto a low tree limb to rest. A minute later, the dog was off like a shot. The cat tore after him, heart pounding, and juggling the thought that he might become the first cat in the state of Connecticut to die of overwork. He was very much considering giving the whole thing up.

Two more clogging miles and he concluded that the dumb dog he was following was genuinely after the coyotes. He could smell them and hear them. What White

Death Two couldn't seem to understand was that the
coyotes had no intention of letting him get within a mile
of them. The cat didn't know how they did it in France,
but here, if you really wanted to surprise a family of
coyotes you had better approach downwind. The cat
called it a night and went home.

He awakened stiff and sore late in the afternoon to
angry humans shouting. The replacement dog at the
neighboring farm, a highly trained German attack hound,
had been killed, which pleased the cat mightily. As he
knew that both the coyote family and White Death Two
had been miles away, his suspects were reduced to White
Death One and Three. On the other hand, he worried
about what would happen if he trailed the wrong dog
tonight and Roger took a walk. Fortunately, Roger was
exhausted, having spent the entire day watching the cat
sleep, which gave the poodle pleasures the cat could not
begin to fathom.

The White Death repeated the same strategy that night
and soon the cat found himself following the designated
hunter, the barrel-chested White Death One, the biggest of
the three. He started off slowly into the night, the cat
pacing him easily. It was a little scary, knowing there was
a fifty-fifty chance that this was the killer.

A mile from the farm he veered toward a wood that
bordered a horse farm with a Doberman pinscher. The
new Doberman pinscher, the cat recalled, the original, a
truly horrible dog, having mislaid his throat. The cat got
too close in his eagerness, and for an eerie second White
Death One slowed and stared in his direction. The cat
assumed the shape of a bent hemlock. The dog kept
moving. When he came to the edge of the woods, close
enough to the stables for the cat to hear the horses
whispering, the white dog suddenly dropped to his belly,

opened his toothsome mouth in a mighty yawn, and went to sleep.

The cat felt his jaw fall. White Death One was a slacker. He wasn't chasing coyotes, he was sleeping. The cat climbed a shaggy maple and stretched out to watch from a limb. An hour after the moon set, the Great Pyrenees got up, loped home, and reported to his colleagues that the coyotes had eluded him.

White Death Three, the one with the scariest light in his black eyes, sneered that One and Two were sorry excuses for hunters. He would make a sweep and settle the coyotes' hash once and for all. White Death One suggested that Three button his lip while he still had one. Both dogs went stiff-legged, hackles rising like wire, and for a pleasant moment the cat thought there would be bloodshed. But White Death Two shouldered between them with a prissy reminder that they had come a long way from a fine French school to do an important job. "This isn't about you or me, it's about the sheep." This made no sense to the cat, but One and Three mumbled abashed apologies and resumed patrol.

So Three was the killer, thought the cat. Lean, rangy Two couldn't catch a coyote in a million years and barrel-chested One was asleep at the switch. Three had a screw loose. Three was going out and killing dogs instead of coyotes. Why, the cat didn't know and didn't care, though it occurred to him that if, as the humans claimed, dogs and coyotes were so closely related they could mate—and there was a truly awful picture—maybe White Death Three just couldn't tell them apart.

The humans had come home late. The pickup truck was still warm. He climbed onto the tire under the front fender and luxuriated in the heat of the ticking engine. He had a marvelous thought. White Death Three could go on for years, killing every dog in the county, while the

humans blamed the coyotes. How pleasant, how lovely.
But what got him onto this subject? He felt a slight
disquiet. Something had ... Oh, moon! Roger. Poor,
dumb, stupid, old Roger. One of these nights White Death
Three would kill Roger. And the cat liked Roger, for some
damned reason he couldn't remember at the moment.
Stupid dog. Wouldn't have a chance, even if it was true
that he had been in the Navy. He said he was a commando
with the Navy SEALS. Strongest bite in the Sixth Fleet or
some stupid thing. Bit the propeller off a submarine. Now
all he did was drop teeth. He hadn't a chance against
White Death Three. Slowly, it all drifted back to the
cat—the soft, fuzzy head, the terrier, the garage.

The pickup engine started with a roar. The cat jumped
up, banged his head hard on the fender and scrambled off
the rolling tire. Moon! He had fallen asleep and hadn't
heard them get in.

"Look out for the cat," the human mother said.

"Damned fool cat can look out for himself. Roger, you
stay up on the porch 'fore them coyotes get ya." The truck
roared down the drive, throwing gravel on the cat, and
when it was quiet enough to hear again, the cat wandered
onto the porch where Roger was mumbling, "I'm not
staying on the porch. I'm going for a walk."

"Yeah, I'll walk with you to the barn," said the cat.

"No, I'm going for a real walk."

White Death Three was out there, and it was no night
for a walk. "Let's just walk to the barn."

"You walk where you want, Cat. I'm going for a walk."

"The coyotes—"

"Did I ever tell you I was a commando?"

"Nightly, for seven years."

Roger didn't hear him. "I could take any three coyotes
they can field."

"What if all five come?" asked the cat, knowing that

there was no way he could explain White Death Three to dumb Roger.

"I would hear them coming in time to get back to the porch, taking you with me. All right?"

"Amtrak Metroliner, southbound," the cat lied.

"I know. I hear it."

They were at the barn and Roger showed no sign of stopping and the cat was wondering what to do with him when White Death One loomed suddenly from behind a feed crib. "Where you going, boys?"

"For a walk," said the cat. "What does it look like?"

"I wouldn't wander too far," White Death One replied. "Least until we finish off the coyotes." Fat chance, Sleeping Beauty, thought the cat.

"We'll keep an ear cocked," said Roger, breezing by the Great Pyrenees. The cat had to admire Roger's sense of self. Dumb, he certainly was, but he was a classy act, taking no guff from some foreign fieldhand. White Death One fell into pace alongside.

"Okay, I'll cover you."

"No need," said Roger.

The cat, thinking of White Death Three roaming the dark and five coyotes roaming the dark, said, "Suit yourself." To his relief, the huge white guard dog stayed with them.

After a mile of walking and sniffing, Roger asked, "Who's watching the sheep?"

"Two's plenty."

The cat's mind was drifting. With the moon down, there wasn't a lot to see. He could smell the coyotes on the wind. And he could hear them, talking quietly among themselves three miles off. He was listening for White Death Three, listening for the sounds of a short scuffle and sudden death as the killer nailed another farm dog.

He felt safe as long as One was here. Three wasn't about to kill Roger in front of One.

One had gotten quiet. He and Roger had been talking at first, trading war stories, Roger going on about some escapade in the Mediterranean and One about wolf tracking. He admitted that he and his colleagues thought the coyotes were a bit of a joke, having tousled with mountain wolves.

"Then how come they're still out there?" the cat had asked and One got very quiet. They had stopped in a small clearing. The cat was picking up strange sounds and went up a beech tree to try to get a fix on them. It was the coyotes, closer now, two miles, and whispering, urgently. The cat climbed higher, until he could hear the conversation.

"It's the white dog, again.The dumb one, Crazy Eyes." Three, thought the cat. Crazy Eyes was Three. Tracking coyotes instead of killing dogs. What in moon was going on?

"If that dumb Crazy Eyes ever learns to attack from downwind, we're in trouble," growled the coyote mother.

"I have half a mind to rip his head off before he does."

"There are easier ways to earn a living, son. Let's go, everyone. Make tracks."

"Damn. Where's Big Chest?" Big Chest would be Two.

"Patrolling the farm."

"Where's Sleepy Head?"

"Sleeping, probably."

"I said make tracks. Head down that stream."

The cat looked down from his tree limb. Roger was sitting on his haunches, smiling at the dark. He had apparently interpreted the coyote talk as the UPS van on a late-night delivery. White Death One was standing behind him, slowly wagging his tail. And he didn't look one bit sleepy.

The cat dropped from the tree, landing on stinging feet.
"Let's go home, Roger."

"In a minute."

"Fight much in the Navy?" asked White Death One.
Roger looked at him. "No." He was moving his jaw side
to side, working a loose tooth with his tongue.

The cat heard the coyotes splashing down the stream
bed, a quarter mile off, which paralleled the deer trail
they were on. Cocking his ears, he heard White Death
Three moving further away, tracking the coyotes in the
wrong direction. You really had to wonder about that
French dog school.

The cat nuzzled up to Roger, rubbed his leg and
whispered very softly, "Roger, this dog is a psychotic
killer. He's killed every dog in the neighborhood and now
he's going to kill you."

"What did you say? Why are you mumbling?"

The cat glanced at White Death One, whose tail was
starting to swish in a weird rhythm. White Death looked
down at him and the cat thought, You know that I know,
you misery. You did spot me tonight. You just pretended
to sleep.

He tried to whisper another warning to Roger.

White Death One snarled, "Why don't you go home,
you little reptile?"

"Don't bother the cat," Roger said mildly. "He can't
help himself."

"What the hell is that supposed to mean?" the cat
demanded.

"Get out of here while you still can," said White Death
One.

"Leave the cat alone," said Roger, standing up and
facing the big Pyrenees.

This stupid dog, thought the cat, is going to try to gum
this killer to death on my behalf. He said, "Roger, I'm

running down to the stream for a drink. Come with me."

"I'll wait."

"Come with me. I can't see too well in the dark."

Roger laughed. "You've got eyes like a cat. Okay, okay, I'll come." They started through the brush, the cat leading at a brisk trot, the Great Pyrenees trailing close.

They were still downwind of the coyotes, but at an angle, and any minute they would catch the dog scent or White Death One would hear them. It was now or never.

The cat bolted to the stream and ran up the bed, leaping from rock to rock. Around a bend, he came face to face with the golden eyes of a hungry coyote.

"Your mother mates with dogs."

The cat spun on his tail and raced back downstream.

They howled after him. The mother coyote forged ahead of her husband and sons, screaming, "I'll eat your liver, cat."

The cat scrambled from mossy stone to slippery log to cold wet gravel, then up the bank, through the brush and smack into Roger, whom the Great Pyrenees had backed against a tree.

The cat was pleased to see the old poodle's instincts were still good, covering his back, but otherwise he looked helpless and utterly bewildered that White Death One would want to hurt him.

Tail thrashing, the Great Pyrenees poised to spring, so intent on murder that he didn't hear the coyotes until they had burst into the clearing. For one long second, no one moved. Then the cat jumped on Roger's back, said, "Jump!" and sunk his teeth in.

Roger gathered his old bones and jumped. The fact was he had made a pretty good shot at the garage, attaining the gutter the second try, and the cat felt that if there had only been a garage there in the woods, he might have made it this time. He jumped so high and so far that the cat nearly

fell off. He saved himself with his claws, causing old
Roger to jump again and leaving White Death One alone
in the clearing with five angry coyotes.

The cat longed to stay for the carnage, but he feared
Roger would get lost and blunder back into it, so he
stayed aboard, nipping the old dog to steer him home,
and sometimes just for the fun of it.

White Death Two and Three were at the house. The cat
waited for the sounds of battle to die down.

"Your partner said he needs some help, couple miles
down the deer path. He said one of you go now, the other
wait five minutes."

Crazy Eyes charged into the night. Three minutes later
Big Chest roared after him.

"I didn't hear that," said Roger, collapsing on the
porch.

"With a little luck, we'll end up with maybe one Great
Pyrenees and no coyotes."

"But I didn't hear him say that."

"Maybe you missed it when the train went by."

JAMES HOLDING

A Visitor to Mombasa

Sergeant Harper of the Mombasa Police was daydreaming about Rebecca Conway when his telephone rang. He reached a long arm for the instrument on his desk. "Yes?"

"Constable Jenkins here, sir. Waterfront Detail."

"What is it, Jenkins?"

"I've got a queer one, sir. Probably nothing in it, but I thought I ought to report it." Jenkins was new to the job and anxious to play everything safe.

"What is it?" Harper repeated.

"Man named Crosby, sir. Works near the end of the causeway, a night watchman. He claims he saw a leopard sneaking across the causeway into town last night. Or this morning, rather. Just before dawn."

"A leopard!" Harper's voice held surprise.

"Yes, sir." Jenkins waited respectfully for Harper's reaction.

It came promptly. "Fellow was drunk," Harper said.

"I thought of that, sir." Jenkins sounded worried now, but continued. "Crosby admits to a couple of pints on the job during the night. But he swears he saw a leopard. Walking across the causeway from the mainland, bold as brass. He couldn't see the cat's spots, it was too dark, but he says he could see the shape all right for just a moment, and he's sure it was a leopard."

Harper said, "We've had no sighting reports this morning from anyone. Which we surely would have by now, if a leopard's on the loose. Anyway, thanks, Jenkins. I'll look into it." He hung up.

Harper leaned back in his desk chair. He damned the sticky heat of his cramped office and the gullibility of all police recruits. A leopard in Mombasa—he snorted. Tsavo, Nairobi and Amboseli Parks weren't far away, of course, but no, the hell with it. He went back to picturing the bright Scandinavian beauty of Lieutenant Conway's wife.

Ten minutes later, his telephone rang again. The constable on switchboard duty said, "A lady calling about a leopard, sir. Insists on speaking to someone in authority."

Harper groaned. "Put her on."

The lady, a Mrs. Massingale, reported seeing a creature she was sure was a leopard at daybreak that morning.

"Where?" Harper asked.

"Right here in Mombasa, Sergeant!" Mrs. Massingale said indignantly. "The least we could expect in this godforsaken city, it seems to me, is protection against wild animals wandering freely about the streets!"

"I meant," explained Harper with exaggerated patience, "just where in Mombasa did you see this leopard?"

"On the old railway line near Mbaraki Creek. Our cottage isn't fifty feet from the line. I happened to look out a rear window this morning at daybreak and there was this black shadow slinking along the ties. I caught its silhouette quite clearly for a moment. It was a leopard."

"Thanks for reporting it, Mrs. Massingale," Harper said. "I'll look into the matter promptly."

"See that you do!" She hung up with a muted crash that made Harper grin.

Two reports. So perhaps there *was* a leopard in Mombasa, unlikely as it seemed. Harper stood up, a tall, solidly built man with a heavy black moustache and an air of general frustration which he made no attempt to conceal.

The frustration was easily explained, even understandable, in a man of his type. He had come late to police work after a long career as a white hunter in Tanganyika before *uhuru*. Now, after being mildly famous in East Africa, he found himself all at once a lowly sergeant of police, reduced to obeying the orders of Lieutenant Conway, a stuffy man, ten years his junior, who was married, damn his eyes, to the most beautiful woman in Mombasa.

Harper stepped two paces from his desk to the city map taped on his office wall. A leopard reported on the causeway just before dawn—he put a fingertip on the map at the end of the causeway. A leopard reported on the railway line near Mbaraki Creek at daybreak—he touched the spot with another fingertip, and regarded the space between his fingertips narrowly. Yes, he decided, it's quite possible.

Suddenly he felt a surge of cheerfulness. Dealing with a leopard was work he knew. Still looking at the wall map, he tried consciously to put himself inside the spotted skin and the narrow skull of a leopard, to think as the cat might think, to forecast the movements of the killer he had come to know so well on a hundred safaris.

Suppose, he mused, the leopard was an accidental fugitive from one of the nearby game reserves. The unexpected sight of a long bridge, deserted and comfortably dark, might well have aroused enough feline curiosity in the leopard to make it venture out upon the causeway. Once there, a drift of scent across the water from dockside cattle pens, perhaps, may have drawn it on in quest of meat. Harper could picture vividly the silent cat, padding cautiously across the causeway, nostrils twitching with finicky distaste at the odors of diesel fuel and rotting refuse that vied with the cattle smell over Kilindini Harbor.

Having crossed the bridge, finding no direct route to the cattle scent that drew him, and suddenly surrounded by the strange effluvia of a large city, the leopard would rapidly become confused and frightened, Harper theorized. The beast's curiosity and hunger would be forgotten in an instinctive urge to find cover quickly in this unfamiliar terrain.

The cat, Harper felt, would therefore turn aside from the wide vulnerable expanse of Makupa Road into the comparative seclusion of the deserted railway line, stepping delicately along the ties through the industrial section of town to Mbaraki Creek, where Mrs. Massingale had caught a fleeting glimpse of him. Thence, it seemed obvious from the map, the leopard might be expected to come out on the bluffs overlooking the sea at Azania Drive, footsore now, apprehension growing as the daylight strengthened, the need for cover reaching panic proportions.

Azania Drive; Harper tried to recall the configuration of the land just there where the railway line bisected the Drive. It was a bleak and lonely stretch of the seaside road, as he remembered it, meandering along the bluffs past an ancient Arab watchtower and bearing little resemblance to the fashionable Azania Drive which also yielded a view of the sea to the Oceanic Hotel, the golf club, and scores of comfortable residences beyond. At that place on Azania Drive, above the ferry, a grove of baobab trees stood, defying the sea winds, Harper remembered.

He nodded to himself, utterly intent, thinking with a sense almost of excitement that the thick twisted foliage of those baobab trees just possibly might offer welcome sanctuary to a frightened leopard.

He turned his back to the map. His next step was clear. He should delegate Constable Gordon in the squad room to go at once and check out the baobab trees on Azania Drive for a stray leopard. Gordon would welcome the action, and he was an excellent shot, too, Harper knew. Yet, after the stimulating exercise of mentally plotting the leopard's probable whereabouts in Mombasa, Harper was reluctant to turn the hunt over to somebody else before he, himself, had even sighted the game. He needn't be in at the kill, he told himself. On safari, he had always turned the final shot over to his clients—he was used to that—but he *did* want to mark down the target with certainty before yielding the kill to another. Aside from his thus far unsuccessful campaign to make Rebecca Conway unfaithful to her pompous husband, this city leopard hunt was the most exciting thing that had happened to Harper since he joined the police force.

Yielding to temptation, he reached for his hat, took field glasses from the shelf under his wall map, and strode into the squad room. "Back in a few minutes, Gordon," he told the constable in passing. "Take over until Lieutenant Conway gets in, will you?" Conway never showed for duty until nine o'clock. Yet who could blame him, Harper thought enviously, with the voluptuous Rebecca to keep him at home until the last moment?

He felt the sweat start the moment he stepped out of headquarters into the compound. He climbed into one of the two police cars parked there, a Land Rover. As he turned out of the police compound and headed for Azania Drive, the sun had already warmed the driver's seat so that the cushions burned him, even through his trousers.

A hundred and fifty yards short of the baobab trees on

Azania Drive, he stopped the Land Rover, parked it beside the road and walked slowly toward the trees. The field glasses hung on their strap about his neck. It was still only a little after eight. Traffic was very light on Azania Drive.

He waited until the road was empty both ways before he stepped from it onto the springy turf that ran like a shaggy carpet along the landward side of the road, solidly covering the acre of ground under the baobab grove. He walked carefully to within thirty yards of the trees, then stopped and brought the glasses up to his eyes and examined carefully the twisted branches and tangled foliage of the baobabs. He saw nothing that looked even remotely like a leopard.

After five minutes, he moved across the road, still well clear of the trees, and walked another fifty yards to a position from which he could comb the grove from a different angle. He swept the glasses slowly from tree to tree, conscious of growing disappointment as they failed to find what he sought.

The glasses were trained on the last of the trees—a gnarled giant closer to the road than its neighbors—when suddenly, with the sense of electrical shock that accompanies an unexpected explosion, he found himself gazing through the magnifying lenses at two merciless yellow eyes which seemed disembodied in the tree's sun-dappled shade.

He breathed an exclamation that was part admiration for the magnificent cat, whose savage stare transfixed him, part satisfaction at his own astuteness in locating the beast.

Carefully he marked the tree and the cat's position in it. Then he withdrew to his Land Rover and drove away, whistling softly to himself and thinking he should have brought a rifle with him when he left headquarters. Still, he hadn't really expected there was a chance in ten that he'd find the leopard in the grove of baobab trees, he justified himself.

All the same, the cat was there!

Harper felt like celebrating, all at once, his frustrations temporarily forgotten. He had brought off a surprising feat, really: tracking a wild leopard ... mentally ... through several miles of sprawling city to a specific lair. His mood was one of exhilaration.

This is what I am good at, he reflected, this is what I was meant to do—not piddling along at a stinking little police job in a dirty city, but working with wild animals, somehow, somewhere, in free, open country, tracking them down and killing them, or working to preserve them from extinction, no matter which, so long as the job was useful and, yes, dangerous. He'd made a horrible mistake when he gave up hunting animals for hunting men. If he could only convince Rebecca Conway to go with him, he'd leave Mombasa tomorrow for Nairobi, Uganda, Australia, India, Alaska—anywhere away from the imperious beck and call of Rebecca's impossible, intolerable husband.

He'd asked her a dozen times to leave the fool she was married to and join him in a new free life somewhere else; but Rebecca only smiled at his pleading, kissed him lightly on the cheek like a sister, called him an aging Lothario (at forty-one!) and quoted Shakespeare at him about preferring to bear those ills she had than fly to others that she knew not of. She was flattered by his passion for her, of course, yet she was too fond of her idle, easy life in Mombasa as Conway's wife to risk it lightly.

Harper decided to drive back to headquarters by way of the center of town. That would give him a little extra time to savor his success with the leopard; to anticipate the soon-to-come thrill of squeezing off the perfectly aimed

shot that would rid Mombasa of its dangerous visitor in
the baobab tree. Fifteen minutes delay in finishing off the
leopard would make no difference to anyone, so far as he
could see. The leopard was treed well off the road. It was
still frightened, edgy, and hungrier than ever, no doubt,
yet posed no threat, Harper knew, to passersby on Azania
Drive unless someone approached its tree.

His memory played back to him one of the warnings he
had always issued to hunters on safari: remember that a
treed leopard, if hungry, frightened, or wounded, will
usually attack anything that moves beneath it. So why
would anyone approach that baobab tree? Harper was the
only person in the city who could possibly have any
interest in it.

The high crenellated battlements of Fort Jesus loomed
on his left above the crimson blossoms of a flame tree as
he passed the Mombasa Club. In the center of the turn-
about, the bust of King George caught the morning sunlight and seemed to wink at Harper as he tooled the Land
Rover around the circle and into Prince Arthur Street.

At police headquarters, he remembered to park his car
in the compound off the street, even though he intended
to use the Land Rover again at once, as soon as he secured
a rifle from the gun case in his office. That was one of
Lieutenant Conway's silly rules, if you like: that the curb
before headquarters must be kept clear and free at all
times, so that if the wooden building ever caught fire,
there would be ample space for the fire-fighting apparatus
to park there!

Thinking of Lieutenant Conway and, inevitably, of
Rebecca, Harper's leopard-inspired high spirits drained
rapidly away. The exhilaration of ten minutes ago had
turned to creeping depression by the time he reached his
office; the elation of winning a guessing game with a
leopard lost its edge. If Rebecca refused him one more

time, he swore to himself, he'd throw up this bloody job, anyway, and go off without her.

He unlocked his gun cabinet and took down one of his old rifles, unused since his last safari five years ago. As a special favor, Lieutenant Conway had allowed him to keep this personal weapon as an addition to the headquarters' arsenal. Harper was glad of it now.

He put ammunition into his pocket, relocked the gun cabinet, and was turning for the door when his telephone rang. Impatiently he paused by his desk, scooped up the receiver and said, "Yes?"

"Some fellow wants the lieutenant," the switchboard man said.

"Then give him the lieutenant," snapped Harper. "I'm busy."

"Lieutenant's not in yet, sir." The constable was apologetic.

Harper glanced at his watch. It was not yet nine o'clock. "Who's calling the lieutenant?"

"He won't say, sir. Says it's confidential and urgent. Native, I believe, and he speaks Swahili."

"Put him on."

The caller's voice was male, low-pitched, sounded very young. "Who is this?" it asked.

Harper said, "Sergeant Harper. Lieutenant Conway is not here. What do you want?"

"The reward, sir," the young voice whispered. "The reward offered by your lieutenant."

"What reward?"

"For arrow poison, sir. For the names of Wakamba doctors who make arrow poison against the new law."

"Oh." Harper remembered that Conway had been trying for six months to discover which of the Wakamba witch doctors were still manufacturing arrow poison, and thus contributing to massive native slaughter of the game in

the reserves. The arrow poison of the Wakamba was made
from tree sap; it smelled like licorice; it left a black
discoloration in the wound; and it was capable of killing
a bull elephant in fifteen minutes.

Harper said, "Have you earned the reward?"

"Yes, sir. I have two names for Lieutenant Conway."

"Who are they? I'll tell the lieutenant."

"No names," the young Wakamba murmured, "until
the reward is given. Not until then."

Harper grinned. "Don't trust us, is that it?"

The boy was silent.

"We'll give you the reward first, in that case. All right?
What's your name?"

"I have no name," said the young voice very formally.
"I am risking death to give the lieutenant this information,
sir. My own people will kill me if they learn of it."

Harper tried it another way. "Where are you calling
from?"

"The Golden Key."

Harper knew the Golden Key, a disreputable bar immediately across the Nyalla Bridge. Used to be called the
Phantom Inn because natives would dress up in sheets
and act the ghost to startle customers. "You a houseboy
there?" he asked.

"No, sir."

Harper hefted his rifle, impatient to go after his leopard.
"How can we arrange to give you the reward if you won't
tell us who you are?"

"Very simple, sir. I will meet the lieutenant in private.
He brings me the reward. I give him the names of the
poison makers."

Harper considered for a moment. "Where do you want
the lieutenant to meet you?"

"Where no Wakamba can see me talking to a po-
liceman." Simple and clear.

"When?" asked Harper.

"Today, sir, please. This morning, if possible. I need the reward very badly, sir. Otherwise, of course . . ." His voice, touched with desperation now, trailed off.

"All right, then," Harper said. "*I'll* meet you and bring the reward, since the lieutenant isn't here just yet. How much were you promised?"

"Ten pounds, sir." Eagerness now. "That will be good. Where shall I meet you?"

The Wakamba boy's simple question seemed to echo and reecho in a strange pervasive way inside Harper's head, and the idea that was born in his mind at that instant seemed to make his heart shift position in his chest. He sank into his desk chair, clutching the rifle on the desk before him with one hand.

He took a deep breath and said, "You know the old Arab watchtower, boy? Below Azania Drive near the ferry?"

"Yes, sir."

"I'll meet you there in an hour. Or Lieutenant Conway will, if he comes here soon enough. You can make it in an hour, can't you?"

"Yes. But remember, please, I dare not be seen, sir. Azania Drive is very public. Is there no more private place we can meet?"

"That's private enough." Harper was brusque. "Don't use Azania Drive to get there, come up the shore line on the beach under the bluffs. No one will see you. No one ever goes there, to the tower."

"Very well," said the soft boyish voice. "I'll be there, sir. One hour."

"Good," Harper said. His hand was sweating on the rifle stock. After he hung up, he dried his palms on the jacket of his uniform. He glanced again at his watch: 9:10. Conway was later than usual today.

He rose and put the rifle back in the wall cabinet. Then, pretending to be busy over a stack of reports, he sat quietly at his desk until he heard Lieutenant Conway's fussy voice in the squad room, greeting Constable Gordon as he passed through to his office.

Harper waited a moment or so before walking into Conway's room.

"Morning, Sergeant," Conway said briskly. "Something on your mind?"

Harper told him about the telephone call from the young Wakamba informer who wouldn't give his name. "Now you're here, sir," he finished matter-of-factly, "I expect you'll want to meet the boy and get his information yourself, since it's your pigeon, so to speak."

"Of course." Conway rubbed his hands together in a gesture of satisfaction that Harper found extremely irritating. He was exultant, his high voice almost a crow of pleasure as he went on. "So the clever lad, whoever he is, has a couple of witch doctors' names for me, does he? Quite a feather in our cap, Sergeant, if we can clear up this arrow-poison business at last, eh? Where am I supposed to meet him?"

Harper said quietly, "At the Arab watchtower below Azania Drive. It's private enough to quiet the boy's fears of being seen, I thought, yet within easy reach for us. You know it, of course?"

"Certainly I know it. An admirable choice, Sergeant. There and back in fifteen minutes without unduly wasting the taxpayers' time, eh? There's an old track down the bluff to the tower's base as I remember it."

"Right, sir. You can park by the grove of baobab trees on Azania Drive and go straight through under the trees to the cliff edge, where the track goes down."

"I must remember to take the boy's money. What time did you tell him you'd be there?"

"As soon as I could. He seemed anxious to get it over with. He's been at considerable risk, he claims."

"I'll leave at once." Lieutenant Conway stood up. "Take charge here, Sergeant." He strutted from the room, calling loudly to the cashier outside to give him ten pounds at once.

That was at 9:20. At 10:15 the call came.

"A motorist on Azania Drive just called in, sir," the switchboard man said. "Says he saw a fellow lying under a tree up there, covered with blood, as he was driving past. Stopped to see if he could help. Got to within fifty feet of the man under the tree and saw he was dead, so he called us."

"Dead!" Harper kept his voice level. "How could he tell from fifty feet away?"

"No face left, sir," the switchboard man said, as though he were reporting a shortage of beer in the commissary icebox. "Bundle of bloody flesh and shredded clothes, the motorist says. As though the fellow'd been mauled by a leopard, maybe." The constable cleared his throat. "Any chance, sir, it could have been the leopard the lady reported earlier?"

"Possible," Harper said. "Where'd he telephone from?"

"The nearest house. He'll stand by until one of our chaps gets there, he says."

"Fine. Hope he has enough sense to keep people out from under that tree where the dead man is. Where is it on Azania Drive?"

"Near the old Arab watchtower. There's a grove of baobab trees just there . . ."

"Right," Harper said. "I'm on my way. Better take a rifle, I guess. Give any calls for me to Constable Gordon."

Surprisingly, when he reached the baobab grove and drew up behind Conway's parked car, there was no one in view nearby save for the motorist, a man named Stacy, who had telephoned headquarters. Greeting Harper's arrival with obvious relief, he said he'd managed to send curiosity seekers—only a handful so far—quickly about their business by telling them there was a wild leopard loose in the grove.

"Good work," grunted Harper, stepping from his car. As though drawn by magnets, his eyes went to the ghastly figure lying asprawl under the nearest tree. Then, in a voice that sounded shocked even to him, he said, "From the looks of that poor chap under the tree, I'd say you were right about the leopard, Mr. Stacy."

Stacy swallowed hard. "I was sick in the ditch when I saw it," he said. "Then I ran like hell and called you."

Harper nodded and reached into the back of the Land Rover for the rifle. "So let's see what we can do about it," he said. "Get across the road, away from the trees, will you, Mr. Stacy, and handle anybody else who may stop to gawk?"

Stacy was more than glad to withdraw across the road.

Harper knew where his target was. For Stacy's benefit however, he was forced to carry on a pretended search of the baobab tree. He moved to various vantage points, left and right of the tree, the rifle held ready. At length, he suddenly raised a hand to Stacy and nodded vigorously, as though he had at last located the cat.

As indeed he had. Even without the field glasses, he had no trouble zeroing in on those blazing eyes turned unblinkingly toward him; and even without the field glasses, he could see quite plainly the streaks and spatters of blood on the savage muzzle. Lieutenant Conway's blood, he told himself with grim satisfaction.

He brought up the gun, steadied his sights on the small target and squeezed off his shot.

Instantly, a squalling cyclone of spotted hide and sheathed claws fell out of the tree, crashing through the baobab foliage. At the crack of the shot, a widow bird rose from the top of a neighboring tree and flapped slowly away, trailing its long black feathers. Harper wondered if that was a sign. When the leopard struck the ground, only a few feet from its mangled victim, it was quite dead.

"You got him!" yelled Stacy from across the road, his voice thin from excitement, "Bravo!"

Harper didn't take his eyes off the leopard, holding the gun ready for a second shot, although he was quite sure the first had done its work thoroughly. He was remembering another of his white-hunter maxims: never approach downed game until you are certain it is dead.

At length he was satisfied. He motioned to Stacy to stay where he was, and stepping carefully on the rough turf, made his way to the baobab tree and the still figures under it. A glance showed him the leopard was quite dead; a head shot of which he could be proud.

He turned, then, toward Lieutenant Conway's corpse, his brain suddenly busy with a variety of thoughts. He must not forget to give the Wakamba boy at the watchtower his reward and settle the arrow-poison business, now that Conway was gone. He must inform Rebecca Conway of her husband's tragic end and console her as best he could. Would he be promoted now to lieutenant, and thus be able to offer Rebecca a continuation of the privileged life she seemed to find so enchanting in Mombasa? Given time, he was sure he could persuade her to marry him—and now, he thought, smiling a little, he had lots of time.

He was wrong. He didn't even have time to raise his eyes to the tree branch above him, or to bring up the rifle, still held loosely in his hand. In the last split second of his life, before pitiless teeth and talons tore his throat out, Harper had time for but a single flash of realization: there had been a *pair* of leopards visiting Mombasa!

DONALD E. WESTLAKE

A Good Story

The big snake moved in its cage, getting hungry. Flat eyes watched Leon walk through and out of the barn; Leon pretended not to notice. There'd been nothing in the mail today, so he was free. He walked past the cages and cotes, past the sawdust-smelling shed where the crates were hammered together, past the long, low main house, with its mutter of air-conditioning, and on down the dry dirt road into town, where he bought a beer in the cantina next to the church and stepped outside to enjoy the day.

The sun in the plaza was bright, the air clean and hot, and when he tilted the bottle and put his head back, the lukewarm beer foamed in his mouth. Stripped to the waist, T-shirt dangling from the back pocket of his cutoff jeans, moccasins padding on the baked brown earth, Leon strolled around the plaza, smiling up at the distant crown of the Andes.

Slowly he sipped his beer, enjoying the sensations. This town was so high above sea level, the air so thin, that perspiration dried on him as soon as it appeared. Eight months ago, when he'd first come to Ixialta, Leon had found that creepy and disconcerting, but now he liked the dry crackle and tingle on his flesh, the accretion of salt that he could later brush off like talcum powder.

Eight months; no time at all. The work he did was easy and the money terrific, and the temptation to just drift

along with it was very strong—that's what Jaime-Ortiz
counted on, he knew that much—but he'd promised
himself to give it no more than a year. Tops; one year. Go
home rich and clean and twenty-four, with the world
before him. Leon grinned, a tall, sloping boy with wiry
arms and the hard-muscled legs of a jogger, and was still
grinning when the car appeared.

Except for Jaime-Ortiz' six vehicles, cars were a rarity
in Ixialta. The dirt road winding up the jungled moun-
tainside was a mere spur from the trans-Andean highway,
dead-ending in this public square, surrounded by low
stucco buildings.

In the past eight months, how many strangers had been
here? A government tax man had come to talk with
Jaime-Ortiz, had stopped for lunch and a bribe and had
departed. A couple of closemouthed Americans had
brought up the new satellite dish, hooked it up and
showed Jaime-Ortiz how it worked.

And who else? A pair of British girls working for the
UN on some hunger survey; two sets of dopers searching
for peyote, going away disappointed; a couple of American big-game hunters who'd stayed three days, shot one
alpaca, and contracted dysentery; and one or two more.
Maybe seven interventions from the outside world in all
this time.

And now here was number eight, a dusty maroon rental
Honda with a pair of Americans aboard. The thirtyish
woman who got out on the passenger side was an absolute
drop-dead ice blonde. In khaki slacks, thonged sandals,
pale-blue blouse, and leather shoulder bag, she was some
expensive designer's idea of a girl foreign correspondent.
The big dark sunglasses, though, were an error; only
Jackie O., in Leon's opinion, could wear Jackie O. sunglasses without loss of status. Still, this was a dream
walking.

The man was something else. Wide-rumped in stiff
new jeans, he wore office-style brown oxfords and a
long-sleeved buttondown shirt. He was an office worker,
a professor of ancient languages, a bank teller, and he
didn't belong on this mountain. Nor with that woman.

Leon approached, smiling, planning his opening remark, but the woman spoke first, frowning as though he
were the doorman: "What place is this?"

"Ixialta," he told her.

"The high Ixi," she said, unexpectedly. There was a
faint roughness in her voice, not at all unpleasant.
"What's an Ixi?"

"Maybe a god." Leon had never asked that question.

The man had draped himself with cameras. Blinking
through clip-on sunglasses over his spectacles, he said,
"Look at those cornices! Look at that door!"

"Yes, Frank," she said, uninterested, and pointed at
Leon's beer. "That looks good."

"I'll get you one."

"And shade," she said, looking around.

"Table beside the cantina." He pointed. "In the shade,
in the air, you can watch the world go by."

"Good." Setting off across the plaza, Leon beside her,
the woman said, "Much of the world go by here?"

"You're it, so far."

Two small round white-metal tables leaned on the
cobblestones beside the cantina, furnished with teetery
ice-cream-parlor chairs and shaded by the bulk of San
Sebastian next door. The woman chose the table without
a sleeping dog under it, while Leon went inside. The few
customers in the dark and ill-smelling place stopped
muttering when he walked in, as they always did, and sat
looking at their thick hands or bare feet. Leon finished his
beer and bought two more. Putting his T-shirt on, he paid
and carried the bottles outside.

Across the way, Frank was taking photos of cornices and doors. The woman had pushed her big sunglasses up on top of her head and was studying her face in a round compact mirror. She had good, level gray eyes, with something cool in them. Sitting across from her, he placed both bottles on the table and said, "I'm Leon."

"Ruth." She put the compact away and looked out at the empty plaza. "Lively spot."

"Come back on Sunday," Leon invited.

"What happens Sunday?"

"*Paseo.*" Leon waved his arm in a great circle. "The boys walk around that way, the girls come the other way, give each other the eye. They come from all around the mountain here."

"The mating ritual," she said, picking up the bottle.

Leon shrugged. "It's the way they do it. All the Indian boys and girls." Across the way, Frank sat in the sunny dust, taking a picture of a stone step.

Ruth drank, head tipped back, throat sweet and vulnerable; Leon wanted to nibble on it. The thought must have showed on his face, because, when she lowered the bottle, the smile she gave him was knowing but distanced. "You're no Indian," she said.

"I'm an Indian's secretary," he said and laughed at the joke.

"How does that work?"

"There's a rich man up here. Owns a lot of land, has everything he wants."

"And he lives here?" The skepticism was light, faintly mocking.

"This is where his money comes from."

"He's a farmer, then."

"He sells animals."

"Cattle?" Confusion was making her irritable, on the verge of boredom.

"No, no," Leon said, "*wild* animals. Jaime-Ortiz sells them to zoos, circuses, animal trainers all around the world. That's why he needs a secretary, somebody to write the letters in English, handle the business details."

She looked faintly repelled. "What kind of animals?"

"All sorts. This whole range around here—Peru, Bolivia, Paraguay—it's one of the last great wildlife areas. We've got puma, jaguar, all kinds of monkeys, llamas, snakes—"

"Ugh," she said. "What kind of snakes?"

"Rattlers. Anaconda. Boa constrictor. We got a huge boa up in the barn now, all ready to go."

She drank beer and shivered. "Some way to make a living."

"Jaime-Ortiz does okay," Leon assured her and grinned at what he was leaving unsaid.

She seemed to sense there was more to the story. Watching herself move the bottle around on the scarred metal top, she said, "And you do okay, too, I guess."

"Do I look like I'm complaining?"

She glanced at him sidelong. "No," she said, slow and thoughtful. "You look quite pleased with yourself."

Was she making fun? A bit defensive through the lightness, he said, "It's an interesting job here. More than you know."

"How'd you get it? Answer a want ad?"

Leon grinned, on surer ground. "Jaime-Ortiz doesn't put any want ads. He doesn't want some stranger poking around in his business."

"You already knew him, then."

"Family connection. Somebody in the business at the other end."

"An uncle," she said and smiled, showing all her teeth, as though he were a kid she didn't have to compose her face for.

"Okay, an uncle," he said, getting really annoyed now. "That doesn't make me just a nephew."

Looking contrite but still smiling, she reached out to touch the tips of two red fingernails to the back of his hand, the nails slightly indenting the flesh. "Don't be mad, Leon," she said. "Take a joke."

Frank and his cameras were still across the plaza. Leon turned his hand, closed it with gentle pressure on her fingers. "I like to joke," he said.

"The wild-animal trainer." She withdrew her hand. "I'd get bored, playing zoo."

"There's better stuff." Suddenly nervous, he gulped beer, and when he lowered the bottle, she was looking at him.

Some instinct of caution made him hesitate. But the English girls had been *very* impressed. And what difference did it make if he talked? The strangers came and went, forgetting the very name of Ixialta. Looking away toward the mountains, he said, "This is also where the coca bush grows. All around here."

"Cocaine," she said, getting it, but then frowned: "What about the law?"

"Around here? You're kidding."

"No, the States, when you smuggle it in."

"That's the beauty," he told her, grinning. "You take your white powder, you see? You put it in your glassine envelopes. You feed your envelopes to your monkey."

"Monkey? But he'll digest it; he'll—"

"No," Leon said. "Because then you feed your monkey to your boa constrictor."

"Oh," she said.

"There isn't a Customs man in the world gonna look to see what's inside a monkey inside a boa constrictor."

"*I* wouldn't."

"The monkey has to go into the snake alive," Leon said,

glad to see her eyes widen. "It takes the snake seven days
to digest the monkey but only two days to be flown to
Wilkinson, the wild-animal dealer in Florida." It was
such a good story that he laughed all over again every
time he told it. "As the fella says, it's all in the packaging."

"Yes," she said, her expression suddenly enigmatic.
She stood, turning away, calling, "Frank! Frank!"

Leon said, "Look, uh . . ."

"Just a minute." She was brisk and businesslike, utterly
different.

Baffled, Leon got to his feet as Frank came trotting
across the plaza, holding his cameras down with both
hands. "Yeah?"

Nodding at Leon, Ruth said, "He's the one."

Frank looked surprised. "You sure?"

"He just told it to me."

"Well, that was quick," Frank said. His manner was
suddenly also changed, less fussy, more self-assured. He
walked toward Leon, making a fist. Leon was so bewildered he didn't even duck.

Someone pulled his hair. Leon jerked, trying to stand, but
was held down, rough ropes holding him to a chair. He
opened his eyes, and Jaime-Ortiz stood in front of him,
along with Paco and a couple of the other workers. They
were all in the big barn, where the air was always cool,
rich with animal stink, the hard-packed earth floor cross-
hatched with broom lines.

Against the far wall, under the dim bulbs, stood the
cages, only a few occupied. A red-furred howler monkey,
big-shouldered and half the size of a man, sat with its
back to everybody, the hairless tip of its long tail curled
negligently around a lower bar, while next door a golden
guanaco pranced nervously, its delicate ears back and
eyes rolling. Further from the light, the big, skinny boa,

pale brown with darker crossbars, its scaly head rearing
up nearly three feet in the air, showed yellow underbelly
as it stared through the bars and wire at everything that
moved.

"Jaime?" Leon tugged at the hairy ropes, tasting old
blood in his mouth, feeling the sharp stings around his
puffy lips. "Jaime? What—"

"I got to be disappointed in you, Leon," Jaime-Ortiz
said. He was a big, heavy man with a broad, round face
and liquid-brown eyes that could look as soulful as that
guanaco's—or as cold as stones. "You," he said, pointing
a thick, stubby finger at Leon. "You got to be one real
disappointment to me." He shook his head, a fatalistic
man.

"But what did I— What's—"

"Little stories going around," Jaime-Ortiz said. He
waggled the fingers of both hands up above his head, like
a man trying to describe birds in flight. "Somebody
talking about our business, Leon. Yours and mine. Making
trouble for you and me."

"Jaime, please—"

"All of a sudden," Jaime-Ortiz said, "these drug agents,
they come to our friend Wilkinson, they got a paper from
a judge."

"Oh, my God." Leon closed his eyes, licking his sore
lips. The rope was tied very hard and tight; he could
barely feel his hands and feet.

"Who would make trouble for you and me and Wilkinson? Leon? Who?"

Eyes shut, Leon shook his head back and forth. "I'm
sorry, Jaime. I'm sorry."

"Friends in New York ask me this," Jaime-Ortiz said. "I
say it's not me, it's not Leon, it's not Paco. We all got too
much to lose. They say they send somebody down, walk
around, see who likes to tell stories."

"Jaime, I'll never, never—"

"Oh, I know that," Jaime-Ortiz said. "You can't be around here no more, Leon. I got to send you back to the States."

Hope stirred in Leon. He stared up at Jaime-Ortiz. "Jaime, I promise, I won't say a word, I'll never—"

"That's right," Jaime-Ortiz said. "You will never say a word. Not the way *you're* going back to the States."

Leon didn't get it until he saw Paco come toward him with the glassine envelope in his hand. "Open wide," Paco said.

DICK STODGHILL

Best Evidence

Martha tells me I shouldn't be vindictive. After all, she says, it happened a long time ago. Perhaps, but I can't help feeling pleased about the way everything turned out. It seems to me that even though it took a while, justice prevailed.

Having the World Series on television again brought it to mind, although the story really began the day we went to a discount store looking for hardware to finish remodeling the kitchen. That would have been ten years before the carpet-tack bandit began dominating the front page of the newspaper.

Martha knows I won't let anything interfere with the Series, not since I missed Don Larsen's perfect game back in 1956. I vowed it would never happen again. Since then I've seen every pitch of every game, won't leave the TV set even during the commercials. Martha understands so she keeps me supplied with snacks and a fresh beer now and then.

Anyway, the first thing we did after buying the house was remodel the kitchen. Even though we were in our fifties we were like a couple of kids fixing it up because it was our first. Up until then a house was just one more thing Martha had always wanted but never had.

I was on the road much of the time during the early years, selling soap and getting transferred to a new

territory every twelve months or so. A year in South
Bend, two in Vincennes, another in Muncie, always on
the move. We'd rent an apartment or a small house but we
never had a place of our own. But someday, I promised
her, we'd settle in one town and then buy that house she
dreamed of.

It was much the same with kids. Martha had planned
on a family, but we kept putting it off just a little longer
until . . . well, the years go by in a hurry.

Even with pets it was that way. Martha always wanted
a little dog but it never seemed like quite the right time for
one. Then one day I surprised her by bringing home a
puppy not long after we moved to Terre Haute. A furry
little fellow, white with black markings. It was love at
first sight with both of them, but only a few weeks went
by before he ran in the street and was hit by a car. After
that Martha never seemed to have the heart for another
dog.

So the day the story began we were looking over the
hardware at the discount store when Martha turned to me
and said, "What's all that racket?"

I hadn't noticed, so I listened carefully and could hear
what sounded like metal rattling a couple of aisles away.
We walked over, curious, and found the noise was
coming from the pet section. There wasn't much to it, just
a couple of tanks of tropical fish and a few cages of white
mice, guinea pigs, other little animals. It turned out to be
a hamster making all the fuss. He was by himself in one of
the cages, just a little guy not much more than a couple of
inches long. His water bottle was empty so he was
hanging on the bars of the cage, rattling the spout against
them, very indignant about the whole thing.

There wasn't an employee in sight, which isn't unusual
in such places. Martha was upset. She walked to another
department, found a woman behind a showcase stocked

with guns and ammunition, and explained the problem. The woman said she'd mention it to someone but Martha told her she was standing right there until the hamster had his water. By then I was getting a little upset myself.

The woman waited a minute or so just to show who was boss, then went over to the pet section, making no attempt to conceal her lack of enthusiasm, and filled the bottle. Martha and I stayed around watching the little fellow drink his fill, chuckling because he was so businesslike and yet still a little put out. When he was satisfied he stood on his back feet, front ones against the bars, and looked out as if to say, "Well, now what?"

Martha talked to him the way she does with little creatures. Birds and animals will stand and listen, almost seeming to understand. The hamster remained stock-still, looking very serious, taking in every word. Martha reached for my hand, pulling me nearer to her. Then she turned, smiling, and said, "Look at those tiny little fingers."

"They're probably toes," I told her.

"No, they look more like fingers."

She straightened up abruptly, a look of concern on her face. "Suppose his water bottle gets empty again? I don't like it the way no one looks after the animals in this place."

I could see what was coming, of course, but there wasn't much I could do but agree with her. The hamster hadn't moved so she talked to him again for a minute or two, then smiled up at me and said, "Let's take him home with us."

Naturally I wasn't going to tell her no. A little later we left with a cage and water bottle, an exercise wheel and a tiny house that looked like a shoe, a box of food, and a book about hamsters. The hamster, too, in a cardboard box the clerk had thrust him into over vigorous protest on his part. We were halfway home before we realized we hadn't bought the kitchen hardware.

I put the cage together, then we transferred him to it very gingerly, both a little uneasy because we didn't know much about handling a hamster. He headed for the shoe and was asleep in thirty seconds. Worn out from the excitement, I suppose, and seeming to be thinking that for a hamster life is just one perilous adventure after another.

After reading the book I agreed with him. And even if all goes well, about a thousand days is all a hamster can expect of life. Of course a hamster doesn't know that.

Our friend had to have a name so Martha decided to call him Chigger because he was so small. Before long that got shortened to Chiggy, on Martha's part anyway.

The book said a hamster will always find a way to escape and it took Chigger three days to make his first. By then we felt comfortable handling him and I was pretty good at picking him up by the nape of the neck, which he hated. After I'd put him down he'd waddle off a little, then sit looking back reproachfully.

Like all hamsters, Chigger would sleep through the day, then be ready for mischief at night. He'd swing on the bars of the cage, run on his wheel—really believing he was going somewhere, I guess—and anything else he could think of to attract attention. Then Martha would take him out and hold him in her hands, stroking him gently, quietly talking to him. He'd sit mesmerized, staring at her with his little black-button eyes, not missing a word. Then he'd walk around her lap, nosing into pockets or trying to work his way down between the cushion and the side of the chair. If you watch them, hamsters are a lot like people, always thinking there is something better just a little beyond wherever it is they happen to be.

We were passing a pet shop one day when Martha said,

"Let's go in." She kept looking at things and saying, "Chiggy would love this." By the time we left we had fifty dollars worth of equipment for a three-dollar hamster. When I mentioned this, Martha said, "He's worth it."

I didn't argue the point.

Chigger enjoyed the new passages and play areas. After investigating all the nooks and crannies he settled on a round plastic ball as his favorite. He'd get in it, we'd put the cap on, and he'd roll around the floor thinking he was out in the big world. Then in the morning we discovered he had moved out of the shoe to a plastic box that was supposed to be an observation tower. It was a foot and a half above the floor but Chigger thought it was a secure burrow deep in the ground.

In no time at all Chigger was one of the family, a happy little guy doing the things he enjoyed. He grew to full size, which still wasn't much, and he kept getting smarter. It tickled me the way he would get excited when Martha would go to the kitchen and open a cupboard or the refrigerator. He knew she wouldn't forget a treat for him—a cracker with peanut butter, a piece of carrot or celery.

Sometimes I'd think about those thousand days and calculate how many of them he had used up. I never mentioned that to Martha, of course.

Chigger had gone through about half his allotted time, not realizing it, when the new people moved into the vacant house next door. Just two of them, a woman of about thirty-five and her twelve-year-old son. It didn't take long to start wishing the kid was back in Indianapolis or wherever it was they came from. He was one of those who doesn't seem to enjoy anything unless it annoys someone or hurts something.

They hadn't been in town more than a month when the kid was in trouble for going to the park a few blocks away and clubbing three ducks to death. That's when we learned his mother made a habit of figuring he was always right and everybody else was wrong. She'd corner Martha and complain that people were picking on her son because he was new in town.

"What do they expect?" I heard her say one day. "Leaving ducks out in a public park like that. Arnie just did what any other boy would do."

"None had up till now," I told her. Her face tightened up and she walked back to the house without another word.

The kid was always shooting at birds or squirrels with an air rifle. One day the neighbor two doors down called the police because he had gone on to bigger things, was out in the backyard trying to pick off a rabbit with a .22. In his line of fire was a year-old girl in a playpen. The kid got the rabbit later with a ball bat.

His mother quit speaking to the neighbor and his wife, not that either of them cared. I know the mother was partially to blame for her son's behavior, but no one will ever convince me this kid wasn't bad from the word go. People who think they don't come that way haven't been around much.

Martha went on trying to be neighborly even though I told her there are times when it doesn't pay. So I wasn't too surprised when I came home one afternoon and found the two of them, the kid and his mother, sitting with Martha in the living room. The women were drinking tea and the kid was wolfing down a plate of Martha's chocolate chip cookies with a glass of milk.

I'd been back about five minutes, balancing the cup and saucer Martha had handed me on one knee because the kid had my favorite chair beside the table with my pipes and tobacco, when Chigger came down for a drink. He was curious about the strange voices, or maybe smelled the cookies, because he stood on his hind legs peering at us from the front of his cage.

"What is that thing, a mouse?" the kid asked.

Martha said he was a hamster, then made me uneasy by going over and opening the door of the cage and taking Chiggy out. She held him in her hands, talking softly, then broke off a piece of cookie and gave it to him.

"Let me see it," the kid said.

I opened my mouth to warn her but before I could, Martha handed Chiggy to him, believing as she always had that there is good in everybody if you treat them nicely.

Chiggy had a wild-eyed look, not being familiar with the hands he was being passed to, and he tried to squirm free. The kid held on to him, though. Too tightly and with a twisted grin on his face. I started to get up but before I could get to him there was a popping sound, then the kid let out a yelp when Chiggy sank his needle-sharp teeth into his finger. The kid dropped Chiggy then, but he didn't run because one of his front legs was doubled back on itself. It had snapped like a twig when the kid deliberately gave it a twist. I scooped him up from the floor just before the kid launched a kick.

The mother gave a yell and rushed over, taking the kid's hand and saying, "Oh, Arnie, you're bleeding." Then she turned on Martha and berated her for "letting poor Arnie have that wild animal."

Martha was white as a sheet, confused, not knowing what to do. She glanced back and forth from the woman to where I stood holding Chiggy in my hands. I didn't share her uncertainty. I ordered the two of them out and didn't bother to spare their feelings in doing it.

Chiggy didn't make a sound. Hamsters seldom do, but we could see he was in pain and, most of all, bewildered.

Up until then his happy little world hadn't included mistreatment or pain.

Martha held him while I drove to the vet's office. A woman veterinarian helped him as much as she could, managing to get the tiny leg pretty well straightened out. But the joint was damaged, she said, and there wasn't anything that could be done about that. We took Chiggy home and he went to sleep in a corner of his cage.

Nothing was the same after that. Chiggy tried to use his plastic runs a few times but he'd get a couple of inches up a tube, then slide back down again. Before long he quit trying. He stayed down in the cage all the time and moved back into the shoe. Once in a while we'd put him in the plastic ball but he'd just sit there, wouldn't try to roll around the way he always had.

It seemed he had lost his zest for living. Even when Martha would hold him and talk to him it wasn't the same. Chiggy would sit quietly but always appeared a little uneasy, probably remembering what had happened before. He gave us his trust, then had been betrayed.

Watching him, seeing how the fun had gone out of his life, was tougher on me than I let on but it really tore Martha apart. She blamed herself, of course, instead of the one at fault.

Then one morning Chiggy was dead. Just why, I don't know. He should have had at least another year coming, but I could tell he was gone as soon as I looked in his cage. Telling Martha was harder than most people would believe. Or understand, probably.

I used a metal file-card box for a coffin, sealed it with furnace tape and buried Chiggy in the backyard. After a couple of weeks I suggested getting another hamster but Martha wouldn't hear of it. I came home one day and found she had packed all the equipment in boxes and stored it in the attic. And I'm sure most people wouldn't understand this, either, but even after all these years she cries once in a while, remembering her old friend.

It was a year and a half ago that the robberies began. There was an unusual twist and the newspaper played it up, began calling the hold-up man "the carpet-tack bandit." It was colorful and the headlines grabbed your attention.

The carpet-tack bandit hit only loan companies, those that keep cash on hand for people who prefer their money fast and green. He'd follow the same routine, go in the door with gun in hand when there were no customers inside. After he had the money he'd rip out the phone lines, then make the employees drop their shoes by the front door before lining up at the back of the room. Before leaving he'd spread carpet tacks all over the floor. By the time the people could brush the tacks aside and get to the door he was long gone.

None of the victims could provide much of a description because the carpet-tack bandit wore a hat with brim turned down, Bogart style, and a Wild West handkerchief mask covering everything but his eyes. They agreed he had a harsh voice and they got to hear enough of it because that was another of his trademarks, cracking wise all the time he was in a place. Something about that seemed to frighten people more than anything else.

It was just a year ago, the night of the third game of the World Series, when things finally turned sour. Up until then the robberies had gone like clockwork. A loan company at the far end of town stayed open one night a week until ten, offering on-the-spot cash for small loans and promising the money by noon the next day for larger amounts. They made a big promotion of it but it impressed me as being a little on the shady side.

The hold-up man hit the place a few minutes before closing time. The manager had left early to catch the end of the Series game, leaving two women behind to wrap things up for the night. One was a girl of twenty, slender and pretty and new on the job. The other was three times her age, an old hand at the business who had been through the robbery routine before. Forty years of poring over figures had left her with eyes that needed glasses a quarter-inch thick. Even at that, anything more than a few feet away was a blur.

The bandit followed the usual procedure until it was time to take the shoes. Then, instead of having them take them off by the door as he always had, he had them do it back of the counter. When it was the girl's turn he got free with his hands. She was already scared senseless and panicked completely when he began pawing her. She started screaming and he tried to silence her but was a little too rough about it, kept twisting her neck until something snapped. Then he tossed her on the floor like a bundle of rags and ran without bothering about the tacks. When the police arrived the girl was dead.

The description given by the older woman pretty well matched that of earlier victims but a positive identification was out of the question. Even if the police had brought the robber in and shoved him under her nose she wouldn't have known him. She did say she might recognize his voice although for once he hadn't done much talking. That, and the different routine with the shoes, had many people thinking he was a copy cat, not the real carpet-tack bandit.

The loan company posted a $5,000 reward, the others in town chipped in to double it. That got results fast. Three days after the murder the police descended on our block like locusts and collared the kid next door. By then he was twenty-one, not much older than the victim and not one bit nicer than the day he arrived in town.

They found a number of things in the house that linked

him to the earlier robberies, plus five boxes of carpet tacks for future ones. On top of that several people identified him, or at least claimed to. Most of the victims couldn't, including the older woman from the office where the girl was killed. Even so the kid confessed to all the robberies except the last, the one carrying a charge of murder. He claimed he had nothing to do with that one.

His mother blamed everything and everybody but her son. Economic conditions, the scarcity of good jobs, the people who had flunked him out of college after one semester without giving him a real chance. Most of all the man at the auto parts store who didn't pay him enough, then fired him for dipping into the till.

She swore that her son hadn't left the house the night of the murder. The two of them said he had had a bad cold and the man at the drugstore a couple of blocks away remembered his mother had been in to buy a few cure-alls that day. It was a weak alibi, and under most conditions a mother's testimony doesn't carry much weight. Considering the lack of solid evidence linking him to the final robbery and the killing, though, it could have tipped the scales in his favor.

That's where I entered the picture. The police talked to everybody in the neighborhood and when they got to me, I contradicted their story. The kid had gone out about nine o'clock that night, I told the detective. I was certain of the time because I had taken a walk downtown and he was pulling out of his driveway just as I got home.

Months went by before the trial. When it began it was questionable whether the state had enough going for it to get a murder conviction, but the prosecutor did a fine job of getting evidence and testimony admitted, some that he had been afraid might be excluded by the judge. And the mother's testimony, being refuted by an impartial witness, hurt more than it helped. It struck the jurors as being trumped-up. In the end it cast doubt on everything the kid said himself, all his protestations of innocence as far as the robbery that ended in murder was concerned.

When it was over the prosecutor said my testimony was the key element in the verdict of guilty. He called it his best evidence.

So now it's World Series time again and Martha, as she always does, sees to it that nothing disturbs me or takes me away from the TV set even for a minute when a game is being played. It was after bringing a beer to me that she said I shouldn't be vindictive.

"Chiggy's been gone a long time now," she said. Then after a minute or two she dabbed at her eyes and hurried out of the room.

That's the first thing she had said about my testimony. From the day that I talked to the detective and then all through the trial, not one word.

She's wrong, though, about me being vindictive. I might have been for a time, now I'm just pleased. I have an idea Martha is, too, more than she lets on. One way or another, justice usually prevails in the long run.

JOAN RICHTER

Intruder in the Maize

She waited until the churning of the Land Rover's heavy wheels on the long gravel drive had faded into the softer sound of tires against murum and then she got up and quickly began to dress. She was annoyed that she had wasted the last hour in a pretense of sleep, but it had been preferable to a confrontation with Jack.

She had heard him get up while it was still dark and go outside. And she had imagined him as he crouched on the rise overlooking the field of maize, waiting, as he had been waiting and watching every dawn for the last two weeks. Sometimes she wondered if he remembered any longer what it was he was waiting for.

She threw a sweater over her suntanned shoulders and left the house by the veranda door, passing the kitchen as she went to tell Kariuki all she wanted this morning was coffee and she would fix that herself later. She walked across the dew-soaked lawn, past the bottle brush tree from whose rose-colored flowers the sunbirds drank their morning fill, to where the shrubs thinned and she could look out across the green valley to the opposite ridge.

Overhead the East African sky was an intense blue, spreading endlessly, with high clouds that rose like white mountains asking to be climbed. Sometimes she wondered if Jack saw any of this, if he realized at all how much beauty there was just outside their window.

She breathed deeply of the cool air. It was dry, but it did not strike her as thin, not even on that first day, a year ago, when they had just arrived. The only time she felt the altitude was when she walked uphill, and then her breath came in quick, short pulls and her chest felt hard and tight.

A cracking of a twig caused her to look down the near slope into the valley where, among the trees and brush, the smoke of cook fires rose. She saw a man making his way up along one of the paths, his dark head bent, so that she could not see his face; but from his dress—the short-sleeved white shirt and the dark trousers—she was sure it was Molo, one of the few farmers in the area who had adopted European dress.

He had a small *shamba* on the other side of the valley where in previous years he had raised potatoes and maize, but this season he had set out his first real money crop—a half acre of pyrethrum, a silver green plant from whose daisy-like flowers an insecticide was extracted. She wondered what the occasion was for his leaving his *shamba* so early in the day.

"*Habari*," she said, using the Swahili greeting.

"*Mzuri*," he replied, but the look on his face did not seem to agree that everything was good.

There were a few more prescribed words for them to exchange before they exhausted her knowledge of Swahili. Then they would switch to English and slowly Molo would come to the point of his visit.

He looked up at the sky. "The rains come soon."

She looked too, but saw nothing that resembled a rain cloud. But, then, both night and day the skies were strange to her. The stars were not the ones she knew, nor were the clouds. She knew only that they were beautiful, more so than any she had ever seen anywhere.

"Is the Bwana at home?"

He called her Memsab Simon, but he never called Jack anything but Bwana.

"He left early this morning on safari." She smiled, still not used to the East African meaning of the word; only rarely did it mean sun helmets and bearers and trekking through the bush; most often it referred to any trip out of town, whether for a day or a week.

"Did the Bwana Red go with him?"

Lately Jack almost never went anywhere without Red, and she did not know whether that made her angry or relieved, whether it was an indication of Jack's lack of trust in her, or lack of confidence in himself. She liked Red—perhaps too much—but she had done nothing to cause Jack to be jealous. Whether Red returned her admiration she had no idea, for he showed no sign; but her ego was mollified by the knowledge that Red was no fool. He had to work with Jack (another sticky point—Jack was the boss, but Red, having lived in East Africa for the last ten years, knew all there was to know).

"Yes, Bwana Red went with him. Is something wrong, Molo? Do you need more seed?"

Jack had come to East Africa on a two-year contract as an agricultural adviser, and one of the things for which he was responsible was the parceling out of seed. It was given on a loan basis, to be paid for when the crop was harvested. It was a precious commodity, doled out on the basis of past records of repayment. Jack had been concerned about stealing, so he kept the sacks of seed locked in a storehouse at one end of the maize field.

That was the one thing she didn't like, the one thing that marred the beauty of the land and the sky; barred windows, locked doors—not just outside doors, but all

inside doors, to closets and pantries, doors that sealed
one section of a house off from another.

"It's different with the seed," she had said to Jack,
though she had not really meant it—but the seed was not
her affair. "But I'll be darned if I'm going to lock up the
pantry every time I leave the house, just so the houseboy
won't help himself to a spoonful of sugar!"

She had pointed to a peg board on the wall. "Look at
that! There must be fifty different keys there. I won't live
that way."

"The house is yours to run as you want," Jack had said.
"But don't come crying to me the day one of them"—and
he had nodded in the direction where Kariuki and his
helper were preparing lunch—"walks off with something
that can't be replaced."

After that she had put the silver that Jack's family had
given them in the wall safe behind the mirror in the
bedroom and left it there. It was too much bother taking it
out in the morning and locking it up again at night.

One day when Red was with them, Jack brought up the
topic again, thinking he would have his colleague's
support; but Red had said, "If I bothered to check, I
suppose at the end of each month I'd find I was out a
pound of sugar and maybe some tea. On a day-to-day
basis Jinja helps himself to a banana or toast that's left
over from breakfast. The banana would rot before I'd get
around to eating it—and what would I do with leftover
toast but throw it away?"

"That isn't the point," Jack had countered. "They ought
to be taught that what's yours is not theirs."

"There's a difference between stealing money and
things of value—and taking scraps of food." Red's voice
had been patient, but not condescending. "When Jinja
washes my trousers, he checks the pockets because I'm
always leaving things in them—cigarettes, screws, keys, a

few shillings. He keeps a basket on the shelf above the tub for all that stuff. I find the shillings there too, along with everything else."

Jack had looked at him narrowly. "Have you ever checked? Have you ever left an odd bunch of change—"

"You mean have I ever tried to trap him?"

Jack nodded.

Red shook his head. "If I did that it would mean I didn't trust him. And he would know, and then the whole thing would break down and I *couldn't* trust him."

Jack had continued the discussion, long after Red would have been happy to let it go. In a final effort to win a point Jack had flashed, "The Africans wanted freedom, now they have to accept the responsibility that goes with it!"

"I couldn't agree with you more," Red had said, "but I don't go along with your methods. You want to *police* them—and that isn't freedom. Sure there are thieves among them—but show me a society that hasn't any. Just once suspect them of thievery without cause, and you will create a thief."

After Red had left them, she had not been able to keep silent. Perhaps she had been too strong in stating her position, for Jack had said unpleasantly, "So you think the Bwana Red is a great hero too." And Jack had turned away . . .

Now Molo shook his head. No, he had not come for seed.

What does he want, she wondered. What has brought him up from the valley at a time of day when he should be working his *shamba*? Although she was better at it than when they had first come, she still found it difficult to read the African face. Joy she could identify, but other emotions—anger, fear, distrust—eluded her.

She prepared herself for more small talk. "The tomato

plants you gave me are doing very well, Molo. Would you like to see them?"

A sudden though almost imperceptible change in his expression made her realize that accidentally she had hit on what he had been waiting for. He had been waiting for her to invite him onto her land.

"I would like to see maize. Bwana says wild pig is coming and eating."

So even Molo had heard of Jack's morning excursions. "You can have my gun," Red had offered. "I bet, whatever it is, comes around dawn. From that rise over there it would be an easy shot."

"I'll get him," Jack had said, "but I won't use a gun."

"Suit yourself, but setting traps can be slow. That's a big field."

"Traps?" She remembered the arrogance in Jack's voice. "I intend to use a bow."

Red had looked up quickly and perhaps the look that crossed his face *had* been one of admiration, though she had not seen it as such. But Jack's satisfied face had been evidence enough of his own interpretation.

"I'm a fair marksman," he had said. "I had some practice in the States."

Silently she recalled the country club's manicured lawn, the steady bull's-eye target.

"A couple of weeks ago I bought a bow from one of Molo's brothers and a dozen arrows. It's a different kind of weapon from what I've been used to, but it sure has zing."

"A little light to do in a pig," Red said, "unless you're an incredibly good shot."

Jack had given him a smug look. "I've got something else that will help it along."

She remembered the frown that had creased Red's

brow. "I'd be careful with that stuff. It's not something to fool with."

"Thanks for the advice. I never did have a wet nurse, and I hardly need one now."

Just the recollection of his retort made her blush . . .

Molo led the way along the ridge toward the maize. She knew that the polite palaver was over. They were getting to the reason for his visit. He turned when they reached the edge of the green field and continued along the north side of the planted area, moving in the direction of the rise, the lookout Jack went to every morning, where she knew he had gone this morning before he'd left to meet Red.

At the rise Molo stopped, and for the first time she noticed that he had his *panga* with him, the machete-like knife whose broad blade was used to cut grass, chop roots, dig potatoes, prune trees, and sever the heads off chickens. It was as much a part of the African farm scene as was the hoe in the States before mechanization. Usually when Molo came to pay a social call or to see Jack or Red on business, he left his *panga* behind. Idly, she wondered why he had it with him now.

He was pointing with it and she followed the dark line of his arm to the end of the blade.

"Pig come out of forest and walk low on belly through maize."

For a moment she could not see the slight furrow in the sea of green stalks, but then her eyes discovered the thin line that traveled straight across the otherwise untouched field.

"You stay here, Memsab Simon."

There was something in the tone of his voice that she reacted to. He was not being rude, but rather protective, and she wondered against what. Or was she misunderstanding completely? Was this like an expression she could not read?

"Molo, you don't think the pig is there now?"

"No, pig is gone."

"Then why, what—"

"It is better you stay. Let me see."

She nodded. Molo might be a guest on her land, but she was still a stranger in his country. With an uneasiness—of what she was not sure—she stood watching him as he descended the small hill and entered the maize. Overhead the sky was the same blue it had been minutes ago, before she had seen him coming up from the valley, with the same white, climbing clouds. There was still no visible sign of rain. It was something else that had thrown a shadow over the day.

The maize was shoulder high, so that when Molo paused and looked at the ground she could not see what it was he was looking at.

What had he found? What *was* he looking for?

He straightened and walked forward, stopping again after a few paces. Then he walked quickly on as though he had seen ahead of him what he had been looking for.

He had entered the field from the side bounded by the forest and was following the path that had been broken for him. As she studied the larger picture she saw that the parting in the maize seemed to lead to the storehouse.

Oh, God, she thought. Some animal found a way into Jack's burglarproof store! Had Jack come here every morning for the last two weeks and not discovered this for himself?

Molo had almost reached the wooden building. As she watched his movements a thought began to form in her mind. Had an animal made that path? Or had it been a man? A man trying to find a way to break into the seed store?

Molo had said something earlier that now made her wonder. "Pig come out of forest and walk low on belly through maize." It was an odd way to describe an animal's foraging.

Molo had reached the storehouse and was standing with his eyes cast down. Then he raised his head and called in Swahili, "Come now."

Hurriedly she started down the slope, slipping as she went, but driven by an impatience that came of waiting, curiosity, and a mounting concern that something was wrong. Her sweater slipped off her shoulders, but she did not stop to pick it up. At the edge of the maize field she put her arms up in front of her face to shield it from the slashing leaves.

She stumbled and looked down at the ground and saw what Molo had seen—a stone smeared with blood and more blood on one of the low leaves. Ahead there were drops of blood, hardly visible on the red brown earth, but unmistakable and vivid against the pale green of the maize.

Had Jack hit his target this morning? Had he only wounded it? She looked around her, trying to see into the impenetrable maize. The wounded animal might be hidden, crouching, waiting to spring at her, or to charge. How could Molo be so sure it was gone?

Her breath was coming in quick shallow gasps when she reached Molo, who was standing in the shadow of the storehouse. Her eyes fell to the ground and she saw a pile of dirt and a hole dug under the foundation; beside them a sack of seed and an abandoned *panga* that had been used to dig the hole.

She took all this in, and more, for at Molo's feet lay an arrow, its shaft bloody, its sharp triangular point sticky. Her hands flew to her face and she heard herself moan. An animal could not use a *panga*, nor could it tear an arrow from its stricken body! The succeeding thought made her cringe and her head twisted between her hands. Jack had shot a man!

All arrows looked the same. Perhaps it wasn't Jack's at all. He had marked his, scoring the shaft. But from where she stood she could not see—the shaft was partially covered with the loosened earth.

With a supreme effort she slid her hands down from her face and brought them to her sides. She had to find out. She had to know. She hesitated, and then with horrified determination she took a quick step forward, her hand outstretched. But almost before she moved, Molo's shadow was upon her and his arm caught her across the chest and threw her to the ground.

A scream choked in her throat as she stared up at him, a black man standing over her, his *panga* raised. It sliced through the air and caught the blood-smeared arrow and tossed it aside.

She saw him stab his *panga* in the ground and turn to her. "I am sorry, Memsab, but the arrow is poison."

He held out his hand and helped her to her feet.

"Even a scratch brings death."

A residue of terror filled her throat and she did not trust herself to speak, for she could not let Molo know what she had thought. She looked at him and pointed to where the arrow lay. The question formed slowly on her lips. "Is it the Bwana's arrow?"

"Yes," he said. "It killed my brother."

Her hand reached out and then fell to her side. What was there for her to say?

"I am sorry, too," Molo said and then she knew that her face did not present the enigma to him that his did to her. "I am sorry that my brother became a thief—and that your husband must die."

Oh, God, she thought, what did that mean? Tribal

vengeance? Could she reason with Molo? If not, she would have to get word to Jack somehow. It was possible that he and Red had not yet left town.

She turned to Molo, hoping she could find some words to reach him, but he had already begun to speak. The words came slowly, thoughtfully, half in English, half in Swahili.

"Before the Bwana came, my brother was watchman for the Bwana Red. He slept at night outside the seed store, the old one which we do not use anymore. No one stole or they would know my brother's *panga*."

Molo's eyes fell to the ground where the multipurpose knife lay. Then he looked at her again. "But then the new Bwana came and everything changed and my brother became a thief." He stopped. It was as much as he could say.

"But why did your brother sell my husband a bow? Why did he give him the poison?"

"The bow he sold because he needed money, and because he thought the Bwana could not shoot well. But he did not give him poison. He would not. The Bwana got poison somewhere far from here, from someone he pay a lot of money."

Suddenly Molo cocked his head, in response to some distant sound. She heard it too. It was the Land Rover returning. She heard it leave the murum road and turn into the gravel drive.

"It is the Bwana Red," Molo said.

She looked, but it was too far for her to recognize who was in the vehicle. It bore down on them coming as close to the field as it could. Then she saw that it was Red driving and that the seat beside him was empty.

She ran toward him. "Where's Jack?"

"In town. What's going on? He sent me out here, said there was something for me to see."

"There was no wild pig in the maize—it was Molo's brother. He'd dug a hole under the storehouse."

Red frowned as he climbed out of the Land Rover. "I guess that's one for Jack's side. I'd have said it would take a lot to make Molo's brother turn thief." A flicker of hope crossed his clouded face. "I suppose Jack caught him in the act?"

She took a breath. "Jack didn't catch him. He killed him."

Red's face went blank with disbelief. "Why? He was a man, not an animal. Why did he kill him?"

Tears seared her eyes, but she fought against them. It was past the time for weeping. She had no answer to Red's question. It was what she had been asking herself.

Molo had come up and was standing with them. Red turned to him. "How did he do it? He wasn't that good a shot with the bow."

"The arrow came here." Molo touched the fleshy part of his thigh. "It would not have killed him—but it was poisoned."

"Poisoned!" Red turned to her. "Where did he get poison?"

"I thought he'd gotten it from Molo's brother. But Molo says no, that he got it somewhere far from here."

"That arrogant—this can only mean trouble for all of us—whites and blacks."

Molo shook his head. "No, Bwana Red. There will be no trouble. My brother is dead. And the Bwana will die. It will end there."

"Molo, old friend," Red said in Swahili, "the viper eventually spends itself. Do not put yourself in danger by seeking its death."

"Do not worry, Bwana Red. The viper has felt its own sting."

She looked from one man to the other. What had they

said? She had caught the proverb, but did not understand its application. She turned to Red. "Why didn't Jack come back with you? Where is he?"

"I left him at the dispensary. He cut himself on one of those damn arrowheads—not bad, but enough to need a couple of stitches. I wanted to wait with him, but he didn't seem to want me around. Now I understand why."

She listened to each word, each progressive syllable, and her realization grew until the horror of it was evident in her face.

Red caught her hand. "God, I'm sorry. I know what you're thinking. But he's all right. It's just a simple cut. You see the poison is applied to the shaft of the arrow, not the tip—for reasons just like this—it's so easy to get a scratch and that's all you need."

She looked at him and shook her head. Then she turned to Molo. "How did you know? How did you know the Bwana would die?"

"Many people were in town, waiting at the dispensary. They brought the news to my *shamba*."

"What's this all about?" Red said, turning to her. "I just told you. He'll be all right."

"No," she said. "No, he won't. You see he didn't know about applying the poison to the shaft—he put it on the arrowheads."

CLARK HOWARD

Plateau

Tank Sherman felt his daughter Delia's hand shaking him gently. "Tank. Tank, wake up. Bruno's dead."

Tank sat up, moving his legs off the side of the cot where he had been napping, fully clothed except for his boots. Bruno? Bruno dead?

"You mean Hannah," he said, automatically reaching for his boots.

"No, Tank, I mean Bruno. Hannah's still alive. It's Bruno that died."

Tank frowned. That was not the way it was supposed to happen. He pushed first one foot, then the other, into black Atlas boots with riding heels. He had owned the boots for eighteen years, and they were as soft as glove leather. After he got them on, he sat staring at the floor, still confused. Bruno dead? How could that be? Bruno was supposed to have survived Hannah. Bruno was young; Hannah was old. And it was on Bruno that the lottery had been held.

"What happened?" he asked Delia.

"I don't know. Doc Lewis is on his way over to check him." She crossed the little one-room cabin to the stove and turned on a burner under the coffee pot. Getting out a cup, she poured a shot of peach brandy into it. "Will they still have the hunt, do you think? Since it's Hannah and not Bruno?"

"No," Tank said emphatically, "they couldn't. Hannah's too old. It wouldn't be a hunt; it would be a target shoot."

When the coffee was ready, Delia poured it in with the brandy and brought it to him. As he sipped it, Tank studied his daughter. She had the dark hair of her mother: thick and black as a crow's wing. And the high cheekbones of her mother's people, the Shoshone. Her light halfbreed coloring and blue eyes she got from him. All her life she had called him Tank instead of Daddy. At nineteen, her body was round and strong. She lived in her own mobile home down the road, and dealt blackjack for a living in an illegal game behind the Custer's Last Stand restaurant. Tank himself still lived in the cabin where Delia had been born. He had been alone for a year, since Delia left; and lonely for six years, since her mother had died of bone disease.

"Are you going down to the concession?" Delia asked.

"In a minute." He held the coffee cup with both hands, as if warming his palms, and smiled at his daughter. "Remember how your ma used to raise hell when she caught you lacing my coffee with brandy?"

"Yes." Delia smiled back.

"She always wanted me to make something of myself, your ma. Always wanted me to do something important. But I guess it just isn't in the cards. If Hannah had died first, like she was supposed to, why, I could have done something important for the first time in my life. Important to your ma, at least, if she was still alive. And to Bruno. But Bruno ups and dies first, so I'm left with nothing important to do. If your ma was still alive, she'd swear on her medicine bag that I arranged it this way."

Shaking his head wryly, Tank drank a long swallow from his cup. At fifty, he was a rangy, well-worn man with not an ounce of fat on him. His face showed the results of a hundred fists, maybe more. Twenty years earlier he had come to town as part of a traveling boxing show, whites against Indians. Dan Sherman, his name had been, but they billed him as Tank because he was so tough. Tank Sherman, after the Sherman tank. A hide like armor. Took punches like Jake LaMotta. But he had taken too many by then. In their little Montana town, a Northern Cheyenne who hated whites had beaten him to a pulp, and when the outfit moved on it took the Northern Cheyenne with it and left Tank behind. Delia's mother had found him sitting behind the 7-Eleven trying to eat some crackers and Vienna sausage he had bought with his last dollar. His lips were swollen so grotesquely he could barely chew, his eyes puffed to slits through which he could hardly see. Delia's mother took him home with her. They were never to part. Delia was their only child.

"Let's go on down to the concession," Tank said when he finished his coffee.

His cabin was on the slope of a low hill, and as Tank and Delia walked down its path they could see a small crowd already beginning to gather at the concession's corral. The concession itself was nothing more than a small barn next to the corral, with a gaudy red sign over its door which read: LAST TWO LIVING BUFFALO—ADMISSION $1. Tourists bought tickets and lined up around the corral, then the barn doors were opened and Bruno and Hannah were driven out to be viewed. They were the last two remaining buffalo in North America.

Now there was only one.

Old Doc Lewis, the reservation veterinarian from the nearby Crow agency, had just finished examining Bruno when Tank and Delia eased their way through the crowd to him.

"What killed him, Doc?" asked Tank, looking down at the great mass of animal spread out on the ground.

"Stroke," the vet said, brushing off his knees. "He was carrying too much weight. Must have been upwards of two thousand pounds."

Tank nodded. "Can't run off much fat in a corral," he observed.

Doc Lewis was making notes in a small book. "How old was he, do you know?"

"Nine," Tank said. "My wife helped deliver him." His scarred boxer's face saddened as he noticed his daughter reach out and pat the dead Buffalo's massive head. Then he glanced over to a corner of the corral and saw Hannah, standing quietly, watching. Unlike Bruno, a young bull, Hannah was a cow and much older: at least thirty. She had thinner, lighter hair than most buffalo, and a triangular part of her neck and shoulder cape was almost blonde, indicating the presence somewhere in her ancestry of a white buffalo. Much smaller than Bruno, she stood only five feet at her shoulders, and weighed a shade over seven hundred pounds.

"I guess this means the big hunt is off, doesn't it, Doc?" Tank asked. It was the same question Delia had asked him, and Doc gave the same answer.

"Of course. There wouldn't be any sport at all going after Hannah. She's much too old."

The three of them walked over to Hannah and, as if compelled by some irresistible urge, all patted her at once. "Well, old girl," Doc said, "you made the history books. The last North American Plains buffalo."

"Maybe they'll put her on a stamp or something," said Delia.

"Maybe," Doc allowed. "They already had the buffalo on a nickel, but that was before your time."

From the barn, a pretty young woman in the tan uniform of a state park ranger walked over to them. White, educated, poised, she was everything that Delia

was not. "Hello, Dr. Lewis, Mr. Sherman," she said.
"Hello there, Delia." She snapped a lead rein onto the
collar Hannah wore. "I just got a call from headquarters to
close down the concession. And to trim Hannah's hooves.
Isn't it exciting?"

Doc and Tank exchanged surprised looks. "Isn't what
exciting?" Doc asked, almost hesitantly. Instinctively,
both he and Tank already knew what her answer would
be.

"The hunt, of course. Oh, I know it won't be the same
as it would have been with Bruno as the prey. But it will
still be the last buffalo hunt ever. That's history in the
making!"

"That," Doc rebuked, "is barbarism."

"Are you saying the hunt's still on?" Tank asked.
"With Hannah as the prey?"

"Of course." She shrugged her pretty shoulders. "I
mean, how else can it be? The tickets have been sold, the
lottery has been held. You don't expect the state to go
back on its word, do you?"

"No," Delia said, "definitely not. Never. Not the state."

"Well, there you are," the young ranger said, missing
Delia's sarcasm entirely. "But, listen, they *have* changed
the rules a little to make it fairer. Bruno was only going to
be given a twelve-hour start, remember? Well, Hannah
gets a full *twenty-four*." She smiled, apparently delighted
by the allowance.

Doc Lewis turned and walked away, thoroughly dis-
gusted. Tank and Delia left also. Walking back up the
path to Tank's cabin, Delia said, "Looks like you're
getting your chance to do something important, after all."

Tank, thinking about his dead wife, nodded. "Looks
like."

*   *   *

When it had become clear that the Plains buffalo had
finally reached the threshold of extinction, when it was
absolutely certain that no new calves would be born
because the remaining cows were too old to conceive, the
state had immediately done two things: penned up the
few remaining members of the species and put an admission on their viewing; and devised a nationwide lottery to
select the persons who would be allowed to hunt, and
take the head and hide of, the last American buffalo. Both
moves proved enormously successful. The Last Remaining Buffalo concession, let by the state to one of its own
departments, the Bureau of Parks, was open nine months
of the year. Managed by park rangers, it operated under
very low overhead, and was the most profitable tourist
attraction in the state. All around the corral where the
buffalo were exhibited, there were coin-operated ma-
chines where for a quarter visitors could purchase cups of
processed food pellets to toss into the corral for the
buffalo to eat. Like peanuts to caged monkeys. Except that
the buffalo refused to do tricks. Despite considerable
effort in the beginning, including the use of a whip, the
buffalo had remained stoic and refused to be trained.
Finally the park rangers had to resign themselves to
simply leading their charges into the corral and letting
them stand there while small children pelted them with
synthetic food. The attraction, nevertheless, was popular.

As profitable as the concession was, however, its earn-
ings were modest compared to the proceeds of the lottery.
In a scheme devised by one of the General Accounting
Office's young financial wizards, two million numbered
tickets had been sold throughout the state and through
the mail nationally, for five dollars per chance. The ticket
supply was exhausted within a month, and the state had
made a quick ten million dollars. Even people who had
no interest whatever in hunting bought a ticket for

investment speculation. Even before the drawing, advertisements had already been run by people offering to buy a winning ticket from anyone whose number was picked.

The drawing, wherein three winners were selected, was by the use of a single, predesignated digit each day from the total shares traded on the New York Stock Exchange. The lucky ticket holders were a piano tuner in Boston, a waiter in Memphis, and a ranch hand in Nevada. The piano tuner sold his ticket for ten thousand dollars to Gregory Kingston, the actor. The waiter sold his for eighty-five hundred to bestselling author Harmon Langford. Lester Ash, the ranch hand, kept his, deciding that the head and hide would be worth far more than the ticket. He was counting on being a better hunter and shot than the actor and author.

Within two hours of the untimely death of Bruno, the three registered owners of the winning tickets were notified to come claim their prize. Hannah, the last surviving Plains buffalo, would be released fifty miles out on the prairie at noon on Friday.

At noon on Saturday, the three lottery winners would be free to hunt her.

By midnight on Thursday, Tank Sherman was ready to go. Hitched to the rear of his Ford pickup truck was a double-stall horse trailer from which he had removed the center divider, creating one large stall. Parking the rig on the prairie some one hundred yards behind the concession corral, he and Delia slipped through the quiet night to the barn, snipped the padlock with bolt-cutters, and led Hannah out. The old buffalo cow was as docile as a rabbit and made no noise whatever as Delia fed her a handful of fresh meadow grass, and Tank slipped a braided halter over her head.

After walking the buffalo aboard the trailer and quietly

closing her in, Tank handed Delia an envelope. "Here's the deed to the cabin and lot. And the passbook to your ma's savings account. She had six hundred and forty dollars saved when she died; it was supposed to be yours when you were twenty-one. Oh, and the title to the pickup is there too, just in case. Guess that's about all."

Delia got a paper bag and thermos jug from her jeep. "Sandwiches," she said. "And coffee. With, uh—"

"Yeah. With brandy." He put the bag and jug on the seat of the pickup, and sniffed once as if he might be catching cold. But he wasn't catching cold. "Listen, take care of yourself, kid," he said brusquely, and started to get into the truck. Then he turned back. "Look, I know I ain't never won no Father-of-the-Year prize, and I never gave you no place to live but that cabin, and I never sent you to college or nothing; but those things don't have nothing to do with caring. You understand?"

"Sure," Delia said. She shrugged. "After all, you did teach me when to fold in poker. And how to change a flat. And how to get a squirrel to eat out of my hand. Lots of girls never learn those things." She had to struggle to control her voice. She was not able to control her tears. But she knew that Tank could not see the tears in the darkness.

"Okay," he said. "I'll be hitting the road then."

He eased the door of the pickup shut, quietly started the engine, and slowly pulled away without headlights.

Behind him, Delia waved in the darkness and said, " 'Bye—Daddy."

When he reached the highway, turned on his headlights, and increased speed, Tank thought: *Okay, Rose, this is for you, honey.*

Rose was Tank's dead wife, the woman who had always wanted him to do something important. Her

Shoshone name was Primrose, given to her by her father because she had been born on a day in early July when the evening primrose had just blossomed. Later, when she moved into town and took up the ways of the white woman, she shortened it to Rose.

Tank always remembered Rose as being beautiful, but she was not; she was not even pretty. Her face was very plain, her eyes set too close together, her nose too long, and one cheek was pitted with pockmarks. Only her hair, lustrous as polished onyx, could truly be called beautiful. But Tank saw so much more of her than was outside; he saw her hopes and dreams, her pride, her nakedness when they made love, her secret joys. He saw everything about her, and it was all of those things combined which made her beautiful to him.

The first time she had shown him the buffalo was three months after she had taken him to live with her. After she had nursed him back to health from the beating he had taken. They got up early one morning on Rose's day off from the sugar beet processing plant, and in her old Jeep they drove thirty miles out onto the raw prairie. There, on an isolated meadow, was a small buffalo herd: three bulls, a cow, six calves. They were the beginning of the last migration, when the ocean of tourists had started driving them north and west from the Black Hills.

"See how noble they look," Rose had said. "See the dignity with which they stand and observe." Her eyes had become water and she had added, "They are watching their world come to an end."

Once, Rose explained to him, there had been sixty *million* Plains buffalo. Their presence on the Northern Plains had been the greatest recorded aggregation of large land animals ever known to man. To the red man of the prairie, the vast herds had been the mainstay of his economy. That single species provided food, clothing, shelter, and medicine for an entire race: the only time in history that such a natural balance between man and beast had ever been achieved.

"Then, of course, the whites came," Rose said. "At first, they killed the buffalo for meat and hides, as our people did, and that was acceptable because the herds were many. Later they killed them only for hides, leaving the carcasses to rot in the sun. Even that act, although it was without honor, could have been tolerated. But then they began killing them for what they called sport. Sport. Fun. Recreation. They killed them first by the tens of thousands. The butcher Cody, whom they called Buffalo Bill, personally recorded more than forty-two thousand kills in one seventeen-month period. Soon they were being slaughtered with total wantonness, by the hundreds of thousands. Today there are only a few hundred left. Most of them are in the Black Hills. But they are slowly migrating back up here again."

"Why?" Tank asked, fascinated by the tale.

"They know the end is nearing for them. A species can tell, you see, when their breed is running out. Each year they see fewer and fewer calves, the herds become smaller and smaller. So they look for a place to end their line. They look for a grassy meadow unspoiled by humans. A place to lie down and die with dignity."

For all the years Tank Sherman knew and lived with the Shoshone woman Rose, she had loved the great buffalo and mourned its diminishing number. As much as Tank missed her in death, he was glad that she had not lived to see Bruno and Hannah, the last two of the breed, penned up and put on display. Or known about the lottery for the privilege of hunting the survivor.

So this is for you, honey, he thought as he headed southeast with Hannah in the horse trailer. He would have about five hours headstart. Possibly two hundred fifty miles. Maybe it would be enough.

Maybe not.

Two hours after dawn, a tall, very handsome man, livid with anger, was stalking back and forth in the empty concession corral.

"What the hell do you mean, *missing?* How can something as large as a buffalo be *missing?*" His name was Gregory Kingston. An Academy Award–winning actor, he was not acting now; he was incensed.

"The state guaranteed this hunt," said a second man. Smaller, plumper, not as handsome, but with a good deal more bearing, this was Harmon Langford, internationally known bestselling author. Like Kingston, he was dressed in expensive hunting garb, carrying a fine, hand-tooled, engraved, foreign-made rifle. "Exactly who is in charge here?" he quietly demanded.

A third man, Lester Ash, the ranch hand from Nevada, stood back a step, not speaking, but observing everything. He wore hardy working clothes: denim, twill, roughout leather.

"Gentlemen," a Bureau of Mines spokesman pleaded, "please believe me, we are trying to get to the bottom of this as quickly as we can. All we know right now is that some person or persons apparently abducted Hannah sometime during the night. The highway patrol has been notified and a statewide search is getting under way at this very moment—"

"Why in hell would anyone want to abduct a *buffalo?*" Kingston inquired loudly of the world at large, throwing his arms up in bewilderment. Now he *was* acting.

"Oh, come, Kingston," said Harmon Langford, "we're not talking about *a* buffalo, we're talking about *this* buffalo. Unlike ourselves, there *are* those," and here he glanced at Lester Ash, "who are interested in this animal not for sport, but for profit." Lester Ash grinned but remained silent. Langford continued, "At any rate, we cannot waste time on *why*; we must concentrate on *where*. Where is our great, hairy prize? And how do we get to it?"

The Bureau of Parks man said, "We should be hearing from the highway patrol anytime now. Every road in the state is covered—"

"What do we do now?" asked Gregory Kingston, directing the question at Langford.

"We must be prepared to get to the animal as quickly as possible after it is located," the author declared, "before some outsider decides to take an illegal shot at it. This part of the country is crawling with would-be cowboys, you know. Pickup trucks, rifle racks in the back window, old faded Levi's: that sort of thing. I'm sure there are a few of them who would like to be remembered as the man who gunned down the last buffalo—"

"Like you, you mean?" Lester Ash said, speaking for the first time.

A smirk settled on Langford's lips. "Yes," he acknowledged. Adding, "And you." They locked eyes in a moment of mutual understanding, and then Langford said, "What we need, of course, is fast, flexible transportation." He turned to the Parks man. "How far is the nearest helicopter service?"

"Fifty miles."

"I suggest we start at once. If we have a helicopter at our disposal by the time the buffalo is located, we can hurry there at once. I presume the state would have no objection to that?"

The Parks man shrugged. "Not so long as all three of you get an equal start. And don't shoot it from the air."

"Of course not. We aren't barbarians, after all," He looked at Kingston and Lester Ash. "Are we agreed?"

"Agreed," said the actor.

"Let's go," said Ash.

Three hours earlier, Tank had parked the pickup and trailer in a stand of elm and gone on foot deeper into the trees where Otter had his cabin. It had still been dark; the eerie void before dawn. He knocked softly at Otter's door.

"Who disturbs this weak old man at such an hour?" a voice asked from within. "Is it someone evil, come to take advantage of my helplessness?"

"Otter, it is Sherman," said Tank. "Your daughter's man before she passed."

"What is it you want?" asked Otter. "I am destitute and can offer you nothing. I have no money or other valuables. I barely exist from day to day. Why have you come to me?"

"For your wisdom, Otter. For your words."

"Perhaps I can give you that, although I am usually so weak from hunger that each breath could well be my last. How many others have you brought with you?"

Tank smiled in the darkness. "I am alone, Otter." Maybe now the old scoundrel would stop acting.

"You may enter," Otter said. "There are candles by the door."

Inside the front door, Tank lighted a candle that illuminated patches of an incredibly dirty and impoverished room. In one corner, an ancient cot with torn, sagging mattress; in another a rusted iron sink filled with dirty pots and pans; in a third an old chifforobe with a broken door hanging loose to reveal a few articles of ragged clothing. Everywhere in between there was dirt, grime, clutter.

Tank did not even pause in the room. He lit his way

directly to a door which led to a second room, and in that
room he found Otter sitting up in a king-size bed, a cigar
in his mouth, a bottle of whiskey at his side. As Tank
closed the door behind him, the old Indian uncocked a
double-barrel shotgun on the bed beside him and put it
on the floor. "How are you, Soft Face?" he asked. The first
time he had seen Tank, the young fighter's face had been
beaten to pulp. Otter had called him Soft Face ever since.

"I'm okay," Tank said. "You look the same."

The old Indian shrugged. "There is no reason for
something perfect to change."

Tank grinned and glanced around the room. It was a
self-contained little world, holding everything Otter
needed or wanted for his personal comfort. Portable air
conditioner, color television, microwave oven, upright
freezer, power generator, small bathroom in one corner,
indoor hot tub and Jacuzzi in another. "How's the boot-
legging business?" Tank asked.

"My customers are loyal. I make ends meet." Otter got
out of bed and put a Hopi blanket around his shoulders.
"Is my granddaughter still dealing cards in the white
man's game?"

"Yes."

"Does she cheat them when the opportunity presents
itself?"

"Yes, if they are tourists."

Otter nodded in approval. "That is good. Even a half-
Indian should cheat the whites whenever possible." At a
two-burner hot plate, Otter set water to boil. "Sit here at
the table," he said, "and tell me your problem."

Tank quietly explained to the old Indian what he had
done, and why. When he got to the part about Rose and
her love for the buffalo, Otter's eyes became misty. When
Tank stopped talking, Otter rose, poured coffee and

brandy for them, and brought it to the table. "How can I help you?" he asked.

"I need a safe place to put the old buffalo. Someplace where she can live out her days in peace, without fear of being hunted and shot. Someplace where she will be able to die with dignity, like your daughter Primrose would want her to die."

Otter sipped his coffee and pondered the problem. Several times he shook his head in silence, as if first considering, then dismissing, a possibility. Finally he tapped a forefinger on the table and said, "Do you remember the place where Ditch Creek runs beside Bear Mountain?"

"In the Black Hills?" said Tank. "Where you used to take us on picnics when Delia was a little girl?"

"That is the place. There is a grassy meadow far above Ditch Creek that belongs to the few remaining people of the Deerfield tribe. It is within the Black Hills National Park, but the federal government deeded it to the Deerfields because there was no road into it and they must have figured the tourists would not be able to get to it anyway. The Deerfield use it for religious ceremonies; it is sacred ground to them. The buffalo would be protected once it got there. But there are only dirt paths leading up to the meadow. I don't know if the buffalo could climb it or not."

"How high is it?" Tank said.

"About seven thousand feet. There is a gravel road to about six thousand, but the rest of the way would be on footpaths. It would have been better if you had stolen a mountain goat. You were never very smart, Soft Face."

"Can you draw me a map?" Tank asked.

"Of course. I am a man of many talents."

Otter got paper and pencil and from memory sketched a map and gave it to Tank. It was daylight now and the two of them walked out to the horse trailer and Tank backed Hannah out to exercise and feed her.

"She is a fine old buffalo," Otter observed. "Only your people would even think of shooting her."

"Just because they're the same color doesn't mean they're my people," Tank replied.

Tank tethered the buffalo to a tree and returned to the cabin with Otter. The old Indian cooked breakfast and they ate together. Then it was time for Tank to leave. Otter walked back to the rig and helped him load Hannah. After Tank got in and started the truck, Otter put a hand on the door.

"In each man's life, there is a plateau," he said quietly. "Every man reaches that plateau. He may be there for a day or a year, or only for a moment. But his time there is the meaning of his life. It is the reason the Great One put him here on earth. I think, Soft Face, that your plateau might be that grassy meadow above Ditch Creek." He touched Tank's shoulder. "Go with the wind, son."

Tank swallowed dryly, nodded, and drove off.

The helicopter was flying a checkerboard search pattern two hundred miles from where the buffalo had been stolen. Harmon Langford sat next to the pilot. Gregory Kingston and Lester Ash occupied jumpseats behind them. All three men scanned the ground below with binoculars.

"This is maddening," Kingston muttered. He tapped Langford on the shoulder. "Tell me again!" he yelled through the noise of the rotor. "Why are we looking in this direction?"

The author yelled back, "The highway patrol reported that a pickup truck pulling a horse trailer filled up with gas in Dayton at four o'clock this morning! The station attendant said the animal in the trailer had a blanket over it and the man driving the truck said it was a rodeo bull! But he thinks it was our buffalo! They were headed toward Gillette! We're searching the area south of Gillette!''

The actor shrugged, as if it were all totally meaningless to him. Lester Ash leaned close to his ear and said, "Highway patrol thinks he might be headed toward Thunder Basin! That's a big grassland area; be a perfect place to set a buffalo loose!"

"I see!" Kingston said, smiling. "Now *that* makes sense!" He patted Ash fondly on the knee. Ash drew back suspiciously.

The helicopter continued to checkerboard, its pilot crossing out squares on a plot map on the console. They flew well into the grasslands, twenty miles deep, and began a random searching pattern, following shadows, wind movement, wild game—anything that attracted their attention. But they did not find what they were looking for. They searched for another hour.

"We'll have to land for fuel soon," the pilot advised Langford.

No sooner had he spoken than they received a radio message from the Parks man back at the concession. "The trailer has been sighted by a Civil Air Patrol scout plane. It's on Route 16, south of Osage, heading toward the Black Hills. It's sure to make it across the state line, so we're requesting the South Dakota state police to set up roadblocks. I'll keep you advised."

"How far is Osage?" Langford asked the pilot.

"Fifty miles, give or take."

"Can we make it?"

"Yes sir, but that'll be the limit. We'll have to refuel in Osage."

"Go," Harmon Langford ordered.

*   *   *

Tank had his CB tuned to the law enforcement band, so he heard the South Dakota state police order go out for roadblocks. They were being set up in Custer, Four Corners, and at the junction of Routes 85 and 16. Pulling onto the shoulder of the road, Tank shifted to neutral and unfolded a map he had picked up at a service station near Sundance, where Otter lived. When he had stopped at the station, the tarp flaps on the trailer had been down so no one could see inside; he was sure it had not been the station attendant who put the law on him. Probably that low-flying two-seater that had come in over him outside Osage.

Studying the map, Tank saw that the locations selected for the roadblocks gave him considerably more leeway than he had expected. Apparently they thought he was going to try to drive well into the Black Hills. He was not; he needed to penetrate them only a few miles before reaching a secondary road that ran north and then east to Ditch Creek. Smiling, he saw that he would miss all three roadblocks. Getting out of the truck for a moment, he lifted one of the trailer flaps and reached in to pat Hannah's thick, hairy cape.

"We're going to beat the sons of bitches, old girl," he said happily.

It had not occurred to him that they might use a helicopter.

At Osage, Harmon Langford conferred by telephone with the authorities responsible for the roadblock. "Of course, I very much appreciate your help in containing this man, Captain, and I assure you that when I write my bestseller about this incident, you and your men will be prominently featured. Now if you'd just be good enough to keep your forces in place and let my associates and me handle it from here, I think justice will be properly served. We really don't consider this a criminal matter; it's more mischief than anything else; a nuisance, but we can handle it—"

Then he talked with the pilot of the scout plane. "Are you keeping him in sight?"

"Yes, Mr. Langford. He's moving up a secondary road toward a place called Ditch Creek."

"Fine. Keep circling and don't lose him. We'll be airborne again in a few minutes and should be there shortly to take over. Of course, I'll expect to see you after this is all over, for photographs and such. The national publicity, you know. Over and out."

As Langford turned to face them, Kingston and Lester Ash saw a look of gleeful triumph on his face. Almost an *evil* look.

"In a very short while, gentlemen," he said, "we should be in position to take our buffalo back. I trust both of you are prepared to deal with this abductor if he resists us?"

Kingston frowned. "What do you mean?"

Langford did not answer. Instead, he picked up his rifle and jacked a round into the chamber.

Watching him, Lester Ash smiled.

Turning off the secondary road into the inclining gravel road, Tank was aware that the patrol plane was following him. But he was not overly concerned. The two men in the light plane could not get to him: no place in the surrounding hills they could land. All they could do was radio his position. And he was too close to his goal now for that to matter. He knew where the roadblocks were; no one from there could catch up with him. Only one obstacle remained in his way.

The thousand feet of footpath from the end of the gravel road up to the meadow.

Frowning, he wondered if old Hannah was going to be

able to make it. A lot would depend on how steep the trail was, and what kind of footing it offered. Good dirt footing was what he hoped for; Hannah's freshly trimmed hooves would slide too much on rock.

At the end of the gravel road, Tank drove the rig as far into the trees as he could. Part of the trailer still stuck out and he knew it could be seen from the air. No matter, he thought, they can't catch us now.

"Come on, old girl," he said as he backed Hannah out of the trailer and rubbed her neck. Studying the terrain above them, he selected the least steep path he could find and gently pulled Hannah onto it. Moving about four feet ahead of her, he drew the halter rope tight and urged her forward. She stepped nimbly up the trail and followed him without resistance.

This might be easier than I thought, Tank told himself hopefully.

The helicopter rendezvoused with the scout plane an hour after Tank and Hannah began their climb.

"Where are they?" Langford asked the air patrol pilot on the radio.

"In those trees on the side of the mountain, sir. You can't see them right now because of the overgrowth. They're probably about halfway up to that grassy meadow on the plateau there."

Langford praised the two men in the plane for exemplary work, dismissed them, and turned to the helicopter pilot. "Set down on that grassy meadow," he ordered.

"I can't do that, sir," said the pilot, who was half Nez Percé. "That's sacred land belonging to the Deerfield tribe. Outsiders are not permitted there."

Langford shifted the barrel of his rifle until it pointed toward the pilot. "I really do want you to land," he said pointedly.

The Nez Percé breed smiled. "I'd be careful with that rifle if I were you, sir. Unless you or your friends know how to fly one of these babies. They go down mighty fast."

Pursing his lips, Langford shifted the barrel back. He reached into his pocket, extracted a roll of currency, and peeled off five one-hundred-dollar bills. "If you could just hover a few feet from the ground. Long enough for us to drop off."

"That," the pilot said, taking the money, "I can do."

The last few hundred feet were the worst, for both the man and the buffalo. The trail, after an easy beginning, had become narrow, steep, rutted, and treacherous. Three times Hannah's hooves slipped on loose rocks or concealed roots, and the big animal went sliding back fifteen or twenty feet, dragging Tank with her. Each time she rolled over onto her side and mooed anxiously as dirt from above displaced and shifted down to half bury her. Each time, Tank had to stroke and sooth her, help her dig out and regain her balance, and patiently urge her forward again.

Twice Tank himself slipped badly, the leather of his old boots reacting just as Hannah's hooves did to the hostile ground under them. The first time he fell, his left foot came out from under him and he pitched onto both knees, puncturing one trouser leg on a sharp rock and cutting his knee badly enough to bleed. The second time, he lost his balance completely and went plunging downhill, sliding helplessly past Hannah, his face, shirt, boots catching the avalanche of loose dirt that followed him. He had the presence of mind to let go of the halter rope, however, and did not upset Hannah with his spill. He slid forty feet; when he straightened himself, he was filthy with dirt stuck to his sweaty clothes and body, and his

face and hands showed nicks and cuts seeping blood
through the dirt. Cursing mightily, Tank clawed his way
back up to where Hannah, watching him curiously,
waited with infinite patience.

Late in the climb, perhaps two hundred feet from the
plateau, Tank thought he heard the roar of a motor. It was
hard to tell, with the thick treetops insulating the ground
from noise, and the constant wind whipping about now
that they were so high. Maybe it was that light plane
coming in low to search the meadow. If so, he thought
craftily, they would find nothing there.

*We're beating them, Rose. Hannah and me. And it's
important. Important that we beat them. Important that
we make that plateau.*

They kept climbing, the man and the buffalo, struggling
against the total environment around them: the height
aloof above them, the ground resistant under them, the air
thin and selfish, the dirt and dust, the rocks and roots.
Blood and sweat burned their eyes, both of them, for
Hannah now had cuts on her old face as well. Foam
coated the buffalo's lips, saliva and tears wet the man's
cheeks.

They climbed until their muscles came close to locking,
their lungs close to bursting, their hearts close to breaking.
With no resource left but blind courage, they climbed.

Finally they made it to the top and together crawled
onto the edge of the grassy meadow.

The three hunters were waiting there for them.

Only when he saw the hunters did Tank Sherman realize
that the motor roar he heard had not been the scout plane,
but a helicopter. As he and the buffalo struggled together
to drag their bodies over the lip of the plateau, both had
fallen onto their knees: Tank pitching forward so that he
was on all fours, Hannah with her front legs bent, great

head down. Both were panting, trying to suck enough oxygen out of the thin air to cool lungs that felt as if they had been singed. For one brief instant, as they knelt side by side, Tank's shoulder brushing Hannah's neck, both their heads hung, it was as if man and beast were one.

Then Tank looked up and saw the hunters. They stood in a row, the sun reflecting on their rifles.

"No," he said softly, shaking his head. "No," a little louder as he got to his feet. "No!" he yelled as he walked toward them.

Harmon Langford, standing in the middle, said, "Stop where you are! Come any closer and we'll shoot!"

Eyes fixed like a madman, jaw clenched like a vise, his big fists closed, Tank stalked toward them. "No!" he kept shouting. "No! No! No!"

"You've been warned!" snapped Langford.

Tank kept coming.

"All right, shoot him!" Langford ordered, shouldering his own rifle and aiming.

No shots were fired. Langford lowered his rifle and looked frantically from Kingston to Lester Ash. "Shoot! Why don't you shoot!"

"Why don't you?" Lester Ash asked evenly.

Langford did not have time to reply. Tank reached him, snatched the rifle from his hands, and hurled it away. Then he drove a crushing right fist into Langford's face, smashing his nose and lips, sending him reeling back in shock.

As Langford fell, Tank turned on Gregory Kingston. "Now just a minute," the actor pleaded, "I had no intention of shooting you—" He threw down his rifle as evidence of his sincerity, but that did not deter Tank Sherman. The old fighter dug a solid right fist deep into Kingston's midsection and the actor folded up like a suitcase, the color draining from his face, his eyes bulging. Dropping to his knees, he pitched forward onto his face, the juicy meadow grass staining it green.

When Tank looked for the third man, he found that Lester Ash, experienced hunter that he was, had flanked his adversary and moved around behind him. It was now Tank standing on the meadow, Lester Ash facing him with his back to the sun.

"We can do it the easy way or the hard way, bud," said Lester. "Either way, that buffalo's mine."

Tank shook his head. "No." He moved toward Ash.

"I ain't no loudmouthed writer or sissy actor, bud," the Nevadan said. "Mess with me and I'll put you in the hospital. That buff is mine!"

"No." Tank kept coming.

"Please yourself," Lester said disgustedly. He snapped the rifle to his shoulder and fired.

The round ripped all the way through the fleshy part of Tank's left thigh and knocked him off his feet. Instincts two decades old still lived in his mind, and as if someone were counting ten over him, Tank rolled over and got back up. Clutching his thigh, he limped toward Ash.

"You're a damned fool, bud," said Lester Ash. He fired again.

The second slug tore a hole in Tank's right thigh and he was again spun to the ground. He moaned aloud, involuntarily, and sat up, one hand on each wound. Pain seared his body, hot and relentless, and he began to choke, cough, and cry. *I'm done for*, he thought.

Then at his feet he saw something white and yellow. Pawing the tears from his eyes, he managed to focus. It was a clump of wildflowers: white petals with yellow nectaries. Primroses.

Tank dragged himself up one last time. He started forward again, weaving and faltering like a drunk man. His eyes fixed on Lester Ash and held.

"Okay, bud," said Lester, "now you lose a kneecap—"

Before Lester could fire, Hannah charged. Massive head down, hooves almost soundless on the thick meadow grass, she was upon Lester Ash before he realized it. Catching him from the left side, her broad forehead drove into his chest, crushing his left rib cage, collapsing the lung beneath it. With his body half bent over her face, Hannah propelled him to the edge of the plateau and hurled him over the side.

Lester Ash screamed as his body ricocheted off the first three trees, then was silent for the rest of the way down.

The Deerfield tribe marshal and his deputy, who rode up to the meadow on horseback at the first sound of gunfire, secured the area and arranged for Harmon Langford and Gregory Kingston to be escorted down to the reservation boundary. They were released with a stern warning never to violate Deerfield land again. Some men with a rescue stretcher retrieved Lester Ash's body, and his death was officially attributed to an accidental fall from the plateau.

A Deerfield medicine man named Alzada, who resided in a lodge back in the trees next to the meadow, was consulted by the marshal as to the disposition of the buffalo.

"If the Great One put the buffalo here," Alzada decreed, "then the buffalo must be sacred. It shall be allowed to graze on the sacred meadow until the Great One summons it back."

The marshal looked over at the edge of the meadow where Tank sat under a tree, exhausted and bleeding. "What about the man?"

"What man?" said Alzada. "I see no man. I see only a sacred buffalo, grazing contentedly. If you see something else, perhaps it is a spirit."

The marshal shook his head. "If Alzada sees nothing, then I also see nothing. Only Alzada can see spirits."

The marshal and his deputy rode back down the mountain.

When they were gone, the medicine man went over and helped Tank into the trees to his lodge.

ISAAC ASIMOV

The Lost Dog

The conversation had turned to pets and both Jennings and Baranov were overflowing with wonder tales of pets they had owned or had known.

I, as a non-pet person, was more than a little annoyed. Having no stories of my own to contribute, I occupied myself in pooh-poohing theirs. I denied that dogs had human intelligence, that horses were gifted with telepathy, and that cats had a sly wisdom that routed their owners every time.

I was sneered at, of course, and finally, out of sheer desperation, I called on Griswold for help. He, to all appearances, had been sleeping soundly throughout the sometimes heated discussion, but I never doubted his capacity to know what was going on despite any state of unconsciousness he might appear to be immersed in.

"Griswold," I said, "did you ever encounter any superhuman animals?"

Griswold's ice-blue eyes opened and one of his formidable eyebrows lifted sardonically. He sipped at the Scotch and soda he had been holding firmly in his hand and said, "I found a dog once."

"A wonder dog?" I asked, suspiciously.

"No," he said, "just an ordinary nondescript mutt."

"If he's not a wonder dog," I said, "then the argument is settled. If, with your imagination, you can't claim you were involved with a wonder dog then I maintain that there aren't any."

"This dog—" said Griswold.

"That's all right," I said, waving my hand at him negligently. "We don't need the story."

This dog [said Griswold] was brought to my attention by Katherine Adelman, a nurse with whom I had been rather friendly in times past. What's more, I still had some youthful fire in me—this was several decades ago—and I was sentimental enough to be willing to listen to her even though at that time, as I recall, I had much of greater moment to occupy my mind.

She said, "There's a man dying in one of my wards and I'm very upset over it."

"I'm sorry," I said, mechanically, though I knew she must encounter death every day. It could be no stranger to her.

"He's a derelict," she said. "He was picked up on the street and brought in. We know practically nothing about him, except part of his name. When we asked him his name, he managed a strangled 'Jeff.' That was all he ever said. After that he just lay there, barely conscious, and then he slipped off into a kind of semicoma."

"Is he being well treated?" I asked, a bit sardonically. The hospital, after all, however high-minded its ideals might be, subsisted on money, and coddling a dying derelict must go against the grain.

"Of course," she said, with a touch of reproach. And then, showing that she quite understood the point I was making, she added, "He won't be much of an expense. He'll be dead in a day or two."

You must understand that in those days the medical profession was not quite as well equipped with devices to keep the soul within the body against the body's will.

People died more speedily and easily, and with greater dignity.

I said, "Why are you concerned, Kate, aside from your general disapproval of death?"

"It's a little thing. As I say, he was found on the street, and I'm sure that he'd gone out, sick as he was, squandering his last strength in the cold and the wet, in order to try to find his dog."

There were tears in her eyes and I grew uneasy. She was an ardent dog lover—that had been an important factor in spoiling our pleasant relationship—and I knew that the matter of the dog would weigh far more heavily with her than anything else would. She was going to ask me to do something, and I might not be able to refuse.

I said, "Did he tell you so?"

"No. He was past talking, as I said, but he managed to scrawl a note on a piece of paper I brought him for the purpose."

"I presume you also brought him a pen."

"Yes, and a board to write on."

"How did you know he wanted all that?"

"He was trying to talk and failing. He could only wheeze and cough in a most pathetic way, and when he made weak, but desperate, writing gestures, it wasn't hard to guess what he wanted. I've dealt with so many dying people, Griswold, I can almost read their minds."

I nodded. "I'm guessing you have the note with you and that you want me to look at it."

"Yes, I do," and she showed me a scrap of paper. "He went into his semicoma while he was writing it."

I don't have that piece of paper to show to you three now, and I rather despair of reproducing the exact wording, orthography, and handwriting, but I shall use the amenities of the Union Club library to produce something that will be close enough for the purpose.

—Here it is.

As you see, it reads:

> PLEEZ MY DORG WAZ
> TAKEN TO THE POND GET
> IT FOR ME PLEEZ I CANT
> DAY WITHOUT I SAY GOODBY
> IT ANSERS TO ITS NAME
> WHICH   IS?

Kate was weeping by now. She said, "He must have been too sick to prevent his dog—unlicensed, I'm sure—from being taken away. I suppose he gathered his last strength to go to the pound to retrieve his dog and then collapsed en route."

I said, "And you haven't been able to find out anything about him? Has he any friends?"

"He's just a derelict. He doesn't live in this area. Neither the police nor the people at the local soup kitchen recognize him. He may be utterly homeless, living out of garbage cans, with nothing but his dog for company. His clothes were rags and he had no effects, certainly no money. I suppose that if we ran a full investigation we might find out something but that's not important. What I need to do is get his dog."

"What good would that do?" I asked, gloomily.

"He killed himself trying to get that dog, Griswold, and now he's going to die utterly alone. No one should die alone."

"Many people have to," I said, trying to console her and feeling that I was only sounding heartless. "How can you get the dog?"

"I went to the pound this morning," she said. "I didn't know exactly when they had picked up the dog and they couldn't identify any as belonging to a particular dying derelict. They knew nothing about it. They just picked up unlicensed dogs. They had over a dozen. It seemed like a hundred to me. I wanted to take them all and bring them to the poor fellow. If he would wake up, he'd know if one were his. —But I could never bring that horde of dogs to his room. I might smuggle in one."

"You'd be risking your job."

"I know. But which one would it be? All I knew was that it would answer to its name but, of course, he never managed to finish the note and write its name. —Did you ever read 'Rumpelstiltskin,' Griswold?"

"Of course," I said. "When I was a child."

"I felt like the princess who was going to lose her baby to the evil little dwarf unless she could guess his name. Except that she had a year to do the guessing and I had only an hour or so. I just kept calling out—Rex—Fido—Spot—every doggy name I could think of and got nowhere. Some dogs barked and yelped and ran about but they just did it generally and weren't responding to some particular name."

"You don't even know if the dog is male or female, do you?"

"No. But after I called Rex, I tried Regina; after I called Prince, I tried Princess. I tried ordinary names—Bill and Jane, for instance. I tried Curly and Genevieve." She looked at me and tried to smile. "I even tried Rumpelstiltskin."

I said, "I take it that didn't work."

"No. Nothing worked. I finally had to give up."

I said, "You know, Kate, the dog may have been put away."

"Oh, no," she said, in obvious pain. "They keep it for several days in case the owner shows up, or someone wants it." Then she said, "I suppose that no one would

want it, though. I keep thinking that that penniless old
man must have had a penniless old dog, if you know what
I mean. Their love for each other was the only possession
in all the world that either of them had, and I must do
something about it."

I nodded. She was a soft-hearted girl. It wasn't her fault
that the world had failed to turn her cynical.

She said, "So I came to you."

"What can I do?"

"Won't you come to the pound with me now? I still
have a couple of hours before my work shift begins."

"I can do *that* if I have to, but what else can I do?"

"You may be able to think of a name I couldn't think of.
Or you may be able to tell which dog is the derelict's just
by looking at it. You know how clever you are."

I said, "I'm not clever enough to pluck a name out of
thin air. Even the princess only got the dwarf's name
because she overheard him announce it."

But the tears were rolling quietly down her cheeks, and
she *was* pretty, and I was quite young, and the memories
I had did their mischief. I said, "Well, let me think."

She waited for me, watching with her big, trusting eyes,
and that gave me no choice. I said, "Very well, Kate. Let's
go to the pound."

We went there and were taken to the department of
recent acquisitions, if I might call it that. It smelled and it
was noisy and I didn't like it. It was the first time I'd ever
visited a pound, as it happened.

I slapped my knees and called out a name—and one of
the dogs went wild. He yelped happily and threw himself
at the mesh barrier trying to get at me, with his tail
wagging into a blur.

I said to the attendant in charge, "I want that dog. It
belongs to a friend of mine. I'll pay for the license and any

other fee required, but I must have it now. My friend is dying."

Kate was wearing her nurse's uniform. She presented her hospital badge with her photograph, and confirmed that it was life and death, and we got the dog.

We raced to the hospital and, with a sympathetic doctor, and quite against the hospital rules, we smuggled the dog into the room in which its master lay dying.

The dog emitted a muffled whine and nuzzled the derelict's hand. The dying man's eyes opened at the touch, and his head turned slightly. He could do no more than smile faintly and his hand trembled as he reached out to pat the dog's head just once. He died, then, with his only friend licking his hand.

Kate took the dog away, then, much against its will. She left it in my charge, but at the end of her shift, she took it over and adopted it.

The dog died a year afterward and, eventually, so did Kate. It was I who sat at her bedside and made certain that she didn't die alone either.

Griswold's eyes were blinking as he finished his drink and he rubbed his nose rather violently.

We did not speak for a while but then Jennings said, softly, "But how did you come to know the dog's name?"

Griswold said, "It was just a guess. The only thing we knew about the man was that his name was Jeff. I had to ask myself: what would someone named Jeff call his dog if his dog was a shaggy, nondescript, unkempt mongrel? Well, there was once a comic strip that maintained its popularity over a period of half a century or more called 'Mutt and Jeff.' Augustus Mutt was, of course, a human character in the strip but might it not occur to someone named Jeff, who owned a mutt, to *call* him Mutt in honor of the strip? It was a long, long chance, but with Kate looking at me, I had to try."

I said, sardonically, "A long chance, indeed."

"Not for you three," growled Griswold. "As soon as I mentioned the dog, I described him as an 'ordinary nondescript Mutt.' Remember? How much more of a hint did you want?"

HOPE RAYMOND

Neighbors

Miss Parsons sat on the back steps, the spring sun warming her thin shoulders. It was the kind of day that makes winter worth surviving. Wisps of cloud decorated a soft hyacinth-blue sky. A red-winged blackbird sang in the reeds that bordered the pond. Beyond him, sailing the breeze-rippled water, a majestic white swan patrolled the marshy shoreline, guarding his invisible mate on her nest at the water's edge. Nearer the house, crocuses bloomed around the old cement birdbath, and warblers chirped to each other in the forsythia. Ulysses the beagle, at her feet, stretched himself out on the new grass and gave a contented sigh.

Miss Parsons, however, was experiencing no lift of the spirit. As she gazed across her own neat yard to the tangled wilderness beyond, her expression was somber. The unthinkable, it seemed, was about to happen.

She had coveted the adjacent lot, which, like her own, ran from the lane down to the pond and seemed somehow to have been overlooked when the surrounding farms were laid out, ever since she and her mother had moved into the little house at the end of the lane years ago, when she had first come to teach at Bayern High. Even then it had been overgrown and of no apparent use to anybody except the birds and rabbits. In those days, though, she had had no spare time to seek out the owner and no spare money to offer when he was found.

Later, when by saving and inheritance she had acquired a little cushion, she had made inquiries and learned that the land belonged to old Mrs. Burger, who spent most of her time in a wheelchair and refused to discuss business. Miss Parsons had been advised to wait and make an offer to the estate later on. She had accepted this suggestion all the more readily because Mrs. Burger had had no children and the probable heir was Betty Vogel, Mrs. Burger's great-niece, a friendly acquaintance; she and Miss Parsons both sang in the Bayern Light Opera Club. No one thought Miss Parsons would have long to wait.

But Mrs. Burger surprised everybody. By the time she finally lost her hold, at ninety-seven, Miss Parsons' mother had preceded her, and Miss Parsons herself was ready for retirement.

When, after a decent interval, Miss Parsons approached Betty with an offer to buy the lot, she received disconcerting news. Although Betty had been left the Burger house and most of the money, the land on Schimmler's Lane had gone to Fred Jansen, a nephew of Mrs. Burger's in Chicago. He was understood to have something to do with wheat futures.

"I don't know him very well," Betty had said. "I don't think Aunt Anna liked him much, and he never came to see her. But he was her brother's son and I suppose she thought she owed him something. George Winters is handling the estate. I guess you could call him and make an offer, and he could pass it on to Fred. I expect Fred'd be glad to sell the lot to you. I don't think he cares anything about Bayern, and who else would want it besides you?"

That question had been answered promptly by George Winters. Mr. Jansen, he said, had asked him to dispose of the land at the best possible price as soon as it was legally his. He had heard from a tavern owner in the next town

who wanted to put up a small resort there. This man
proposed to clear the land completely and erect a building
big enough for Saturday night dances. With a large
parking lot, boats for rent, and, naturally, a bar. Of course,
George said, Mr. Jansen would be just as happy to sell to
Miss Parsons if she would care to match the tavern
keeper's price. He named a sum that was more than Miss
Parsons could have raised if she had bankrupted herself.

Miss Parsons was appalled. She had bought her house
in the first place because she liked privacy and peace, and
had worked hard to get the place the way she liked it.
Now, when she was ready to enjoy it, this. She could look
forward to trespassing drunks. Constant auto traffic. Curious strangers peering at her from the pond. Casual
vandalism.

Fighting a rear-guard action, she had appealed to the
town authorities to zone the tavern out or buy the land for
a nature reserve. But times had been hard in Bayern.
Everyone sympathized with Miss Parsons, but no one
wanted to discourage any enterprise that might bring
money into the town, and as for buying parks, she knew
very well that there were potholes on Main Street and the
high school needed a new roof.

Betty Vogel had offered to intercede for her with Fred
Jansen. She would tell him, she said, that Aunt Anna
would have liked Miss Parsons to have the land if he
didn't want it himself. Miss Parsons had had very little
faith in this appeal to sentiment, but she had nothing to
lose by letting Betty go ahead.

Betty had just telephoned with a report. Fred Jansen
had called her from Minneapolis the previous day to ask
when the estate was likely to be settled. She had pled
Miss Parsons' case, but he had been completely unrespon-
sive. According to him, things were not going well in the

futures markets, and he needed to get all he could from
the land.

"Personally, I think he's just being a pig," Betty had
said. "If only it was his daughter. I know her. She's nice,
and she's married to a surgeon, she doesn't need money.
I'm real sorry."

Miss Parsons had felt, somehow, that she could assim-
ilate this final blow more easily if she went outside. But
her mind refused to deal with it. At her feet, Ulysses
muttered a little, and she managed to formulate the
thought that he wouldn't like it if they had to move to an
apartment. She had decided some time ago that if the
resort was definitely coming she would sell out and move
into town. With a prospective neighbor like that, she
couldn't expect to get much.

The sound of an automobile approaching down Schimmler's Lane made her pull herself together and rise to her
feet, prepared for visitors. People who drove down the
lane were usually on their way to see her.

The noise of the engine cut off before she reached the
front yard, and no car was in sight. While she was still
asking herself whether she had been hearing things, a
pudgy, balding stranger dragging a small kayak on a
wheeled carrier came trudging down the lane. Perhaps it
was the peculiar picture he presented that disturbed the
normally friendly Ulysses, who had followed her to the
front yard. His lips drew back from his teeth and he
growled in his throat.

The man hailed her as soon as he came within voice
range.

"This the Burger property?" he said, gesturing toward
the tangle of underbrush.

"That's right," said Miss Parsons. With one hand on
Ulysses' collar, she advanced to meet him.

The man propped the carrier against a tree and pulled

out a handkerchief, with which he wiped his brow. He
looked pasty and out of condition, Miss Parsons thought.
She wondered why he had dressed in a business suit if he
planned to go boating.

"I just inherited it," said the man. "Kind of a godforsaken spot, isn't it? Guess I shouldn't complain. Never
expected old Anna to leave me anything. We didn't get
along. Thought as long as I was driving through anyway I
might as well have a look at it. Got a pretty good offer for
it, better than I was expecting, and thought there might be
something more here than I realized." A sly look crossed
his face. "You never know, do you? Lawyer tells me the
guy wants it for the pond frontage and the best way to see
that is from a boat. So I rented this." He gestured toward
the kayak. "Hope I can still work it. Haven't used one
since camp. Lawyer says it's marshy down by the shore
but there's a path leads to the remains of an old dock that
I can take off from. That right, do you know?"

"You must be Mr. Jansen," said Miss Parsons. "I can't
tell you about the path, I haven't been down it lately. I'd
be trespassing, wouldn't I?"

Something about her tone seemed to arrest Jansen.
"You the lady wanted to buy the land?" he said.
"Couldn't match the other offer?"

"I'm a teacher," said Miss Parsons. "We don't get rich.
I would have offered more if I'd had more. I don't want a
tavern for a neighbor."

Jansen's gaze swept over her neat little house and
garden, her well-weeded lawn, and a flash of compunc-
tion crossed his face. Then it settled again into a hard
geniality. "Too bad," he said. "But business is business,
isn't it? That the path to the dock I passed a few feet
back?"

"I believe so," said Miss Parsons. She hesitated a

moment, and then, as if forcing herself, went on, "Better be careful down by the marsh."

Jansen gave her a knowing look. "Trying to scare me off?" he said. "No quicksand or water moccasins around here. Well, thanks for your help. I better get going." He seized the carrier again and headed back toward the path.

Miss Parsons gazed after him a moment, as if wondering whether to add to her warning. Then she shook her head slightly and turned toward the house, Ulysses beside her. She felt she had been fair.

When the deputy sheriff drove up the next day, he found Miss Parsons kneeling beside the petunia bed in her front yard, a little pile of weeds beside her. She rose to her feet as he got out of the car. Ulysses, digging furiously under the hedge for a putative rabbit, paid no attention to him.

"Morning, Miss Parsons," said the deputy respectfully. He had had her for American History at Bayern High ten years earlier.

"Good morning, Carl," said Miss Parsons. "What brings you out here?"

"Seems there's been an accident in the pond," said the deputy. "They wanted me to ask you if you saw anything."

"An accident?" said Miss Parsons. "Well, you'd better come in if you want to question me." She led the way into the house and established him at the polished dining table. "Now, what did you want to ask me?" she said.

Carl hesitated. He was finding it difficult to take charge of the interview; he was used to thinking of Miss Parsons as Authority. But he pulled himself together. "Thing is," he said, "Bill Dorfman over the other side was out on his hill this morning, checking on his cows, and he saw something floating in the pond, looked like a kayak upside down. So he got his canoe out of the barn and paddled over, and there was this kayak, and a man lying in the shallows. Bill towed him over to his side, where it was easier to get him ashore, and worked on him for a while, but it didn't do any good. So he called us and we came out. The man was dead all right. Stranger to Bill, he said. We checked his wallet. Name's Jansen. Comes from Chicago. Lives in a hotel there. The office is trying to locate some family. We'll have to make a report. First thing is, what was he doing in the pond? Bill said he didn't see him go by his place. Wondered if you'd seen him."

"A Mr. Jansen with a kayak came down this way yesterday," said Miss Parsons. "He said he'd come to look at the land he inherited up the lane." She described her visitor.

"Sounds like him," said Carl. "Alone, was he?"

"As far as I know," said Miss Parsons. "Although I didn't see his car—from the sound, he parked it further up the lane, and I suppose he could have left somebody in it. But he spoke as though he were alone, and he had a one-man kayak. And if he'd had a companion the person would have given the alarm, surely."

"Nobody came here?" said Carl.

"Not a soul."

"Bill says he didn't see anybody either. And nobody called us."

"Why do you think there was somebody with him?"

Carl looked unhappy. "Thing is, the doc doesn't think he drowned. Says it looks more like a heart attack, but not a peaceful one. There are bruises on his face and arms, like somebody'd been beating up on him with a stick or something and he tried to shield himself. May have been fright that put him out, the doc thinks."

"Are you saying this unfortunate man was murdered?" said Miss Parsons.

"Well, helped along, you might say."

"Good heavens," said Miss Parsons.

"Yours is the only house that overlooks the pond," said Carl. "You didn't see anything, I guess?"

"I was working inside all afternoon," said Miss Parsons. "Ulysses didn't bark. Of course, he doesn't always. He's not a very good watchdog, I'm afraid." She spoke with gentle regret, but no sign of fear that Carl could notice. He had worried that the thought of a lurking menace might frighten her.

"I'll have a look at that patch next door on my way out," he said, getting to his feet. "Not that it'll do any good. If there was anybody there, he's long gone."

"You should find Mr. Jansen's car there," said Miss Parsons.

"Saw it on the way in," said Carl. "He'd pulled off the lane under a tree. I'll have a look at that too."

"Be careful down in the marsh," said Miss Parsons. "You don't know what you might run into."

"Oh, I don't think we'll have to do much down there, except to see where he started out from," said Carl. "Too wet and tangled for anybody to hide in, Bill says."

"I dare say that's right," said Miss Parsons, following him toward the door.

Carl opened it and then paused on the threshold. "Well, thanks," he said. "If you think of anything or if you need us, give us a call. If you wanted to come into town for a day or so, just till we're sure there's nobody hanging around, lots of people'd be glad to have you. Nedda and I would, only it's kind of noisy with the baby."

Miss Parsons smiled at him. "That's very kind of you, Carl," she said. "But don't worry. I'll be all right." She closed the door gently behind him.

As he headed toward the path to the old dock, Carl cast

a final look back at the little house. He had heard about Miss Parsons' efforts to buy the land; everybody in Bayern heard practically everything. If Jansen was indeed the man who had inherited it, this death might turn out very convenient for her, and she had certainly taken it calmly. It was hard to believe, but could she possibly have . . .? Then he shook his head. Miss Parsons was about five-foot-two and probably weighed ninety-eight pounds after Thanksgiving dinner. Jansen, although not in the best of condition, had been considerably bigger and stronger. There was no way . . . Carl gave a sigh of relief. He simply could not imagine himself arresting Miss Parsons.

A month went by. Miss Parsons planted her vegetables and attended her committee meetings. The sheriff's office continued its investigations. The crocuses faded and the tulips came out.

On a particularly balmy day, Miss Parsons drove her subcompact into Bayern to do some errands. In the post office she ran into Carl.

"Have you found out yet what happened to poor Mr. Jansen?" she said, after they had exchanged greetings.

"Oh, we're dropping it," said Carl. "We checked back on where he'd spent the night—it was a business trip—and he was alone then, and he got gas in town here just before you saw him and he was still alone. And there haven't been any strangers showed up in the area. Doc says he got the bruises before he died, but it might not have been down at the pond. He might have been in a fight somewhere. We couldn't pick up any traces of one, but you can't always. Something like that happens in a tavern, say, they'd just as soon not talk about it. We're calling it a natural death from heart failure. His daughter, she's satisfied about it—says his doctor told him be careful, but he wasn't."

"I see," said Miss Parsons. She was quite sure that there had been no bruises on Jansen's face when she had spoken with him, but she had no intention of saying so. "Well, that must be a relief to you. How's the baby?"

The baby, it seemed, was fine. Miss Parsons must come and see him someday. Miss Parsons promised to do so soon, and passed out of the post office. An old pupil, observing her as she headed down Main Street toward the stationery store, noticed how light her step was. Outside the bakery she encountered Betty Vogel.

"Oh, Nell!" said Betty. "I've been meaning to call you. I've got good news and bad news."

"Tell me the bad news first," said Miss Parsons.

"Well, I've talked to Helen, Fred Jansen's daughter, you know, she's his heir, and she doesn't want to sell that land to you. The good news is she doesn't want to sell it to anybody else either. She and her husband'll keep it—might build a weekend cottage there later on. She'd be a good neighbor—I'm sure you'll like her. And that'd be a lot better than a tavern, wouldn't it?"

A small but genuine smile appeared on Miss Parsons' lips and spread to her eyes. "A great deal better," she said. "I'd like to have the land, of course, but it'd be nice to have a good neighbor, too, now I'm getting older. Thanks, Betty."

On the way home, she sang softly to herself. As soon as she had stowed away her purchases, she took a loaf of sliced bread from the refrigerator, pulled on a pair of rubber boots, and, accompanied by Ulysses, made her way down to the pond, where the whole swan family was now on display, with the proud cob in the lead, four tiny, fluffy beige cygnets paddling valiantly after him, and the pen in the rear. Parting the reeds, she clumped to the shoreline and began throwing out bits of bread. As the cob changed course and headed in her direction, followed by his family, Ulysses whined softly and began to back away. The cob looked graceful and harmless now, but earlier in the season Ulysses had explored too close to the swans' nest and had encountered a slashing beak, a neck like a bull whip, and mighty wings that could break a man's leg with a blow. Gifted with agility and a sound heart, he had escaped safely, but he had no desire to meet the cob again.

Miss Parsons fed the swans the entire loaf of bread. It was the only way she could think of to thank them.

MARGARET MARON

On Windy Ridge

Waiting is more tiresome than doing, and I was weary. Bone weary. "Seems longer than just yesterday those two went up to Windy Ridge," I said. "Two went up, but three were there, you know."

"Now what's that supposed to mean, Ruth?" asked Wayne.

Wayne's my cousin and a good sheriff. What he lacks in formal training, he makes up in common sense and a knowledge of the district that comes from growing up here in the mountains and from being related by birth or marriage to half the county. Our grandmothers were sisters and we've run in and out of each other's houses for forty years. I knew he was wondering if my queer remark came from tiredness or because I half believe some of the legends that persist in these hills.

He walked over to the deck rail and looked down into the ravine, but my eyes lifted to the distant hills, beyond trees that burned red and gold, to where the ridges misted into smoky blue. The hills were real and everlasting and I had borrowed of their strength before.

When I built this deck nearly twenty years ago, I planned it wide enough for a wedding breakfast because Luke Randolph and I were to be married as soon as he came home from Vietnam. It was May, wild vines grew up the pilings, and the air was heavy with the scent of

honeysuckle and wisteria the day Luke's brother Tom
came over with the crumpled telegram in his hand.

The hills haven't changed since then, but the red cedar
planks have weathered to silver-gray and Wayne looked
at me uneasily across their width.

"You're not going ghostie on me, are you, Ruth? This
isn't the first time a man's been shot up on Windy Ridge,
and it won't be the last. Hell, Sam's already put in two
complaints."

Feisty Sam Haskell owns a small dairy farm on the edge
of Windy Ridge, and trying to keep his herd from being
shot out from under him every year makes him a perennial source of tall tales. In exasperation once, he'd painted
C-O-W in bright purple on the flank of every animal. Two
were promptly shot.

Wayne sighed. "That's what puzzles me. Gordon Tyler
was a furriner, but Noah knew better than to go into the
woods the first day of deer season when all those city folk
show up, blasting away at anything that moves without
waiting to see if it's got two legs or four. Why'd he go?"

"Gordon wanted to try his new rifle, and he talked
Noah into it," I said.

Yesterday had been one of those perfect October morn-
ings with barely a hint of frost in the air. We'd just
finished a late breakfast here on the deck: Noah Randolph, who was Luke's nephew, my niece Julie, and me.
Julie had bubbled like liquid sunshine that morning, her
red hair flaming like a maple tree. After a summer of
flirting around with Gordon Tyler, she'd finally decided
that Noah was really the one she wanted to marry, and
her brand-new diamond sparkled in the crisp air.

Noah was so much like my Luke—a mountain man, tall
and solid, with clear brown eyes and a mane of sandy
hair. Not handsome. His features were too strong and
open. But a good face. A face you could trust your life

with. Or trust with a niece who's been your life for fifteen of her twenty years after her parents died in a plane crash.

They were arguing over the last cheese biscuit when Gordon Tyler came up the side steps carrying a gleaming new rifle. Dark and wiry, he moved with the grace of a panther, and most women found him magnetic.

"I never liked Gordon," I told Wayne.

"Then why did you encourage him?"

"Because Julie didn't appreciate Noah. Remember how I dithered over Luke so long? Wondering if I loved him only because no one more romantic was around? It took that damn war—knowing he could be killed—to make me realize. Julie was me all over again, and Gordon had money, glamour, and the surface excitement she thought Noah lacked. I thought if she got a good dose of Gordon, she'd wake up to Noah's real value."

"It's usually a mistake to play God," Wayne said.

Which was exactly what I had thought as I fetched Gordon a cup from the kitchen and urged him to pull up a chair and how about a slice of ham? I knew I'd acted shabbily in using him to help Julie finish growing up, and I tried to ease my conscience by being overly hospitable when the pure and simple truth was that I wanted Gordon Tyler to go away. To get off our mountain and out of Julie's life now that he'd served his purpose.

Until then, I'd rather enjoyed the seasonal influx of wealthy people who bought up our dilapidated barns and farmhouses and remodeled them into sumptuous vacation homes. Old-timers might grumble about flatlanders and furriners and yearn for the days when Jedediah's store down at the crossroads had stocked nothing more exotic than Vienna sausage, but it's always amused me to step around a flop-eared hound sprawled beside the potbellied stove and ask Jedediah for caviar, smoked oysters, or a bottle of choice Riesling.

Now I felt like one of the old-timers, and I wished all flatlanders and furriners to perdition, beginning with Gordon Tyler, who'd bought the old Edditston orchards as a tax shelter and play-pretty last year. We'd heard he'd inherited right much money, and he never mentioned any commitments to work beyond occasional board meetings up north. That gave him a lot of free time. Especially after Julie caught his eye this summer.

Julie said she'd been frank with him about Noah, but I was sitting across from Gordon when Noah and Julie announced their engagement out at Taylor's Inn, and something about the way he went so white and still made me think he really hadn't expected it. The moment passed, though, and he was the first to jump up and offer a toast.

Before the engagement, Gordon had barely noticed Noah; yet in less than two weeks he transformed himself from Julie's rejected lover into Noah's good ol' pal. When Noah could get away from the farm he'd inherited from Luke, they even went squirrel hunting and fishing together.

"It always sort of surprised me that Gordon could shoot so well," said Wayne, "him being a city boy and all."

"Gordon never did anything in public unless he could do it best," I said bitterly. "He always had to win. By hook or crook."

"He won the shooting medal fair and square," Wayne observed.

"Only because the Anson boy couldn't enter."

"Come on, Ruth! You don't think Gordon had anything to do with Tim Anson's falling through his barn roof, do you?"

"I don't know what I think anymore," I said crossly. "Gordon was up there with him, pointing out the rotten spots he wanted reshingled. Maybe he didn't know that section of roof was so far gone. All I'm saying is that Tim's the best shot around, and Gordon didn't enter the match till after Tim had broken his arm."

"No, honey," Wayne said gently, "you're saying a lot more than that."

Wayne has known me all my life. Did he realize I'd spent the last twenty-four hours brooding over all that had happened since Julie and Noah became engaged?

When Gordon had interrupted our breakfast on the deck, I'd marked down the faint unease his presence aroused as a product of my own guilt pangs. Unlike Noah and Julie, I wasn't happy that he'd taken their engagement so well. Good-natured resignation seemed out of character.

Yet, as I brought out a fresh pot of coffee, there was Gordon showing Noah his new rifle. All morning the surrounding woods had reverberated with gunshots as deer season opened with its usual bang, and Gordon was anxious to test the gun. "It should stop a whitetail," he said.

"Oh, it'll do that," Noah agreed dryly. His big hands held the expensive, customized Remington carbine expertly, and as he laid his cheek against the hand-carved stock and sighted along the gleaming barrel, a strand of brown hair fell across his eyes. Julie brushed it back with a proprietary hand, her ring flashing in the sunlight.

Gordon's eyes narrowed, but he smiled and said, "I know you don't like to go out opening day, but this may be my only chance. I'm flying to Delaware tomorrow on business, and there's no telling when I'll get back. Of course, if you're afraid to come, I can go alone."

"Common sense isn't fear!" I snapped, and Julie said, "Noah's staying right here. Too many fools show up the first day."

If we'd kept our mouths shut, he probably would have

put Gordon off; but with both of us jumping in, Noah naturally stood up, touseled Julie's red-gold hair, and told her to quit acting like a bossy wife.

"How far do you feel like walking?" he asked Gordon.

"Why don't we try Windy Ridge? I saw a nice buck up there the other day."

As Noah grabbed his jacket and started to follow Gordon down the steps, he looked back at Julie. There were times when she could look very tiny and crushed, as if all the sunshine had gone out of her life, and she was doing it then. I'd have sworn that even her hair had gone two shades duller. Hurt tears threatened to spill over her sandy lashes, and Noah returned, wiped her eyes with his handkerchief, and gently cupped her face in his strong hands.

"Quit worrying, honey. I'll wear my orange hunting cap. Nobody's going to take me for a deer, so cheer up and give me a kiss."

Brightness flowed back into her and she kissed him so thoroughly that it took an impatient horn blast from Gordon in the driveway below to tear Noah away.

"You be careful, Noah Randolph!" Julie called. She saw me grinning and smiled ruefully. "Was your Luke as pig-headed as Noah?"

"Never," I lied airily. "Any Randolph can be led around by the nose if you know how."

"Yah! And cows can fly," she gibed, but she was content again and it did give us a chance to work on the wedding. By mid-afternoon we were well into the invitation list when we heard a car door slam on the drive below.

Julie pushed the papers away and rushed to the rail to peer over. Mild disappointment in her voice, she said, "It's only Cousin Wayne. Gordon's with him, but where's Noah?"

I joined her at the rail and as soon as I saw Wayne's face, my arms went around her instinctively, as if I could shield her from what I knew he would say.

The next few moments were a blur of kaleidoscoping time. I heard Wayne's words, but they seemed overlaid by those other words twenty years ago.

". . . some trigger-happy hunter (*Vietcong sniper*) . . . up on Windy Ridge (*on midnight patrol*) . . . happened so quickly . . . I'm sorry, Julie." (*Luke's dead, Ruth.*)

"I was up ahead in some thick brush," Gordon said shakily. "There was another party working the west slope, but we didn't think anyone else was up as high as we were. I heard the shot, and when Noah didn't answer, I ran down and found him lying there. Someone went crashing through the bushes. I fired my gun and yelled at him to stop, but he didn't. Thank God for those guys on the west slope. I didn't even know they were there until I heard their dog bark."

One of them was a doctor from Asheville, and he had stanched the wound and applied first aid while the others rigged a stretcher. Together they got him down from the ridge and into a truck. Using CB radio, they had called for an ambulance that met them halfway into Asheville. Even so, it didn't look good.

"He's lost too much blood," Wayne told me quietly.

While Gordon drove us to the hospital, Wayne remained behind to direct the hunt for whoever had shot Noah. It was a forty-minute drive, and Gordon kept blaming himself all the way. "If he dies, it'll be my fault," he kept saying.

"He won't die!" Julie said fiercely.

"Whatever happens, it won't be your fault," I told him. "Noah's a grown man. He went with you of his own free accord."

                    *   *   *

Tom and Mabel Randolph were in the intensive care waiting room when we arrived, along with her sister and some cousins. The news had traveled fast.

Noah was still in surgery, we were told. There was nothing to do but wait. "And pray," said Mabel Randolph, her eyes swollen from so much crying. "Please pray for him."

Time dragged. There was a snack area next to the waiting room, and hospital volunteers kept the coffee urn filled. More kinfolk arrived to share the wait and to offer the homely comfort of fried chicken, ham biscuits, and stuffed eggs. Everyone kept trying to get Julie and me to eat, but Julie couldn't seem to swallow either.

Six hours after Noah had been rushed into surgery, the doctor came to us, still dressed in his operating greens, the sterile mask dangling from his neck. Clinically, he described the path the bullet had taken through back and lung, just missing the spinal column, but nicking the heart and finally coming to rest in the left lung.

He talked about shock and trauma and blood pressure that wouldn't stabilize, and Mabel Randolph listened numbly until he'd finished, then said, "But he'll be all right, won't he?"

The doctor's eyes dropped and I liked him for that. Till then, he'd been so full of facts and figures that he could have been talking about soybean yields or how he'd gone about mending a stone wall. But he still had enough feeling that he couldn't look a dying boy's mother straight in the face and tell her, sure, he was going to be just fine. "Maybe, if he makes it through the night," he told Mabel and his voice trailed off.

He seemed relieved when Wayne's sturdy form advanced across the waiting room. "Here it is Sheriff," he said, and gave Wayne a small packet. "I tried not to scratch it any further."

It was the slug he'd removed from Noah's lung, and Wayne passed it over to one of his deputies, who left in a hurry for the state lab.

"We blocked the roads and impounded every gun that came down the mountain," Wayne told us. "Then we did a sweep to make sure nobody was hiding up there."

By morning, Noah's threadhold on life was stretched cobweb thin and Wayne had the lab report. Noah had been shot with a .30 caliber bullet.

Now, I like to trail along behind a pack of bell-voiced coon-hounds on a moonlit night, and I can knock a possum out of a persimmon with my .22 as well as anybody, but such things as calibers, rifling, bores, and grains were beyond me. All I knew was that after the roads were blocked, every gun that came down from Windy Ridge, even Noah's old Winchester and Gordon's new Remington, was impounded, and all the rifles that could shoot a .30 caliber load were test fired.

No match.

"What about the three men who helped carry Noah out?" I asked.

"All cleared," Wayne said.

It had been a long, tense night, and when he offered to take Julie and me home, I was ready to go, but Julie wouldn't be budged.

She promised to nap on one of the empty couches if I'd bring her some fresh clothes that afternoon when I returned. We left with Gordon trying to persuade her to go down to the cafeteria with him for breakfast and Mabel telling her she needed to keep up her strength for Noah's sake.

As we drove home along winding mountain roads, Wayne said, "We found his white handkerchief up there where he fell, Ruth. Warm day like yesterday, a man works up a sweat tramping the woods. Guess he forgot and pulled it out to wipe his brow."

I looked puzzled so he spelled it out for me. "Say you've never done much hunting; say you've got an itchy trigger finger, and you spot something white, flickering in the underbrush. You gonna wait till it turns around and shows antlers? Hell, no! A patch of white means a whitetail deer to you, so *bang!*"

At home, I showered and lay down, but tired as I was, sleep was a long time coming. I drifted in and out of troubled dreams in which Noah blended into Luke—Luke in his army uniform manning a lonely sentry post in a thicket of red-berried dogwoods and golden poplars. I saw the Vietcong sniper snaking through the underbrush and tried to cry out, but Luke couldn't hear me. He fell slowly into the leaves, and the sniper covered his face with a white flag.

"But Luke doesn't have a white flag!" I cried, and came awake as the telephone rang.

It was Julie with a list of small items she wanted me to bring. She said they'd persuaded Mabel Randolph to let Gordon take her home for a few hours while she and Tom kept the vigil. There was no change in Noah's condition.

"No change is probably a good sign, don't you think?" Julie quavered. "It means he's holding on."

I said it did seem hopeful, but my heart grieved for what she still might have to face.

My dream of Luke had left me too restless and disoriented to sleep again. Instead, I found myself pacing the deck as I had twenty years ago, until—like twenty years ago—I got into my car and drove aimlessly, until despair finally eased off again and I realized that I was at the end of one of the old logging trails that crisscross Windy Ridge.

The trees had begun to shed, and a cool gust of wind stirred the fallen leaves. I got out of the car and walked up a slope where Luke and I had often walked together. Squirrels chattered an alarm, a pair of bobwhites exploded into flight at my feet, and, from further up the ridge, a dog greeted me with sharp, welcoming barks.

I thought I knew every dog in the area, but I couldn't place the pointer that came crashing down the hillside so recklessly. For some reason, dogs lose all dignity with me. I'm not particularly fond of them, but through the years, I've become resigned to having them act the fool whenever I'm around. This one was no exception. He came prancing through the leaves, paw over paw, as if I were his long-lost friend, and tried to jump up and lick my face.

"Down, boy!" I said sternly and he sat obediently enough. He was white with the usual rust-colored markings, flop-ears, and intelligent brown eyes. His long, thin tail whipped the air to show me how happy he was for company, and I remembered that Gordon said he'd heard a dog bark just before Noah was shot. This dog, probably. He wasn't wearing a collar, but I was willing to bet he belonged to the party that helped Gordon with Noah, though I'd never heard of anyone using a pointer to hunt deer.

"Your people go off and leave you in all the excitement?" I asked, scratching behind his floppy ears.

More tail-whipping and another attempt to wash my face.

It was so peaceful there that I sat down on a nearby tree stump and let silence wash over me. The dog sprawled at my feet, his big head resting on my shoe. Bluejays played Not-It in the treetops, and scarlet maple leaves drifted down around us. Beyond the ridge, I heard the lazy tinkle of Sam Haskell's cowbells. It seemed unreal that Noah's

life could halt amid such peace and beauty. Winter winds
had stripped these flaming trees and spring rains had
reclothed them in green twenty times since Luke and I
had raced each other up these slopes looking for chinqua-
pins or wild violets, and now Luke's nephew might soon
be gone, too.

I buried my head on my knees and the dog nuzzled my
ear sympathetically. When I stood at last, I heard him
frolicking on the rise above me.

Those city hunters had given Noah Good-Samaritan
help; I could at least keep their dog for them. He answered
my whistle with a woof but didn't reappear.

Wayne told me he'd closed Windy Ridge to hunters, so
we had the woods to ourselves, I thought. Except for the
cowbells and birds and the sound of the dog running
ahead through dry leaves, the place seemed silent and
watchful.

I followed the dog up past a clump of red-leafed
dogwoods until we were just below the last steep incline
to the crest. Pulling myself around an outcropping of
rock, I was startled to realize that this must have been the
very spot where Noah fell. The ground was scuffed, and
cigarette butts and bits of paper from an instant camera's
film pack lay discarded from where Wayne's deputies
had photographed the site.

Then I heard the dog bark further up. He had stopped
by a large fallen log; and when I approached, he pawed at
the hollow end and whined as if he'd cornered something.
Field mouse or chipmunk, I hoped. It was a little late for
snakes, but you never know.

I found a stick and raked aside the leaves that stopped
the hole. As I probed, my stick touched something soft
that crackled almost like dry leaves. Gingerly, still thinking of timber rattlers, I pulled it out.

The bundle was long and heavy, wrapped in several

layers of waterproof plastic, and it was worse than
rattlesnakes. Even before I unwrapped it, I think I knew it
was a rifle that had been bought for just one reason.

Abruptly, I was pushed aside, and Gordon Tyler
snatched the gun from me, his eyes blazing with anger
and fear.

"How the devil did you know?" he cried. "You weren't
even here."

"The dog—" I said.

"What dog?" he snarled. "You came around the rocks
and went as straight to that log as if you'd watched me
yesterday."

I looked about and the dog was nowhere in sight; but in
the horror of the moment, one more oddity didn't register
because I was suddenly remembering.

"Noah couldn't have pulled out a handkerchief! He left
his with Julie. You dropped one there after you shot him
Gordon, to make Wayne think some trigger-happy fool
saw a flash of white."

"And this evening, he'll think you stumbled across the
killer hiding up here and got yourself shot for meddling."

The rifle barrel gleamed in the sunlight as he swung it
up to aim. After that, everything seemed to happen in
slow motion. The gun swung up; but before it could level,
there was a blur of white and brown fur springing for
Gordon's throat, then both plunged backwards onto the
rocks below.

By the time I slipped and skidded down into the ravine,
the gash on Gordon's temple had quit bleeding and there
was no pulse.

I thought the dog would be nearby and I whistled and
called, fearful that he might be lying somewhere among
the rocks, hurt and dying, too.

Eventually, I had to give up and climb out of the ravine;
yet, though dazed from my brush with death and from

learning that Gordon had shot Noah deliberately, I was vaguely soothed by a sweet fragrance and was even able to wonder what autumn-blooming plant could so perfume the air.

Now Wayne and I waited on my deck and watched twilight deepen the blue mountains while Gordon's body and Gordon's gun were examined in distant laboratories.

At dusk, one of Wayne's deputies stopped by. "Sorry, Miss Ruth, but we looked under every log and rock in that ravine and there's no sign of your dog."

"I appreciate your looking, but he wasn't mine," I said. "He belonged to those other hunters yesterday."

"They didn't have a dog with them," Wayne said gently. "I asked. And Sam Haskell says he hasn't seen any stray pointers up that way, either."

I shrugged and didn't argue. Gordon had denied the dog, too. Maybe I was getting senile.

Once more, Wayne called the lab, and this time he learned that a test bullet from Gordon's second gun matched the one removed from Noah's lung. Ten minutes later, the medical examiner phoned to report that Gordon's death was from a broken neck and, no, except for the gash on his temple, no other marks; certainly no teeth marks at his throat.

The phone rang again and this time it was Julie. "Noah's blood pressure's stabilized and they think he's coming out of the coma!"

Her voice sparkled with radiant thanksgiving, and a huge weight rolled off my heart.

I've heard that people often don't remember the actual moment when they were hurt; but someday soon I will ask Noah whether or not he heard a dog bark just before Gordon fired at him. *Something* up there had thrown Gordons' aim off just enough to save his life.

Yet, even if Noah doesn't remember, it won't really matter because I suddenly identified the sweet fragrance I'd smelled earlier. All around me, trees and vines flamed with October colors; but in that ravine up on Windy Ridge, the air had been heavy with the honeysuckle and wisteria of May.

EDWARD WELLEN AND JOSH PACHTER

Stork Trek

It was not especially chilly, not yet, but somehow the big white bird knew it was time to begin its annual journey to the south. It did not know that fact in the way we humans know of knowing, but deep within its genes and chromosomes, coursing irresistibly through the microscopic labyrinth of its nervous system, leaping forward across the millions of synapses in its way, a demanding chorus of ancient voices cried: *Now!*

Old Annie Dekkers bobbed to and fro in a tired old rocking chair which had itself been old when she was still a girl. Then, suddenly, the sky outside her window exploded in a brilliant blur of sun-sparkled wings as the graceful bird soared up and away from the wagon-wheel nest that crowned her unused chimney. A youthful smile danced across her dry, cracked lips. How lovely to see the creature in flight again! She did not sorrow to see it go. It would be back, she knew, in the spring. It came back every spring, had done so for a dozen years and its father and mother before it. Where did it go, she wondered, when it left the quiet comfort of her farm? South was the only answer she could feel sure of. South. She frowned, now, troubled at last. The bird would be back in the spring, yes, that much was certain. But this next time, this next spring, when the bird returned, would *she* be there to greet it?

The farmhouse dwindled and disappeared below, as powerful wingbeats carried the white bird aloft. As always, the first hours of its journey were pleasant, peaceful. Only later, far away, when the storms began, would the trip become a struggle.

A great city appeared in the distance, drew closer, a place of tall buildings and much noise and filthy air. There was, though, a tranquil oasis of leafy trees and rippling waters in the heart of this city, a spot forgotten by time and civilization, where monkeys chattered in a jungle-like environment and polar bears paced back and forth to the delight of small children. It offered an inviting foretaste of the serenity that awaited at journey's end, and had it been a few hours later, the bird might well have stopped there to pass the night. But it was still broad daylight and the bird felt vibrantly alive. It was enjoying the whisper of wind that ruffled its pinfeathers as it thrust strongly against the thermal air currents that helped it in its gliding flight, and so it kept eagerly on.

As it passed, a second bird—almost identical to the first, except for the angular black stain on its forehead— rose up from the oasis to join it. Though nothing we humans would call messages or symbols was exchanged, an unspoken thought was in the air between them: how good to have company to fly beside on the long and often lonely pilgrimage to the south! Below and behind them, a tall man in a severe black suit stood next to the squat brick building atop which the second bird maintained its nest, a thin hand shading his eyes as he watched them recede from view. The man was smiling, like the old woman at the farmhouse, but this smile was filled with evil and with greed.

On an empty street at the southern edge of the city, a younger man with unkempt long hair and a small gold earring affixed to his left earlobe felt something soft and liquid drop onto the shoulder of his badly weathered black leather jacket. His mind was elsewhere, and he moved to brush off the mess without thinking. At the feel of it, though, he jerked his hand away in horror. *"Getver-demme!"* he swore and, looking up, shook his fist in futile anger at the two large birdshapes that, silhouetted against the autumn sunshine, winged purposefully southward toward the distant horizon.

"The stork is under way," said Gerard Valkenier, brushing crumbs from the legs of his black trousers and rising to greet the lanky South African who had just appeared in the doorway of his office in the squat brick Bird House of Artis, the Amsterdam zoo. "It took off about an hour ago. I watched it go, and then I came back here and called you at your hotel."

"So it's begun, then," said Kuypers, pronouncing the Dutch words slowly and with a distinct Afrikaans accent.

"Yes," Valkenier nodded, "it's begun."

The two men sat in facing armchairs, and Valkenier helped himself to another *negerzoen* from the bag he had picked up that morning from the bakery across from the main gate. "It ought to reach the Kruger Wildtuin in about three weeks," he said, "and it will winter there until sometime around the middle of March. So now it's your move. When you're back in Johannesburg and you've acquired the diamonds, all you need to do is pack them in the capsule and attach it to the bird's leg, just as I've already shown you. The stork will do the rest of the work. If past performance is any guide, it should return here by the beginning of the second week in April."

"With no borders, no customs, and no export or import duties to worry about. I like it, I like it very much. There's only one thing I *don't* like. What if there are *fifty* of those damned white birds hanging around the preserve when I get there? How will I know which is the one that summers up there on your roof?"

"I've explained that already," Valkenier said patiently, "the first time we met." He popped another candy into his mouth and chewed it noisily. "I painted a small mark on our bird's forehead, with indelible black, a V for Valkenier. With a decent pair of binoculars, you'll be able to spot it from a hundred meters off."

Kuypers grinned. "That's right," he remembered. "That's good." He reached for the bag of sweets, hungry at last, but he was too late. His partner was swallowing the last of them, and licking his lips with a darting motion of his sharp pink tongue.

Dirk Kuypers flushed the toilet and washed his rough hands thoroughly. A metal plaque next to the aluminum basin said, FOR THE CONVENIENCE OF THE PASSENGERS WHO WILL FOLLOW YOU, PLEASE WIPE OUT THE SINK WITH YOUR USED PAPER TOWEL BEFORE DISPOSAL, but he ignored it and returned to his seat, leaving the basin full of scummy water.

The stewardess was just coming around with her wheeled trolley, and he ordered himself a miniature bottle of jenever and drank it neat from the flimsy plastic cup the woman gave him.

What a caper, he thought, as he had thought so often this last week in Amsterdam. What a delicious and foolproof scheme!

They were ten thousand meters above the Mediterranean, just south of Gibraltar and arrowing straight for the looming bulk of Africa at a little less than six hundred kilometers per hour.

On the underbelly of the aircraft, a hatch door swung open on hinges that had been oiled much too assiduously by a mechanic at Schiphol Airport who had his mind on his girlfriend, and Kuypers' waste fell through. It froze almost immediately in the sub-zero temperatures at that altitude, and looked strangely attractive as it built up speed, a ragged block of greenish ice flecked interestingly with shiny black droplets of still-liquid oil from the hatch door.

By the time it had dropped to only five hundred meters, the block of ice was traveling at terminal velocity; scant seconds before plunging into the emerald waters of the sea and melting away to nothingness, it struck and killed a white stork who had not even been aware of its approach.

A second stork survived uninjured. Several drops of oil splattered wildly at the projectile's impact with its companion, though, leaving a curiously V-shaped marking on the snowy white background of the remaining bird's forehead.

The creature did not understand the tragedy of the death it had just witnessed—not, in any case, as we humans understand tragedy—but at some deep level of its awareness it mourned at the prospect of continuing its long journey alone.

The knife thrust took the miner completely by surprise. His cry of anguish was lost in the empty vastness of the veldt, and the expression of horrified betrayal that spread across his coal-black face even faster than the warm crimson bloodstain soaked the white cotton shirtfront at his belly was seen by no one but his assassin.

Dirk Kuypers wiped his blade clean on the stiff brown grass, and returned it to the sheath that hung from his belt. The leather pouch of uncut diamonds for which he had just committed murder went into his rucksack, along with his bug spray and his cigarettes and his packet of cheese sandwiches.

He headed back toward the waterhole where he had left his Jeep without another glance at the body, kicking his way through the scrubby tangle of karroo bushes and zigzagging to avoid the dangerous *kopjes* that were bright-red anthills. His sharply defined shadow marched on before him.

One might make a haiku of that, he thought, and turned soft images around in his head as he walked:

> We travel by twos
> Till the final darkness falls,
> My shadow and I.

A good one, that. He would try it out tonight, when he was back in the city with his mates around him and the lager flowing freely.

In Amsterdam, Gerard Valkenier took a huge bite of his chocolate *moorkop*, and sighed contentedly as the sweet whipped cream caressed his tastebuds.

He wiped his mouth carefully with a paper napkin, then picked up a red felt-tipped pen and marked an X through that day's date on the wall calendar that hung behind his desk. It was the eighteenth red X he had drawn, beginning just after the South African had left his office the afternoon the bird had taken flight.

Any day now, he told himself dreamily, as he reached for another bite of his pastry. Any day.

Kuypers sleeved his face and tasted the salt sweat on the edge of his tongue. He rubbed his stinging eyes, then for the nth time scanned the desolate landscape of the Kruger Wildtuin with his binoculars. Whichever way he looked the veldt stretched out in dry distances to drown his presence and dwindle all creatures to the size of ants.

Where *is* the damn bird? he asked himself. Every day

for a week now he'd been sneaking over the chainlink
fence that bordered the wildlife preserve, and some
internal pressure gauge told him he was beginning to
push his luck. If the keepers didn't catch him, and lock
him up for trespassing, the lions would surely get him
sooner or later.

The rhinos did not worry him so much. Though the
rhino has brute strength to match its nasty temper, it is
dim of sight and even dimmer of wit. If it misses on its
first charge, it does not think to turn and try again; it
plunges on until it runs out of steam, and then it stops.
All Kuypers would have to do if a rhino should threaten
him was step out of its path at the right moment, and that
would be that. The lions, on the other hand, were a
different matter . . .

Enough of this train of thought. Kuypers shook his head
to clear the stuffy cobwebs from his brain. Concentrate on
the stork. It will come.

That long Dutch drink of water certainly seemed to know
his business: there were, indeed, storks arriving, and just
where Valkenier had told him he would find them. This
had to be the birds' ancestral home. Prehistoric men had
scratched their artwork deep into the surface of a nearby
stone, so that one could still make out—despite time's
cruel eraser—faint birdshapes gliding fluidly across the
stone. Some things never changed. Or, at least, there were
long-lasting patterns of built-in behavior which—

A streak of shadow smoothly coursing the rough ground
made him lift his gaze to the sky. False hope: only another
cursed vulture on the lookout for game—or, rather, for
gaminess.

The bloodshot sun's slow metronome had swung toward dusk; soon all the sky's day-flying storks would
land to spend the night, however short of journey's end
they might be. If Valkenier's bird didn't show up soon,

Kuypers might as well call it quits for the day and come back again tomorrow.

At that moment, as if it were a piece torn from an earlier hour, a sudden whiteness floated down into this darker time. Kuypers spotted it coming in, a large white stork, and as it landed he moved closer to bring it within range of his fieldglasses. He adjusted the fine focus and—yes, the black spot was there on its forehead, a bit faded but definitely visible in the dying light of the afternoon!

He hummed softly to himself as he broke out the tin of dried locust and grasshoppers he had brought along for the purpose of luring the bird within reach. Slowly he crept toward it, sowing the insect bait between himself and the stork with carefully small movements of his arm. Valkenier had tamed, if not domesticated, the creature, so Kuypers' manshape should not frighten it off, if all went well.

The bird did not flap away, but neither did it approach at once the tasty morsels leading back to the manshape. Perhaps it had suffered some mishap in its long and arduous passage, some battering or buffeting that had made it extra cautious. Certainly it *looked* weary, its proud stance giving way to the heavy pull of the earth.

Then hunger gave it strength, and with delicate gluttony it snapped up the trail of insects, following it back to Kuypers till at last it was eating out of his palm.

In an instant he had it, grasped the weakly struggling creature in his firm yet gentle hands. Careful, careful. All he needed to do was snap a leg or break a wing, and the game was lost.

Using his back and hunched shoulders to shield his face from beak and wing, he banded the metal capsule to one leg as Valkenier had taught him. Engraved into the metal in tiny print were the words: PROPERTY OF NETHER-LANDS ORNITHOLOGICAL SOCIETY. IF FOUND, PLEASE RETURN

WITH SEAL UNBROKEN TO N.O.S., BOX 4234, AMSTERDAM,
NETHERLANDS, FOR CASH REWARD. This way, if anything
should happen to the bird on its way back to Holland,
there was still a chance that the diamonds would go
through.

The Netherlands Ornithological Society, indeed! How
did Valkenier think these things up? The man was a
genius!

There. With the capsule attached, Kuypers' part of the
job was finished. Now it was up to the bird. He threw it a
Churchillian V to match the crude marking on its forehead, then turned away, stepping accidentally between
the spokes of an old wagon wheel baked into the soil.
Some fallen-by-the-wayside relic of the Great Trek of the
Boers, the wheel. Its trail reached back through time to
the days when the pioneers had yoked up their oxen and
driven them across the veldt. And here it had lain in wait
for him, all those years, to catch his foot where two of its
spokes met the hub and twist his ankle viciously.

Kuypers swore: his foot was jammed solidly in the
narrow angle of the spokes. It seemed easier to pull a
spoke loose than to work his hurting foot free, and the
brittle old wood gave way with a screech like the protest-
ing hinges of a long-rusted gate.

No, it was not the wood that screamed after all. It was
Kuypers himself, screaming in pain as his balance shifted
and his foot slid further beneath the remaining spoke and
took his full weight.

Gasping for breath, his ankle afire with agony, he dimly
realized that the loosened spoke still hung loosely in his
hand. He flung it angrily back over his left shoulder, and
heard a dull whump as it connected with some object
behind him. Then came an irritated snort from the same
direction, and Kuypers turned his head at the sound.

There was a rhino not ten meters away from him, its

head down, its foreleg clawing at the ground. His un-
guided missile had hit it and offended its primitive sense
of dignity. Though the beast's sight was poor, it had
gotten a fix on him by smell, and suddenly it was
charging.

Kuypers struggled frantically to pull his trapped foot
free. He succeeded at cost of shattering pain, but not in
time to hobble out of the rhino's path. Nor was there time
for him to draw his knife, for all the good that would have
done him; the beast's leathery hide would have turned
the blade aside harmlessly.

The horn caught him in the very spot where he had
stabbed the black miner when stealing the diamonds, but
the sudden pain of the wound was so intense that the
irony of it escaped him.

Tossed high, he landed back on the wheel as the rhino
pounded on into the distance and dissolved in a cloud of
its own dust. He lay there in the empty veldt, bleeding his
wasted life away, as the stork with the metal capsule on
its leg looked on, its long reddish beak parted slightly in
what a fanciful observer might have taken for an expression of sympathy.

A faint cry bubbled from Kuypers' lips, like the sorrow-
ing wail of a bagpipe's final notes. The stork, curious
now, approached the broken manshape nesting on the
half-buried wagon wheel. It rubbed its forehead almost
tenderly across the South African's palm, as if absolving
him from the sin of having mistreated it. Its touch brought
Kuypers back briefly from the business of passing on into
the one great shadow, and he turned his head painfully to
gaze at the innocent creature. Through tear-filled eyes he
noticed that the black mark on its forehead was no longer
shaped like a V; it was smeared now, and formless. He
forced his weakening neck muscles to bend, and saw that
his palm was stained with oil.

It was the wrong bird, he realized, the wrong damn
bird!

High overhead, a trio of hungry vultures circled patiently, maintaining their vigilant holding pattern, waiting for the figure sprawled out beneath them to stop its
thrashing about so they could settle down to their dinner . . .

After a long and bitter winter—a winter so unusually cold
that, for the first time in years, there were ice skaters on
her canals—spring came at last to the city of Amsterdam.

In thousands of window boxes crocuses and narcissi
and the inevitable tulips bloomed; in thousands of back
gardens, pear trees pushed forth their first tentative
blossoms. A flotilla of glass-enclosed tour boats replaced
the skaters on the vast network of intersecting canals;
recorded voices described the sights in Dutch, English,
French, and German as the tourists breathed patterns of
mist on the glass walls and snapped pictures of the
Skinny Bridge and the narrowest house in Holland and
the stately gables along the Herrengracht. In the Lei-
desplein, the skating rink was disassembled and trucked
away to a warehouse for storage, and in its place a
hundred white tables sprang up like mushrooms, surrounded by rings of metal chairs and crowned by gay red
and white Campari umbrellas; white-jacketed waiters
bustled about with frantic energy, serving coffee and beer
to a population that seemed to have just awakened from a
five-month hibernation.

There was rain, of course, and an occasional promising
glimpse of the sun. There were bicycles everywhere, and
street musicians crawled up from the shelter of the Metro
stations to fill the air with song. In the Vondel Park, dogs
ran free and Frisbees flew and white lines of smoke
wafted lazily from the bowls of pipes packed with shag

tobacco or Lebanese hashish or some hopeful mixture of
the two.

Indoors there were meetings, many meetings, as the
anti-nuclear groups and squatters and homosexuals and
punks and feminists broke out their signboards and
paints and brushes and began their preparations for the
long round of protest marches that lay ahead of them all.

On the roof of a tall white building not far beyond the
city limits, a gull sat proudly on its spacious nest of grass
and reeds and feathers. There were four speckled eggs
beneath it, and soon those eggs would hatch. Then there
would be hungry mouths to feed, hungry bellies to fill.

To the gull, it was simply a time for babies. But to the
city of Amsterdam nearby and the flat Dutch countryside
all around, it was spring.

Gerard Valkenier caught himself licking his fingers automatically, and felt shock at the realization of what he had
let go to waste by his lack of attention at the critical
moments. A fine state of affairs, a sad commentary on the
state of his mind, when a connoisseur of his standing
missed out on the delights of a freshly prepared *Tom-
poes*! He tried to summon up the delicate flavors that his
senses must at least subliminally have registered, but
their traces were already too faint. There was your true
ghost at the banquet—the failure to engage to the full
one's tastebuds, one's olfactory mucous membrane, one's
retinal cells. What a waste! And another day wasted, too.
His window showed him evening making ready to settle
across the city.

Time flies, he thought. Time flies, but does my stork?

There had been no word from Kuypers the entire
winter, no word at all, and Valkenier feared that something must have gone terribly wrong with his plan. Day
after day, while the pile of progress reports and purchase

requests and invoices demanding his attention grew higher and higher on his desk as if to chart his mounting anxiety, he had sat in his lonely office just like this, searching the framed oblong of sky beyond his window for the flash of white that would be his stork returning at last from the south.

What could have gone wrong? Had Kuypers failed to obtain the diamonds? Had he been caught trespassing in the game preserve? Neither explanation answered the questions raised by the bird's continued absence. Well, then, what else? Had the damned South African injured the stork while trying to attach the capsule to its leg? Or had the bird fallen prey to the Wildtuin's predatory teeth and claws? Or had some unexpected other disaster befallen it on either leg of its long and arduous journey?

Valkenier clenched his fists, a thousand catastrophes tearing torturously at his mind.

He was completely helpless. All he could do was sit here and wait, try to convince himself that the bird would arrive tomorrow, get up and go home to another sleepless night after first stopping at the post office, just in case the capsule of diamonds had come to roost in the box he had rented in the name of the mythical Netherlands Ornithological Society.

And, of course, pay a call on the *bakkerij* across from the gate as he left, to replenish his dwindling supply of sugary treats. They were, these days, his only remaining pleasure—and now even *that* small comfort was being denied him!

Savagely, Valkenier tore the topmost leaf from the calendar pad on his desk. Time flies, he thought again, then chuckled mirthlessly and stopped himself from crumpling the sheet and tossing it angrily into his wastebasket. Instead, he folded it into a paper airplane and sailed the flimsy craft across the room. Time flies, he thought with a bitter smile as the airplane flew through the open window and a fit of wind caught it and swept it high over the zoo.

Playful air currents teased the plane through a long series of climbs and dives. It was several minutes before it ran out of fuel and crash-landed into the riotous purple of a rhododendron in full bloom; on its final approach, its jet-black shadow swooped hawklike across the wire mesh of a dovecote, startling the birds into a confused flutter of terror.

Annie Dekkers lay helplessly in her great brass bed, her withered hands clasping fitfully at the thick down quilt that held her prisoner. She had sewn the quilt herself, every stitch, in the fall of the year she had married poor Fokke, but now the rheumatism had left her so weak that she could not even manage to move it aside and swing her thin legs over the side of the bed and grope her way downstairs to fix herself the cup of tea she craved so badly.

It must be close to three by now, and Lien would be back from the shop at half past five. Dear Lien. A sweet and wonderful daughter, a true comfort to old Annie in these tiring, tiring times. How Lien had failed so dismally with her own child, that horrible grandson of hers, that Roel, was a mystery Annie had never been able to solve.

But it was Lien who lived with her and cared for her, not Roel, *dank zij God*, and she could wait for her tea until her daughter's return. There, it was already three, the bell from the church tower in the village sounded loudly through the window of her bedroom, the window dear Lien had so thoughtfully opened for her that morning before she left, so she could breathe the lovely spring air and watch the birds as they decorated the sky with the confident brushstrokes of their passing.

Perhaps today her beloved stork would come back to her. Perhaps today it would—

As if by magic, the lines engraved on Annie Dekkers' tired face disappeared, dissolved into a suffusion of joy that transformed her from a dying old woman to the happiest of farm girls.

Outside her window, the great white bird approached. She followed its flight with glistening eyes as it drew closer and closer, larger and thrillingly larger. She held her breath in an ecstasy of terror as it glided out of sight at the top edge of the window, until at last she heard the familiar rustling sounds of the bird settling back down onto its nest atop her chimney, the old wagon wheel poor Fokke had set there the year before he died.

"You've come back," she sighed contentedly, Fokke and Lien and her tea at once forgotten, her voice the coo of a child at play. "You've come back!"

The pimply hoodlum in the worn leather jacket absently fingered the small gold hoop depending from his left earlobe and gazed out the window of the bus at the cows grazing in the meadows that stretched off into hazy distances on either side of the road. The sun was shining, which made him think of the pier of Scheveningen and the luscious German *mädchens* who were out there panting with hunger for a hot young *kerel* with his kind of style. But that whole scene cost money and plenty of it, while he'd shelled out practically his last *stuiver* for a seat aboard this crummy yellow bus. Hell, he didn't have enough *poen* left over for *one* admission to the pier, forget about the funds required to entertain a delightful young *fraülein* or maybe even twins, the way he dreamed.

He turned away from the window with a scowl, and wrapped himself tightly in the awful unfairness of his life.

All the damned *gastarbeiters* had to do was stand in line at the GAK for an hour a week in order to lie to the bored civil servant about how diligently they were out there searching for work, and the government would shower enough WW on them to keep them and their lousy twenty-seven-children families in *pisang goreng* or whatever it was they ate for the rest of their lives. Surinamers, Moroccans, Turks, Moluccans—the *regiering* looked after them all without a squawk. But here he was, Holland-born and Holland-bred, and if *he* should dare to show his face around the GAK office he'd have a dozen filthy *smerissen* crawling all over him and no mistake. And it wasn't even fair! All he'd meant to do was *startle* that old fool at the tram stop, just a joke, give the guy a quick scare and have himself a couple of laughs. It wasn't *his* fault the *ouwe oelewapper* had panicked and jumped right into the path of an oncoming streetcar. They couldn't possibly blame that on *him*—and yet of course they would, the bastards. He was lucky he'd had the common sense to take off as soon as he saw the old man go down.

The bus rumbled heavily to a stop—*his* stop, he realized at the last possible moment—and the rubber bumpers on the rear door sucked at his arm as he squeezed past them.

He was in no mood for a half-hour trudge down the muddy country roads that led from the village center out to Oma's, but he didn't have much of a choice. There was no other bus he could take, he didn't have money for a cab, and no one was likely to pay any attention to his thumb, not in *this* dimwitted backwater, not with his shoulder-length hair and his one gold earring and his scruffy tough-guy clothes. Muttering angrily, his tight black boots already pinching his toes, he set off for Oma's.

The old bitch had never liked him, he knew, not since

he was a kid and he used to sling pebbles at the creepy bird of hers at every opportunity. The last year or so before he'd finally chucked the small-town life and run off to live in the city, that was the only reason he'd allowed his nag of a mother to drag him out there for a visit—so he could lob rocks at Oma Annie's darling *ooievaartje* perched up there on the roof as if it owned the damn house. It made him sick to think that he had crawled out here today to beg her for help—him, Roel Olpers, with his tail between his legs! But he was down on his luck, on the run from the law, and she was his only hope. She pretended to be nothing but a poor old widowed farm wife, the *vuile trut*, but the whole family knew about that supposedly secret hoard she kept stashed away in the chimney. Who did she think she was kidding?

Ah, there was the house, and—unbelievable!—there was that stupid bird in its nest. He scooped up a stone from the ground and drew back his arm to let it fly—then checked himself and dropped it with a curse. A stork on the roof brought good luck, they said; maybe Oma Annie would be a little more likely to help him out if this once he left her pet alone.

"Roel," the old witch cried when she saw him, when he'd let himself into the house and found her upstairs in bed, loafing away the afternoon. "What are *you* doing here?" Grudgingly she offered him her cheek, and he swallowed his disgust and brushed the papery skin with his lips.

"I'm in trouble, Oma." he said. "I need money, as much as you can spare. I've got to go away for a while. I—"

"Money?" The word exploded from her mouth like a gunshot. "You don't come to see me for years and years, and then suddenly you turn up here and ask me for money?"

"You bet I do," he raged. "And don't tell me you

haven't got any, either! Do you think I'm such an idiot I
don't know about that famous pile Opa Fokke left you
when he died?"

He stormed over to the fireplace and reached up inside
the black mouth of the chimney to feel around for the
treasure trove he had so often heard the grownups discussing in secretive whispers when they thought he was
sound asleep. His grandmother was shrieking some nonsense behind him, but he was able to ignore her—until
she tore away her ragged blanket and flung herself at his
back with the last of her waning strength. Her weight was
negligible, yet still she knocked him off balance and
threw him up against the mantelpiece, jarring a decade's
accumulation of soot loose within the chimney and filling
the room with a dense black cloud.

Blinded, he staggered away from the mantel to tumble
over the old woman, who lay gasping hoarsely on the
floor. Her body broke his fall, but his fall did not break her
body, not quite. She clawed at him with feeble fingers,
screaming shrilly, and he slapped her across the face with
the full force of his hand.

Then, at last, there was silence in the room.

The soot slowly settled and, when he could see again,
the first thing he saw was Oma Annie on the floor.

She was not moving

She was not breathing.

She was dead.

And everywhere in the thick black dust from the
chimney, his footprints and fingerprints stared up at him,
accusing him.

It's not my fault, he thought wildly. It isn't fair!

Outside the window, the chimes of the village's church
bell sounded across the fields. It was five o'clock. His
mother would be there in half an hour!

He searched the room frantically, desperately, and at

the back of a cluttered closet he found at last an ancient upright vacuum cleaner. He dragged it around Oma Annie's body to the outlet by the chimney and plugged it in. But he flipped its rusty toggle switch in the wrong direction by mistake, and instead of sucking *in* air, the damned machine began to roar air *out*, an electrical dragon exhaling its noisy, stale breath into the room.

By the time he thought to turn the switch the other way, the vacuum cleaner had blown an enormous cloud of soot back up the shaft of the chimney. The cloud blasted through the loose construction of the stork's nest above, and Annie Dekkers' *ooievaarje*, terrified, spread its wings and flew away forever, its body black and sluggish with the weight of the soot.

Roel, busy vacuuming away the evidence that tied him to his grandmother's death, neither saw nor heard it go. When the room was cleaned to his satisfaction, he silenced the dragon and went back to the chimney. Feeling around inside it, he discovered a loose brick in the far wall. There was a deep cavity hollowed out behind it, and within that opening his fingers touched metal. A box. He pulled it gently free and opened its lid—and stared in wonderment at his Opa Fokke's legacy.

Not cash, not stocks or bonds, not jewels.

Gold coins.

Hundreds of them.

Gold!

It was Thursday night in the city, *koopavond*, the one evening when the stores stayed open late to accommodate those shoppers who worked during the day.

In the area up and down Damrak and Rokin and the Kalverstraat, from the Centraal Station at one end to the Munt Tower and the Leidseplein at the other, the city was bright with neon and alive with activity. The shops, the *bruin cafés*, the restaurants swirled with the comings and goings of bustling crowds.

Only in the Jordaan, one of Mokum's oldest sections, was it quiet. An auto showroom, a *melkboer*, a couple of snack bars were open for business, but otherwise the district was dark.

There were several battered trashcans at the end of the alley that ran along one side of the showroom, invisible from the mouth of the alley because of the magnificent new sportscar that was parked there. But the gull did not need to see the cans to know they were there; its keen sense of smell guided it unerringly to the spot. It dropped from the sky to light on the rim of the fullest can, and began at once to pick busily through a layer of discarded advertising circulars toward the tasty scraps of unfinished sandwich beneath.

Two men deep in conversation turned into the alley from the direction of the showroom entrance. "Good luck with it!" the older man said cheerfully, and shook the other's hand with a firm and friendly grip. The customer, looking affluent in an immaculate cream-colored suit, a bright gold coin gleaming richly from his left earlobe, took the keys the salesman held out to him and climbed eagerly into the driver's seat of his new car.

But the young man with the earring had never driven a stick shift before, and he accidentally shifted into reverse instead of low. As he eased his foot from the clutch, the car bucked backwards and smashed into the garbage cans behind it. The driver muttered an exasperated curse and raced around to inspect the damage he had caused.

He was interested only in the car, of course, and never even noticed the mangled body of the dead gull in the crumpled trashcan that lay on its side at the back of the alley.

*   *   *

Gerard Valkenier picked despondently at his dinner. He had ordered frogs legs, but the waitress had brought him someone else's chicken livers by mistake. He had thought of complaining, but what did it really matter? What did *anything* matter any more? The stork was almost a month overdue, and he was certain by now that it was never coming. What had gone wrong? Why hadn't he heard from Kuypers? And what was left for him now, except to try to pick up the pieces of his undistinguished career at the zoo?

As he gazed sadly out the window by his table, a majestic black stork winged by. But for once in his life he was too depressed to admire the simple beauty of a bird in flight.

Birds, he thought miserably, and lifted his knife and fork to attack the defenseless bits of chicken on his plate.

And then he froze, goosebumps rippling across his skin.

A *black* stork?

But there *are* no black storks! *All* storks are white! This black one must be a mutant of some sort, a previously unknown species, an aberration as rare and important as, say, that albino rhino Smedts was so insufferably proud of!

My God, he thought, I'll be famous! This is even better than the diamonds!

He slapped a hundred-guilder bill down on the table to pay for the meal he had hardly touched and bolted out of the restaurant without waiting for his change. The bright-eyed watersnipe on the banknote seemed to watch him go, its soft brown feathers glittering in the overhead lighting.

Fred Bogaard and Ad van de Polder sat in their dumpy Kevertje, waiting patiently for the street ahead of them to

clear. The protesters had been parading slowly through
the intersection for more than ten minutes now, and their
ranks showed no signs of thinning out anytime in the
near future. Bogaard and Van de Polder were in no hurry,
though, and they were both sympathetic to the marchers'
point of view. If they hadn't been on duty, in fact, Van de
Polder at least would have been out there carrying a
placard himself.

"I like that one," he said, pointing past the windshield
at three braless young women in thin T-shirts holding up
a banner that read IN EUROPA STORT HET VAN DE REAGAN.

"The message or the messengers?" Bogaard smiled.
"Hey, what's that one supposed to mean?"

"Which? You mean SS-20, EUROPA-0?"

"No, no. To the left. No, you can't see it anymore, he's
just turned away. But it's that kid in the army jacket,
looks like an American escapee from the sixties. The sign
he's carrying says PERSHING 1-5314. What do you think
that's all about?"

"*Geen idee.* Maybe they've figured out where they've
got the missiles siloed, and those are the location coordi-
nates or something. Hey, look at that one. WE ALL HATE
JAN. What's that doing *here*?"

"Got me. Poor Jan, whoever he is."

The driver of the sportscar in front of them chose that
moment to lose his patience. He leaned on his horn and
kept right on leaning.

Bogaard and Van de Polder exchanged long-suffering
looks.

"What do you think?" Van de Polder sighed. "Shall
we?"

"Might as well," said Bogaard. "That is what they pay
us for."

The Volkswagen's doors swung open simultaneously
in a fluid movement that looked as if it had been practiced

a thousand times before, and the two men stepped out.

"*Tjongejonge,*" Bogaard murmured, shaking his head at the badly dented rear fender of the brand-new sportscar.

As they approached the driver, Van de Polder had to shout to make himself heard over the blare of the horn and the background din of the demonstration.

"What's your hurry, there, sir? Don't you think these folks have a right to—"

The driver heard him then, and turned to find the two of them hovering over him, tall and confident in their royal blue uniforms. His hand jerked away from the horn button as if it had bitten him. His white suit and large gold earring shone brilliantly in the afternoon sun, but the expression on his youthful face was one of fear.

"Well, well, well," Van de Polder grinned, his voice lower now and clearly amused, "if it isn't Roel Oplers. And in a lovely new car, too. Last time I laid eyes on you, Roel, you could barely afford to ride the tram. What happened, *makker,* you win the Lotto?"

"And speaking of trams," added Bogaard, "we've been hearing some nasty stories about you the last couple of days, Roel. I think we're going to have to ask you to come along with us for a little chat, once this street opens up."

From above, an acrid blob of white dropped onto the shoulder of the driver's beautiful suit, and the two policemen burst out laughing.

Roel Oplers looked up to see a sleek black shape sail regally across the sky. Last time it was a white bird, spoiling his black leather jacket. This time it's a black bird, ruining his new white suit. Why were they against him? Why were they all against him? "*Getverdemme!*" he shouted, shaking his fist at the bird in impotent fury.

A hundred demonstrators took up the cry, screaming "*Getverdemme!*" at the top of their lungs, threatening the heavens with their tightly clenched fists.

*   *   *

There, below, an empty nest! A bit small, perhaps, but that could be fixed. The stork swooped down eagerly. It was tired, and ready to rest.

No, it saw, as it came closer, the nest was not empty after all. There were eggs in there, four of them, four perfect eggs abandoned and in need of love. They were gull eggs, but the stork neither knew nor cared. They were eggs, that was all that mattered, and it was a lost and lonely creature in search of a nest.

It landed, and settled itself comfortably atop the eggs.

It could not experience emotion, of course—not as we humans experience emotion—but all the same it was happy, in its own gentle way.

Valkenier paced back and forth in his Churchillaan apartment like a caged animal, exploding with frustrated energy. Somewhere in or near the city was a unique black stork, the find of a lifetime, and he had no idea how to go about tracking it down. Damn, damn, *damn!*

Well, there was nothing to be done about it. He might as well go back to the Bird House and start digging into that pile of paperwork on his desk. Perhaps that would keep him from thinking of killing himself.

"Did you see it? A stork. A *black* stork! It's moved into that gull's nest on the roof of Building B."

"A stork? You don't say! *Jee*, won't our gull kick up a fuss when it comes back and finds out someone else's muscled in on its eggs!"

"Did you say a *black* stork, Ed? I never saw me a black one before."

"Me, neither, now I think about it. A black stork . . ."

"Maybe we'd better ring up the newspapers or somebody and let them know it's here, don't you think?"

"Sure, there's an idea!"

"Maybe they'll name it after us!"

"The Bijlmer Bird, I can see it all now. *Geweldig!*"

Valkenier slammed down the phone and grabbed for the camera that was always ready in the bottom drawer of his desk. He raced downstairs to the parking lot and laid a black streak of rubber on the pavement as he screamed off toward the zoo's main gate.

The sky was sprinkled with fleecy white clouds, though off to the west a gray thunderhead was beginning to form. Valkenier wound through the city streets as quickly as the afternoon traffic would allow, then left them behind him and picked up speed for the last few kilometers out to the Bijlmerbajes.

The gate guard was expecting him, and pointed across the yard to Building A, where an excited knot of officials were waiting for him.

They led him proudly to the roof of the building and took him to its northern side. One story below them and fifty meters to the north was the roof of Building B; from their vantage point atop Building A, they had a clear view of the nest and its occupant. Valkenier raised his camera to his eye, and its long telephoto lens drew the scene even closer.

And, yes, incredible as it seemed, the bird in the nest was a dark gray, an almost *black* stork!

Breathless at the sight of it, he set his f-stop and shutter speed and rolled into focus and started shooting.

And then the gathering storm clouds broke open and a shower blew quickly toward them. Valkenier lowered his camera and turned to go.

As the first drops hit him, his mind was already racing with plans for his next visit, for many visits, with lots of film and his video camera and portable VTR, and perhaps he should rent an Arriflex for sixteen-millimeter coverage as well.

He turned back for one more look at the bird—and stared horrified at the soot streaming from its feathers in the rain. As the blackness washed away, revealed beneath it was an ordinary white stork.

His jaw dropped open.

Again, he thought dully, they've done it to me again.

As he stood there, glued to the spot, the chill rain coursing down his cheeks like tears, the stork struggled upright and spread its wings to shake off the heavy water and the last of the soot.

There was a slight bulge visible on one of its legs, in a place where no bulge ought to have been.

For a moment, it was as if Valkenier's heart stopped beating. Then, with a trembling hand, he brought the camera back to his eye and stared hopefully through its telephoto lens.

"My diamonds!" he shrieked. "My diamonds!"

"Diamonds?" said the warden at his elbow. "What's all this about diamonds?"

Roel Opers paced the narrow confines of the cell, his mind awhirl with vindictive dreams of revenge on those two lousy cops, on the arrogant prosecutor and that so-smug judge; on his mother and his dead *oma* and the whole damned system. Sitting on his bunk in the corner with his head sunk pitifully in his hands, Gerard Valkenier was lost in his own private thoughts.

Two guards strolled down the corridor outside. "Get a load of those birds," said the elder to the younger, who had just been reassigned to the prison that morning. "That *zenuwpees* with the hole in his ear's been in there for two weeks now, and the other one for eight or nine days, and I haven't heard a peep out of either of them in all that time. Real silent types, the both of them."

But beyond the bars of the window on the far wall of the cell, there was much peeping to be heard. On the roof of Building B a proud mama stork had her beak full, feeding the quartet of noisy baby gulls that surrounded her in her nest.

GAHAN WILSON

A Gift of the Gods

Spring always sneaked up on the children in Lakeside. The winters were so convincing and so durable that we eventually forgot about other possibilities, about a chance of change.

Then, always without warning, there were tender new leaves on the bushes surrounding the apartment buildings; a fresh, clayey smell of earth everywhere; birds picking up broom and mop fragments for making nests; summer vacation becoming an actual possibility; the bravest new flies crawling out from their hiding places along the edges of windows and wandering on the sunny panes—and the children began taking ruminative walks, going places they wouldn't ordinarily go and observing things they would ordinarily ignore.

It was the time of exploration come again, and the taste and feel of new adventure were everywhere, infusing the world and none of the implications of any of it were lost on Henry Laird.

He had been walking, for no conscious reason, along the broad quietness of Harmon Avenue, gazing at the fine old trees and the low hills of the lawns and the looming bulks of the old mansions that lined its sides, when he found he had come to the little park that sat at the end of Main Street and faced the great spread of the lake.

The park was a small jewel of design, with its gardens

gracious even now, before their real blooming; and its budding trees, waiting for their new leaves, stood composed in smooth, stylish curves and clumpings.

In the center of the park, or, rather, just enough off its center to make its location more interesting, was a small Grecian temple of the open, pillared style. Henry climbed the western steps and stood on the porch like a lost prince come at last to his kingdom.

The air from the lake wafted as gently over his face as a deliberately loving stroke, so he pulled his wool cap from his head in order to let the breeze caress more of him. He closed his eyes for a long moment and after some time let them flutter open. At first, he looked about dazedly, enjoying the faint, odd, golden gleam that everything about him had taken on; but then he began to observe his surroundings in some detail, looking around in the manner of one who has returned home after a long and hazardous voyage.

It was then, for the first time, that he saw the greasy paper sack.

A thing as ugly as that had no business being in such surroundings. It belonged in a dingy alley next to garbage cans. It was not proper that such an object be in such a place as this. Henry advanced to the brown sack and, after a moment's hesitation over its really spectacular filthiness, bent down and picked the thing up with both hands.

It was nowhere near as heavy as its bulk seemed to indicate. Although it was jammed full, almost to bursting, it could not weigh a full three pounds. A rich animal reek exuded from the sack, and Henry peeked down into its gaping mouth and saw that it seemed to be stuffed full of grayish black hair. He would remove the disreputable, odious thing.

But just before he left the park—just before he stepped

from its grass to the sidewalk that would lead him back into the twentieth-century maze of concrete and asphalt that made up the basic webbing of this modern world—he became aware of being observed.

Something, he knew it, something with shiny, dark eyes was watching him, was carefully taking his measure as a hunter does of a rabbit or a lion of a zebra colt; and it was thinking, he could feel it in his own mouth, how Henry Laird would taste if you sunk your teeth into his shoulder until the skin split and the muscles tore and the blood spurted into your maw. And it was enjoying the taste, enjoying it very much.

So Henry quit the little park with more speed than he ordinarily might have used, and he was very glad when he reached his apartment building with his shoulder still unsplit and whole, and he was even gladder when he had gained the safety of his bedroom, having gotten past his mother, who, thank God, was busy making Jell-O with fruit in it and so hadn't caught as much as a glimpse of him or what he bore.

In his room, on his desk, the sack looked even worse than it had before. Its splotchings were more numerous and varied now, it seemed, and the disreputable, furtive look of it, its sullen poverty, made it stand out starkly against its present comfortable surroundings.

Henry took hold of the long, dark hair that poked from the sack's mouth, and when he tugged, it slithered forth and cascaded smoothly to the floor almost like liquid, like thick blood or oil. Henry tossed the sack aside and went to his knees, smoothing the fur with his hands, spreading it out; and then, with a silent gasp and a widening of his eyes, he saw what he had got.

From its head (for it certainly had a head) to the sharp, curving claws of its hind feet (for it had them, too), it was a kind of nightmare costume made of, as far as Henry could see, one single pelt for all its six-foot length and the wide stretch of its arms or upper legs.

It was animal skin, no doubt of it, bestial for certain, and yet there was an extremely disquieting suggestion of the human about it, too. It seemed to have been scalped from something between species, something caught in the middle of an evolutionary leap or fall.

The ears were animal in shape, pointed and high-peaked, with the wide cupping given to wild things that they might better hear their prey or would-be killer padding in the dark, and yet the placement of them, their relation to the forehead, was entirely human. And was that a nose or a snout?

It was hard to say, too, whether the appendages at the end of its arms or forelegs were claws or hands, since they had something of the qualities of both. The cruelty in their design strongly suggested an anatomy too brutal to be human, yet the thumbs and the forefingers were clearly opposable, and there was something about the formation of the palms that denied their being exclusively animal.

Of course, in their present condition, these last were neither hands nor claws; they were gloves. Large gloves— far too large for the hands of Henry Laird, for instance— but gloves all the same.

Henry held his left hand over the left glove of the costume. Yes, it was far, far too small to fill that hairy, clawed container. The fingers of them were inches too long. If he slipped his fingers into them—it was a strangely disquieting thought that made all of his own skin tingle and crawl—the gloves would dangle limply hollow from the first knuckle.

Still, Henry would try; and he moved his hand down in a kind of slow swoop to where the skin gaped in a slit just under the costume's palm and slid his hand in, noting

how smoothly and effortlessly it seemed to glide; and
when it was in, entirely in, the glove, with an odd noise
something like a cat's hiss, shrank in against the fingers
and back and palm of Henry's hand until it fit him like a
second skin.

Henry gave a kind of muffled shriek, stifling it with his
unclad hand, and then pulled frantically at the glove. He
expected a horrible resistance, but no such thing; it slid
off most cooperatively—shot off, really, since he had
pulled so hard—and when Henry saw that his hand
seemed none the worse for having worn it, he slipped the
glove on and off again a few more experimental times.

Now it seemed that Henry's wearing of the glove had
permanently affected it, for it remained his exact size,
whether he had it on or not, which meant it was now
ludicrously small for its opposite partner; so Henry, after
giving the matter a little thought, slipped his other hand
into the other glove with identical effect and the end
result that the two were now precisely the same size—
which is to say Henry's size.

The implications of this singular phenomenon gave
Henry a clear challenge that very few boys his age could
have resisted, and certainly Henry did not; and so, after
going very quietly to the door and peeking out of it and
listening carefully to make sure that his mother was still
immersed in making fruit Jell-O, Henry picked up the
costume and, with just a slight grating of his teeth and
squinching up of his face, slipped it on.

He started with the legs, slipping into them as he would
into pants, and gasped slightly as they shrank instantly to
accommodate his size, again with that catlike hissing
sound; and then he hunched into the arms, and they,
hissing, fitted to him; and then there was a very alarming
moment when the torso of the costume curled around his
own and shrank to coat him smoothly, this with the

loudest hissing of all; and then, by far the worst, the whole thing sealed up, the openings withering down to slits and the slits healing to unbroken skin, until his whole body was covered and wrapped with the dark grey pelt.

Except for his head, that is. Henry had left the head for the last, just as he would have done with a Halloween costume.

He walked over to the mirror set into the door and gazed at himself in wonder, his pink face staring above the dark, hairy body, a mad scientist's transplant. He moved his arms and legs, experimentally at first, and watched their reflections make little, cautious movements. He reached out with one hand to touch the mirror and thrilled when he realized that he was actually feeling the glass not through the skin, as one does when wearing a glove, but *with* the skin!

After a time of touching and moving and carefully watching, Henry reached up behind him, groping for the mask, which was dangling down his back like a hood, and took hold of it and, very slowly and cautiously, watching anxiously all the time, slipped it over the top of his head and then his forehead; and then, closing his eyes—somehow, he did not want them to be open when they would be blind and covered—he pulled the mask completely down until the fur of its neck met the fur of the costume's chest, and he shuddered violently when he felt, with his lids still firmly closed, the whole business squeeze gently in, molding itself to the flesh of his face; and only when the catlike hissing had faded away entirely did he dare open his eyes.

There, facing him from the mirror of his own bedroom, with his desk covered with homework and a hanging model airplane for its background, was a monster—a small monster, true, but no less frightening for that.

Henry crouched a little as he studied his reflection. It seemed more comfortable that way. He moved his face closer to the glass. The nostrils worked as he breathed.

He lifted his head slightly and inhaled deeply and found he could smell the Jell-O his mother was making way off in the kitchen more clearly than he would ordinarily be able to do if he put his nose close enough to the pot to feel the heat.

He looked back at his reflection and studied his eyes intently. They were his eyes, no doubt of that, though the blueness of them was strange in their present setting. Then he opened his mouth and nearly fainted.

It was in no way the mouth of Henry Laird. It had fangs, for one thing, for the most obvious thing, but the differences did not stop there. All its teeth were as sharp as needles, every single tooth; and moving in and around them and lapping over them, constantly on the move, was a long, lean, curling tongue. Not Henry Laird's tongue. Not even a human tongue.

Without giving any thought to it, Henry pulled the skin costume from his head, his arms, his whole body, and threw it on the floor.

Again he studied himself in the mirror, touching his forehead, feeling his arms, wiggling his fingers; and then, only after all those preliminary tests, he opened his mouth and nearly cried aloud in his relief in seeing nothing more formidable in it than the ordinary incisors and molars with the occasional filling put here and there by Dr. Mineke, the family dentist, because of Mounds bars and licorice.

The skin was returned to its filthy paper sack, the sack was stuffed into the rear of the bottom drawer of his bureau and Henry took the most meticulous shower of his life and scrubbed his mouth three times in a row with Stripe toothpaste.

*   *   *

About ten that night, when Henry was just about to go to bed and had almost convinced himself that there was nothing waiting in his room, the doorbell rang and his father got out of his easy chair with a grunt and pushed the button by the doorbell so that he could talk with whomever it was downstairs and said, "Yes? Yes? Who's there?"

At first, there was nothing but breathing from downstairs; then they all heard a voice, Henry and his father and his mother—a deep, growly sort of voice.

"I want it back," the voice said, muffled and distorted.

"What?" asked Henry's father. "What did you say?"

"You give it back," the voice said, louder; and this time you could hear the saliva in it, the drool. "It's mine, you! They gave it to me, see?"

"Look here," said Henry's father, "I don't know who you are or what you're trying to say."

"Who is that, dear?" asked Henry's mother. "What does he want?"

Now there was only breathing, heavier than before and with the hiss of spittle.

"You're going to have to speak up," said Henry's father. "I can't make out a word you're saying."

But now the breathing was gone and there was only the sound of rain, near and insistent as it battered and spattered against the windows of the apartment. Henry quickly gathered up his books from the table where he had been doing his homework.

"Hello? Hello?" said Henry's father, pressing impatiently on the LISTEN button. "I think he's some drunk."

Henry started down the hall, holding his schoolbooks to his chest.

"Whoever he was, he seems to have gone," said Henry's father, and the rain, which had suddenly grown much fiercer, began throwing itself against the windows in alarming, angry-seeming gusts.

"Well, he certainly doesn't sound like anyone we know," said Henry's mother, and his father, chewing his lip a little, casting a glance or two at the front-hall door of the apartment, settled again into his easy chair.

Lying in his bed, staring up at a ceiling too dark to be seen, Henry listened to the roaring wind and considered the situation.

Outside, in the wet wildness of this awful night, prowled a being dangerous to Henry and his family. It would not do just to give back what was asked for. Wearing the skin had roused something in Henry that knew all that and relished what it now made necessary.

When it seemed from the stillness of the apartment that his parents were asleep, Henry rose, carefully and quietly, padded across the floor to his bureau, extracted the skin from its double confinement of sack and drawer and slipped it on.

The cat hissings merged into one smooth, unbroken cry when he donned the costume all at once, going from a kind of throaty purr to a final yowl of triumph as the mask sealed on, but all blended into the sound of the rain. Henry was sure his parents had heard none of it.

His passage through the apartment to the kitchen was so near to silent that even his hearing, heightened astoundingly by its joining with the high-peaked ears of what he wore, was unable to detect any of it save for the tiniest clicking as he turned the back-door lock. He took a deep breath, opened and closed the door as quickly and softly as he could, and he was standing in the wind and pelting rain on the apartment's back porch.

He rested his claws—for they were claws, not hands— on the wooden railing of the porch and peered down and

around three stories below at the apartment's huge backyard.

There were occasional lights mounted here and there,
none too solidly from the wild way they swayed in the
wind: some on posts, spewing their swaying beams on
parked cars; some fixed to the brick walls of the building,
making a dancing shine on dark, wet windows or creating
ominous shiftings of shadows in the depths of basement
entrances; but none of them did much to dispel the dank
gloom all about.

Henry lifted his snout and inhaled deeply and quest-
ingly and got a wild medley of night odors: rain and
cinders; something strong blown in from the lake; a nest
hidden on a nearby roof whose smell of new eggs and bird
flesh made his mouth, with its needle-sharp teeth and
long, lolling tongue, water—but not a whiff of his enemy.

He began to trot quietly down the rain-slicked wooden
steps, glancing sharply about with his incongruous blue
eyes as he moved.

He did not stop at the foot of the steps—there was a
revealing pool of light from a lamp—but ducked quickly
into a sooty patch of shadow before he crouched and
sucked in great pulls of air, analyzing each one carefully
before turning an inch or so to sample again. Then,
suddenly, he froze and blinked and inhaled again without
moving, this time even deeper, and a snarling kind of
chuckle came from his throat, and his teeth were bared in
a human, if singularly cruel, grin.

Bent low, ducking craftily from shadow to shadow,
Henry dodged his way nearer and nearer to the wide gap
in the wooden fence that led to the alley in back of the
building.

He pressed himself against the wall, listening with his
animal ears and feeling the rain exactly as though it were
falling on his own bare skin. He could make out the motor

of a far-distant car; someone in an apartment was playing
dance music on a radio and humming to it; there was a
muffled mewing from a covered nest of kittens; and there
was the harsh, slurred breathing of his enemy.

He was near. His smell was mixed with garbage smells:
moldering oranges and lamb bones gone bad mingled
with a hot hate smell, a killing smell out there in the dark.
He was very likely watching the opening in the fence.
Henry slowly backed up along the fence away from the
opening until it joined a porch. After a listening pause to
make sure the enemy had not moved, he stealthily
climbed the porch's side, which gave him a perch just
overlooking the alley.

The tar of the alley gleamed like black enamel in the
rain from the light of the bare bulb mounted over the rear
door of the apartment building opposite. The first sweep
of his glance seemed to indicate that the alley was
innocent of anything save a tidy army of garbage cans
beside the building's concrete landing and a less respect-
able accumulation of cans and rubbish just outside the
backyard of a private house further down, but a squinting
second look showed an ominous bulk hunkered down
between the second batch of garbage and a low wooden
fence.

Silently, hurrying as fast as he could so as not to give
the enemy time to mull things over and change position,
Henry made his way through his building and around the
block so that he could approach the alley fence of the
private house from its rear. Once in the house's backyard,
he dropped to all fours and inhaled deeply. He grinned
again, and this time the grin was significantly less human
than it had been before. His prey was still there.

The impulse to rush with all speed so that he might
throw himself at once upon his enemy and rip his skin
and drink his spurting blood was so devastatingly strong

that the flesh of Henry's flanks rippled suppressing it. He hunched down, puffing from the effort of wresting control from the sudden killing urge. He could not let such a thing master him. A blind scurry forward might undo all his cleverness so far. He had done well as a neophyte; he must continue to do so.

But still the smell of the enemy, the rich meatiness of it, was maddening. It seemed he could even detect the pulsings in the veins and arteries!

He forced himself into calmness, hunching low into the wet grass. He took a deep snuff of the earth scent in an attempt to clear his head and then began to work his way slowly and silently forward toward where the pile of garbage and his victim were lumped together on the fence's other side.

But as he drew nearer, he became aware of some confusion. It seemed the garbage stench was growing stronger than his victim's. Then it crossed his mind that that might well have been the reason that place had been chosen. He was, after all, dealing with someone far more experienced than himse——

Then there was a terrific shock and a sidewise lurch, and Henry's head exploded in a searing blast of light followed by a great, black rushing that threw him into a confusion of motion, not himself moving but himself being moved, roughly, brutally, and he screamed because of the awful, horrible pain—someone was tearing the skin from his face, ripping it off him, roots and all, and now his scalp and now the flesh of his neck—and he screamed and screamed and cried out, "Please, please stop!" but the tearing of the flesh from his body did not stop, only went on and on; and with each violent ripping and rending of himself from himself, the raw agony burned over more and more of him, until he was nothing but a scorched, stripped leaving thrown aside.

He lay naked on the wet grass, confusing his tears with the rain running over his body, and was profoundly grateful for the tears and the rain, for they were cooling and healing the rawness of him so that he was becoming aware of something other than pain, aware of the night and of movement before him.

There was the enemy before him, the victor, not the victim, huge and smelling—even to Henry's human nose, the stench of him was clear enough—hunched down and pulling this way and that at something in his hands.

"You spoiled it, you little bastard!" the enemy sobbed and, leaning over, huge and dark in the night, sent a pale fist lashing out and knocked Henry's head back painfully against the fence. "You f——d it up, you little prick!"

Henry curled closer into himself and for the first time realized that the thing the enemy was tugging at was the costume. He did it with such absorption and violence that at one point his hat fell from his head and the rain streaked his long, black hair in curling ribbons down his furrowed forehead without his noticing.

The enemy's eyes were shiny and black, as Henry had sensed they were back in the park with the Grecian temple, and his teeth, though human, seemed much more pointed than the norm, the canines longer and sharper. All were bared in alternate snarling and sobbing, for the enemy was desperate. At length, he threw the costume down in fury and then lunged at Henry, taking him by the shoulders and shaking him hard enough to make his teeth rattle.

"It's all gone small, you little son of a bitch!" he shouted into Henry's face, and the stink of his breath made Henry gag. "What did you do, hah, you f——r? How did you make it shrink, you shit?"

"I put it on!" Henry sobbed, his head bouncing crazily as the enemy continued to shake him. "I put it on!"

A crafty look sprang into the enemy's face. He held Henry still for a long second, staring closely at his face.

"Yeah," he said. "Yeah, I remember. It changed when they gave it to me!"

He threw Henry hard against the fence and clawed up the skin, holding it spread open before him like a huge, soggy bat.

"Yeah," said the foe to himself, his wet face gleaming, his long canines shining. "Yeah!"

Then, with a growling chuckle, he lifted the costume's arm, pushed his huge hand into the skin glove of it and grinned wider and wider until it seemed that all of his teeth, his not really human teeth, were showing. The glove had stretched easily, and that which had been a small claw when Henry wore it was now something like a grizzly's paw.

He held his hand wearing the glove high into the rain in savage triumph, the rest of the costume trailing from it like a shaggy banner, and then he thrust it in front of Henry, waving it as a fist under his nose.

"You wait, you little piece of shit!" he crowed. "You wait till you see what I do to your face with this!"

He pulled on the other glove with equal ease, then stood and stepped into the hairy costume with his long, powerful legs, roaring with laughter when they slid in smoothly. A great flash of lightning made Henry blink, and when he opened his eyes, it was to see the costume curling around his enemy's chest, fitting it with a loving closeness.

His foe looked down at him with a grin of hate that made Henry shudder, and then, as a sudden crash of thunder made the ground jump, the grizzly paws took hold of the costume's mask, pulling it over the brutal, laughing face, so that the following volley of crackling lightning showed the monster standing there complete, towering awesomely over Henry, striding toward him, bending down and picking him up with a paw clutching either side of his throat. "I got you now, you little f——k!" the monster said, and Henry felt his weight making the long claws dig into his neck as he was swung in a high arc close to the hairy face grinning with fangs of such a fearsome length and sharpness that he almost vomited at the sight of them.

Then the monster suddenly froze position, and as Henry watched, the ghastly maw's grin made a weird, rapid transition, faltering, twisting and finally turning to a wide gape of dismay.

"Naw!" his enemy snarled. *"Naaaw!"*

And then came a shocking crash of thunder, loud enough to make the very ground of Lakeside shudder, and as it pealed and pealed, rolling round in the sky, Henry saw the monster's eyes bulge impossibly, and then the paws released him with a spastic gesture and he landed with a hard thump on the ground to stare up in astonishment.

Lit by endless lightning, all sound of him drowned out by the ceaseless, merciless, air-flung cacophony, the monster pranced wildly in a crazy dance, arms and legs swinging like a mad jumping jack's, and from the gape of his horrible jaws and the spewing of blood and saliva, his screams must have been bloodcurdlingly ghastly could they have been heard.

But they could not; thunder censored all—and so it was in a kind of earsplitting silence that Henry saw the monster's eyes bulge more and more until the roundness of them projected entirely outside the sockets of the mask, and then they were violently ejected in a double spray of blood, and Henry found himself staring unbelievingly at the extraordinary sight of his blinded enemy beginning to shrink before him!

At first, the process was uneven, one huge paw shriveling at a time, an arm bunching oddly and then shortening in a jerky telescopic fashion; but then, almost as if getting the feel of it, the whole creature began to reduce itself in step, so to speak; and as Henry watched in appalled fascination but with an undeniable undertone of profound satisfaction, he saw the being crushed down by stages, dancing and screaming all the while, kept alive and conscious by some horrendous magic until it was no larger than he had been while in the costume—until, that is, the costume had returned itself to a perfect fit for Henry Laird. Only then, and not before, was the suffering of his enemy terminated and the creature allowed to drop to the rain- and blood-soaked grass on which it had danced these last awful minutes.

Its murderous readjustments completed, the costume opened its various slits and slowly disgorged Henry's enemy, now only a shapeless, glistening redness, washing itself carefully in the pouring rain after it did so. When it was entirely free of all traces of its recent tenant, and not before, it slithered smoothly over to Henry's curled and shivering legs, very much as a cat would work its way to the side of a beloved master, and, snuggling close to him, waited to see what he wanted to do next.

EDWARD D. HOCH

The Problem of the Hunting Lodge

"**I** think I promised to tell you about the time my folks visited me here in Northmont," Dr. Sam Hawthorne said as he poured the brandy.

"It was the start of deer-hunting season in the autumn of 1930, and I was thirty-four years old. I'd been practicing in town for eight years and it had become more of a home to me than the Midwestern city where I grew up. That was a difficult thing to explain to my father . . ."

We'd always done a great deal of hunting in my youth [Dr. Sam continued], and I suppose it was only natural that my father, Harry Hawthorne, who had retired from the profitable dry-goods store that was his life for nearly forty years, would decide to visit his only son in New England and get in a bit of deer hunting at the same time. My mother came with him, of course, and I was happy to see them both. I hadn't made a trip back home since the previous Christmas, just after Sheriff Lens' marriage, and this was only the second time in my eight years here that they'd come to Northmont.

I met them at the train station and went to help Dad with their baggage.

"You'd think we were staying a month instead of five

days," he grumbled. "You know what your mother's like when she travels." Though it was white now, he'd kept most of his hair, and he still had the vigor of a much younger man. My mother, by contrast, had always been on the frail side.

I led them to my new Stutz Torpedo and listened to my father's words of grudging approval. "The doctoring business must be pretty good these days for you to afford a car like this."

"I got a good deal on it," I explained, "from another doctor who needed the money."

"It's too bad about the car we gave you for a graduation present," my mother said, climbing in the front seat.

"It burnt up. I was lucky I wasn't in it," I said, shutting the passenger door and going around to the other side.

We stopped by the office first and I took them inside. "Mom, this is my nurse, April. As I've told you, she's a great help to me."

April had never met my parents and she fussed over them in her best manner. Sheriff Lens dropped by just as we were leaving and gave my father a vigorous handshake. "I'll tell you, Mr. Hawthorne, that son o' yours would make a fine sleuth. He's helped me out on more cases than I care to count."

"Oh?" My mother looked alarmed. "Do you have much crime here, Sheriff?"

"More than you'd think possible," he said with something like pride in his voice. "We needed the gumption of somebody like Doc here to deal with 'em. He's got a mind like that fella Einstein!"

"We'd better be going," I mumbled, embarrassed as always by the sheriff's praise.

"What're you goin' to do while you're here?" he asked my father.

"Oh, a little deer hunting, maybe."

"Good weather for it."

"There's a fellow lives near here that I've been corresponding with," my father said. "Ryder Sexton. I thought
we'd drive over and see him one day."

"Oh, Sexton's a hunter, all right! You should see his
collection o' weapons!"

"I'm anxious to. He's written me about them."

Sheriff Lens licked his lips. "I'll give you some advice,
go see Ryder Sexton right away—today or tomorrow.
Maybe he'll invite you to hunt on his property. He's got
some woods an' a pond that're the best deer-huntin' spots
in the whole county. He's even got a little huntin' lodge
built back on his land, near the pond. He uses it for duck
huntin' too."

"Thanks for the tip," my father said. "Be seeing you,
Sheriff."

I'd planned a quiet evening for them, but after the
sheriff's advice Dad insisted that I phone Sexton after
we'd had dinner at my apartment. I knew the man only
slightly, though when I put my father on the line it was
clear that they were excited at the prospect of a first
meeting. The upshot of it was that I agreed to drive my
parents over to Sexton's house the following morning.

"I have to see a patient at nine," I told them as I
prepared the bed in my spare room, "but I'll be back here
to pick you up around ten. Sexton's place is about a
twenty-minute drive from here."

Ryder Sexton was the last of our county's old land
barons, if the term could ever be used properly in this
area of New England. He owned some three hundred
acres of property. There were farms that large, of course,
but Ryder Sexton was no farmer, not even the gentleman
sort. He'd made his money in munitions during the war,

and though he no longer had an interest in the Sexton
Arms empire his name was still linked to it.

The following morning was crisp and unusually clear
for mid-November. I drove along the rutted back roads,
pointing out the farms and landmarks. "This fenced-in
property is the beginning of the Sexton place," I said.

"It certainly is large," my mother remarked. "Harry,
you always knew how to make friends with rich folks."

Father sputtered in mock protest. "I read a letter of his
in the *American Rifleman* magazine and wrote him about
it. I never knew if he was rich or poor, and I sure never
connected him with Sexton Arms."

"He bought this place a few years ago after he sold the
company," I explained. "He spends part of the year in
Florida and in New York, but he's always up here during
hunting season. Sheriff Lens told me about his collection
of primitive weapons."

Ryder Sexton himself came to the door to greet us,
wearing a fringed deerskin jacket and riding britches. He
was a tall, imposing man with a ruddy complexion and
steel-gray hair worn in a short military fashion. Seeing
him with my father made me think somehow of a reunion
of Army officers from the last war, though I knew that
Sexton had been busy on the home front and my father's
military service had been confined to the local draft
board.

Sexton nodded a greeting to me, but he seemed genuinely pleased to meet my father. "I look forward to your
letters, Harry. They're more sensible than most of the
stuff in the daily papers. And this must be Doris," he said
to my mother. "Welcome to Northmont, both of you.
Come in, come in!"

I'd never met any of Sexton's family and I was surprised
when a young woman appeared with an armload of fall
flowers and was introduced as his wife. "There's sup-

posed to be a frost tonight," she explained, "so I've been gathering up the last of them."

Her name was Rosemary, and I guessed her to be maybe thirty years younger than her husband, who was pushing sixty. She was probably a second wife, and attractive, with a direct, friendly manner. I tried to remember if I'd seen her about town, but I didn't think I had—which wasn't surprising, since the Sextons were here only part of the year.

"How's the deer hunting in this area?" my father asked when we were settled down in the paneled living room before a large open fire. "I'd like to give it a try while I'm visiting."

"Fine right now," Ryder Sexton assured him. "Couldn't be better. In fact, I'm going out with a few people tomorrow morning, if you'd like to join us. We hunt here on the property, down by the pond. I have a bit over three hundred acres, with lots of woods. I even have a small hunting lodge down there."

"That's mighty generous of you," Father answered with a smile, quickly accepting the offer.

"You too, Sam," Sexton added, including me as an afterthought. "Your mother can come and stay here at the house with Rosemary while we're out."

I mumbled something about appointments with my patients, but I knew I'd be able to arrange it. The idea of hunting with my father again, as we'd done so many years ago, overcame my momentary distaste for slaughtering deer. "What time will you be starting?"

Sexton thought a moment. "Early. Be out here by seven if you can. My neighbor, Jim Freeman, is joining us and Bill Tracy is coming out from town. Maybe I'll invite Sheriff Lens too. That'll make six of us in all."

Bill Tracy was a real-estate man who'd had some dealings with Sexton, and Jim Freeman was a successful farmer. I knew them both quite well, and had recently doctored Freeman's daughter for the usual childhood illnesses.

"We'll be here," Father assured Sexton. "Now what about your collection? I'm itching to see it."

Ryder Sexton chuckled and led us to an adjoining den where two walls were almost covered by tall glass-doored cabinets. Inside were a number of items, mainly made of wood, and our host gave us a quick description of each. "I've been collecting primitive weapons for years, and though we're here for only a portion of the year I decided this was the best place to house my collection. This first is a cord sling. One of those stones was placed in that pouch and the thing was whirled over your head and released. That's how David killed Goliath. This pellet-bow from India has the pouch fixed between its two strings."

"Unusual," my father murmured. "I never saw one of those."

"These are throwing-sticks used by Australian aborigines. And of course you're familiar with the boomerang. Here's a collection of darts, javelins, and throwing spears. Jim Freeman next door will tell you how he dropped darts from airplanes during the war.

"Notice this wooden spear-thrower from the South Pacific. The spear fits into this socket and the thrower acts like an extra joint in the arm. Eskimos use something similar for harpoons. Here we have some Patagonian bolas, with three balls connected by thongs to a common center. They're generally used to entangle the prey."

I looked ahead at the next cabinet. "These swords seem more recent."

"They're ceremonial swords from the western Pacific islands," Sexton explained. "Notice this club. It's been edged with sharks' teeth to make it quite deadly. I sometimes use it to dispatch wounded deer. And here are some shields of coconut fiber from the same area." He might have gone on for another half hour if his wife hadn't interrupted to say, "Here's Jennifer!" Out the window I saw a young woman in her twenties walking a bicycle into the side yard. "Come on," Mrs. Sexton urged us, "I want you to meet my sister."

We trooped outside and she introduced us as her sister stowed the bike away in an unused henhouse. "Jennifer, this is Harry and Doris Hawthorne—and their son Dr. Sam Hawthorn, from town. They're visiting him this week, and Harry is a friend of Ryder's."

Jennifer seemed delighted to meet us. "Rosemary insisted I come and stay with them for a month, but I really like to see people around. After living in New York, I've become too much of a city girl, I guess."

"You seem quite at home with that bicycle," I remarked.

"Ryder says I mustn't take it on the trails back in the woods. He's afraid a hunter might mistake me for a deer." She pouted prettily. "Would you mistake me for a deer?" she asked me.

"I might," I conceded.

Our departure was delayed by the arrival of Jim Freeman from the neighboring farm. He'd walked over through the fields, a big lumbering man who'd always reminded me more of a wrestler than a farmer. "Weather forecast says we might get a little snow tonight," he told Ryder Sexton. "You gonna run the hose out to your huntin' lodge to keep your water from freezin'?"

Sexton nodded. "I suppose I should." He turned to my father and explained. "I have a tank of water in the lodge for necessities. It comes in handy for brewing coffee or

mixing drinks, doing dishes or even flushing the outhouse."

"All the comforts of home," my mother remarked
dryly. She'd never thought much of hunting, and I
remembered how in my youth she'd badgered my father
for taking me out to shoot pheasants on a Sunday afternoon.

Ryder Sexton kept a hundred yards of hose coiled
around a drum out in back of the barn and he started
dragging one end with him as we walked down to his
lodge. "I'll show you where we'll be in the morning," he
said. "I'll leave the water running slowly all night and
then my tank won't freeze up."

He turned to his neighbor. "There'll be six of us in the
morning, Jim. Harry and Sam are joining us, and I thought
I'd invite Sheriff Lens too."

"Fine."

We strode between two oaks and over the crest of a
small hill. Below us, some fifty yards away, was a crude
shelter made of rough boards with a roof of tree branches.
It stood near the edge of a pond, still and quiet in the
morning sun. Sexton gave a yank on the hose and pulled
it down the hill, trailing it after him through the short
grass. It wasn't much thicker than a garden hose but many
farmers bought it in hundred-yard lengths for irrigation
purposes.

The hunting lodge was larger inside than it had first
appeared, with room for all of us to crowd in easily.
Rosemary Sexton and her sister Jennifer had followed
along, and with Sexton, Freeman, and my folks and me,
that made seven of us. The ceiling was low above our
heads, but I could stand and walk without stooping.
There were firepots, crude chairs, and a table, together
with gun racks and even a small icebox where food and
beverages could be kept. A metal tank full of water was

attached to a shelf along one wall. Sexton ran the end of his hose into it.

"It holds thirty gallons—almost the size of a barrel," he explained, directing his words to my father. "The hose goes in the top. I'll turn the water back on at the pump, just enough to keep it flowing all night. And I'll open this faucet a dribble. The drain empties into the pond."

"There are quite a few holes in your wall," I commented.

"Those are gun holes, Sam," my father was quick to explain. "Right, Ryder?"

"Sure are! Tomorrow morning a couple of us will wait here while the rest of you drive the deer toward us. Then we'll fire through these gun ports and catch 'em as they cross that open space."

"Sounds good to me," Father said enthusiastically.

"It would," my mother muttered.

Jennifer gave a little groan. "Looks as if you and I are going to be cooking venison, Rosemary."

Sexton's wife snorted. "They haven't killed them yet. My money's on the deer."

We strolled back up the hill and watched while Sexton turned on the pump and regulated the flow of water through the hose to the crudely built hunting lodge. Then Freeman headed back across the field toward his farm and I got my folks back to the car. "Seven o'clock," Ryder Sexton called out after us.

That night over dinner my mother admitted that Ryder and his wife seemed nice enough. "For deer hunters," she added.

Father laughed. "I don't think the wife hunts, Doris. Don't tar her with the same brush as him."

"I have to stop by the office," I told them, "in case April left me any messages."

"You go ahead." Mother started gathering up the dishes. "Your father and I better get to bed early anyhow if we're supposed to be up with the chickens."

"Before the chickens, Doris," he corrected her.

I drove down to the office and found only one message of any importance. A farm injury had hospitalized one of my patients, and I drove over to Pilgrim Memorial to see how he was doing. As I was leaving, I ran into Bill Tracy. Bill was always well dressed, with a stiffly starched collar that made him look more like the town banker than a real-estate man. I'd never known him to hunt before, and I had to mention it to him.

"My hunting's no stranger than yours, Sam. How come you're going out there?" he countered.

"My folks are visiting and Dad's corresponded with Sexton. He invited us both to come along. We were out there looking around this morning. It's quite a place."

"Is his sister-in-law still there?"

"Jennifer? Yes, she was around. Lovely girl."

Bill Tracy slid a finger beneath his starched collar. "I think I saw her over at the Freeman place one afternoon last week as I was driving by. I couldn't be sure, though. It might have been Mrs. Sexton. They look a little alike."

"Not close up. Maybe it was one of Freeman's daughters."

"Naw, I recognized that bike Jennifer rides, parked around the side of the house." He winked at me. "And she told me she was bored with country life."

"She implied that much today," I admitted.

"Well, I'll see you in the morning, Sam. Keep your eyes open and you might spot something more interesting than deer."

I was still thinking about that when I got home and found my mother sitting up by the window with a cup of hot chocolate. "I need to relax before I can sleep," she told me. "Not your father, though. He's already snoring in there."

"How's his health, Mom?" I asked, settling down on the sofa by her side.

"Good enough for his age, I suppose. He saw his doctor about some heart palpitations last month. Keep an eye on him during the hunt tomorrow, Sam."

"Of course."

She sipped her hot chocolate and sighed. "I've never liked him hunting. You neither!"

"I haven't hunted in nearly twenty years—not since the last time with him. I'm going along tomorrow because I think he wants me to."

"He likes to think you're still his boy, Sam."

"I guess I always will be. And yours too."

"No, no." She shook her head. "You're a man now. You should be married, with a family."

"I know, Mom."

"When you wrote me about that wedding last Christmas I thought for a minute it was yours."

"Sheriff Lens got married. And he's a lot older than me."

"Don't let it slip by you, Sam. Don't spend all your time treating ill people and doing this detective work of yours and wake up one morning to find you're an old man without anyone to love you."

"Hey," I laughed, "this is pretty serious stuff! Come on, it's off to bed for both of us. I've got the alarm clock set for five-thirty."

"All right," she agreed, and gave me a kiss on the cheek. "But think about what I said."

I lay awake for a time after that, listening to the snoring from the next room and wondering if my mother had anyone to love her.

*　　*　　*

The morning alarm wakened me from a deep dreamless sleep, and I peered out the window to see a thin coating of snow over the landscape. It was still dark as I heard my folks moving to and from the bathroom and getting dressed.

"Good morning," I called out to them, "we got about a half inch of snow overnight!"

"Good deer-tracking weather!" my father called back.

"Sure is! I'll get us some breakfast."

The road to the Sexton place was virtually deserted as we drove out an hour later. Only a few tire tracks had broken the white mantle of snow, and when we turned into the Sexton driveway I realized that one set of these belonged to Sheriff Lens, who'd arrived ahead of us. The sun was up now, and the sheriff stood by his car with a deer rifle at his side, chatting with Sexton and Jim Freeman.

"Isn't this snow-cover great?" Ryder Sexton exclaimed as he greeted us. "The deer won't have a chance!"

Jennifer came out of the house with wrapped sandwiches for everyone and Rosemary Sexton hurried out behind her to welcome my mother. "Come in the house where you'll be warm—and safe."

Another car pulled into the driveway behind my Stutz and Bill Tracy climbed out, carrying his rifle in a fancy leather case. "Good morning, all!"

I introduced him to my parents and he accepted a sandwich from Jennifer. Then Sexton began issuing orders. "You'll spread out in a half circle with the pond and the hunting lodge as the focus. Stay clear of each other so's you can cover a wider area, then start converging toward the lodge, driving the deer that way. Sam, how about if you stay in the lodge with me?"

I remembered my promise of the previous night to keep

an eye on Dad. "I think I'd rather be out in the field if it's all the same with you."

Ryder Sexton shrugged. "Sure. I'll stay down there alone and pick 'em off like in a shooting gallery. Five of you can probably cover a larger circle anyhow."

We tramped back through the shallow snow to the pump house, where he turned off the water he'd had running since the previous night. "Jim, stay here till I disconnect the hose and then reel it in for me. I don't want anyone tripping over it and spoiling a good shot."

While Freeman stayed, the rest of us headed for the lodge. Jennifer, wearing only a thin jacket over a sweater and men's workpants, was in the lead with Sexton. "Are you hunting too?" I called out to her.

"I wish they'd let me!"

I fell in step with Sheriff Lens while Bill Tracy brought up the rear with my father. "How's the wife, Sheriff?"

"Good, Doc. I'd better bring home some meat for the table, though, or she'll never forgive me for takin' a whole day off!"

"Damn," Sexton grumbled from up ahead. "I'd forget my head if it wasn't screwed on!" He muttered some instructions to Jennifer and then paused at the top of the rise overlooking the hunting lodge. "And, Jennifer, on your way back tell Jim to start winding up the hose when I give the signal."

"Sure," she said, and started back.

"I like your boots," I told Sexton, admiring the sleek glisten of the new leather.

"Bought 'em in New York. Look at the tread on them!" He showed me the soles, then for the first time he noticed my rifle, an old Winchester I'd had for years. "If you don't mind my saying so, Sam, that's not much of a weapon for deer. I've got an extra up at the house if you'd like it."

"No, no, this is fine for me. I leave the fancy shooting to my father."

"All right, if you say so." He turned to Dad and Bill Tracy and the sheriff. "Look, this little rise pretty much protects the house from stray shots, but even so let's try to keep from firing in that direction. A rifle slug carries a long way and I don't want any broken windows. Or dead wives." He chuckled a bit at the last, to show it was meant as a joke. Then we waited at the top of the rise as he walked down across the virgin snow toward the lodge. He carried the rifle in his right hand and one of Jennifer's sandwiches in his left, stepping over the hose to enter the doorway.

I could see him through some of the gun ports in the lodge walls, pulling the hose from his water tank and dropping it in the doorway. "Pull it in!" he shouted, and I relayed the signal back to Jim Freeman at the pump house. Freeman started turning the drum, collecting the hose as it snaked back through the snow.

When Sexton saw that Freeman had rejoined us, he called out, "Start your circle now. Watch for deer tracks, and drive 'em this way. I'll be ready, and I'll have the coffee brewing too!"

We headed off across the fields, with Tracy and Freeman moving out to the east while the sheriff, Dad, and I fanned out in the opposite direction. I managed to keep my father in sight, and once when he spotted deer tracks I ran over to check them out.

"It's a deer, all right," I agreed. "A big one too, from the looks of it." I trudged along at his side, not bothering to resume my former position. We were on the trail together now, as we'd been so many times in my youth.

He must have been thinking the same thing. "Brings back the old days, don't it."

"Sure does, Dad."

"Your mother tell you about my heart?"

"She said you've had a few problems. Are you taking some pills?"

"Sure, sure. I'll live to be a hundred. After all, my son's a doctor, isn't he?"

"I only wish I lived nearer to you. What would you think of moving east?"

"To New England? Not a chance! We're Midwesterners. You were too, once."

"I know. But it would be hard to go back now."

"I don't know. Do you think your life is any better here?"

"I enjoy it."

"You like men like Sexton for patients? Rich men?"

"He's not my patient. He's your friend, remember."

"Your mother thinks his wife's not happy."

"Why's that?" I asked, guiding our route through the woods so we stayed in line with the deer we were tracking.

"Oh, Rosemary Sexton made some remark about hunting, and about how her whole life seems to be lived around her husband's whims. Doris thought she sounded a little bitter."

"Most women in Northmont would love to trade places with her."

We came upon fresh deer droppings in the snow and my father signaled for silence. "Quiet now," he whispered. "We're not far behind him."

We came out of the woods, moving around a clump of underbrush, and I saw Sheriff Lens off to the left. He waved and pointed straight ahead, at something we couldn't see. Then suddenly a deer broke from cover about two hundred yards ahead of us, running in the general direction of Sexton's lodge.

"Look at the rack on him!" my father breathed. "Might be a twelve-pointer!"

The deer started to turn toward us, and Sheriff Lens raised his rifle for a quick shot. The range was too far for any accuracy, and he must have realized that. He lowered his weapon as the deer changed direction again.

"The wind is from our direction," my father said. "He probably scents us."

"If Tracy and Freeman are in position we've got him trapped. The only way out is past the lodge where Sexton will nail him."

We hurried now, breaking into a trot to keep up with the fleeing animal. Presently the pond came into view, and then the lodge. I could see Freeman just coming over the hill on the other side, and after a moment Bill Tracy appeared too, back toward the house. Both men had seen the deer and had their weapons raised.

"Why don't they shoot?" Sheriff Lens wanted to know, trotting over to join us.

"The buck is so near the lodge Sexton can kill it with an easy shot," my father said. He had his own rifle ready, but the deer kept running, straight as an arrow. It scooted across the clearing, passing not twenty yards from the lodge.

There was no shot.

Then, before anyone realized what was happening, the big buck ran through the shallow water at the edge of the pond, outflanking Freeman. The farmer turned, dropped to one knee, and fired a quick shot. We saw the spout of water where the bullet hit beyond and behind the fleeing deer's path, then it was gone, into the woods beyond the pond.

"What in hell happened?" Tracy yelled, coming down to join us.

Freeman hurried over too. "Why didn't Sexton get him?"

"I don't know," my father replied, and I didn't know either. We all just stood there, staring down at the hunting lodge. There were still only Ryder Sexton's footprints leading into it, but a little column of smoke showed that he'd started the fire for coffee.

My father started down across the snow, following the deer's trail till it passed the lodge, then dropping off to enter through the doorway.

He reappeared almost at once, calling up to me. "Come quick, Sam, something's happened! I think he's been murdered!"

I warned the others to stay where they were and went to have a look.

Ryder Sexton was sprawled in the center of the lodge, near the table. He lay on his face and the back of his head was bloody. Nearby was one of the clubs edged with sharks' teeth, from his collection of primitive weapons.

"He's dead, all right," I confirmed. "That thing probably killed him instantly."

"But who, Sam?" my father asked.

I walked to the doorway and called to Sheriff Lens. "I need you, Sheriff, but walk carefully. We don't want to disturb any footprints."

"There aren't any footprints, Doc—except Ryder's own. I been all around the cabin. And the outhouse is empty."

I looked out on the pond side and confirmed what he'd said. The lodge was near the water here, but there were still some ten yards of unmarked snow separating them. Despite my warning, Tracy and Freeman had followed us down, but it didn't really matter. Ryder Sexton's were the only tracks into the lodge, and there were no tracks going out. Whoever had killed him with the primitive club had done it by remote control.

"Someone will have to tell his wife," Jim Freeman said, staring down at the body.

"Who could have done it?" Tracy asked. "A tramp passing through the woods?"

"A tramp who didn't leave footprints?" I asked. "All we saw were the tracks of the deer. Did any of you see footprints?"

They all shook their heads. None of them had. I went outside and knelt in the snow, examining the tracks that Sexton had left. Then we all went back up to the house together, where Sheriff Lens broke the news while we stood grimly by. Rosemary Sexton simply stared at us, uncomprehending. *"Dead?* What do you mean *dead?"*

"We heard a shot," Jennifer said. "Was it a hunting accident?"

"He was killed by a blow on the head," I said. "We don't know who did it."

Rosemary Sexton collapsed.

When Jennifer and Jim Freeman helped carry her to her room, I got my bag from the car and gave her a mild sedative. Sheriff Lens was already on the telephone, instructing the operator to ring his deputies and have an ambulance sent out for the body.

I came back into the living room and went over to my mother, who was sitting white-faced in a chair. "What happened, Sam?" she asked me.

"I'm trying to find out," I replied. "Tell me, were either of the women out of the house while we were gone? Mrs. Sexton or Jennifer?"

"No," she answered, then immediately corrected herself. "At least I don't think they were. Rosemary was baking a cake for later and she was in the kitchen part of the time. Jennifer was upstairs for about ten minutes. I suppose either of them could have been out without my realizing it."

I squeezed her hand and went upstairs. Jennifer and Freeman were still with Rosemary. I found another bedroom at the back of the house that faced in the direction of the hunting lodge, but a big red barn stood between the house and the lodge, blocking my view of it.

"Trying to figure out how it was done?" a voice behind me asked. It was Jim Freeman.

"I know it seems impossible, but he is dead. I had a nice theory that the club might have been fired from here, like some sort of mortar shell."

Freeman came over to the window. "This is Jennifer's room. Do you think she did it?"

"I have no idea. I was just checking the view."

Freeman nodded. "During the war I was with the Air Corps in France. They were actually dropping darts, called fléchettes, out of planes onto enemy soldiers."

"That's what I mean. Darts can be dropped from planes, people can be stabbed with arrows. Perhaps clubs can be fired from mortars."

"Not too likely, though," Freeman said.

"No," I admitted, "especially since the roof of the lodge has no large openings in it." I thought of something else. "Have Mrs. Sexton or her sister ever visited your place?"

"Why do you ask?"

"It would be natural, since you're neighbors. Bill Tracy told me he thought he saw one of them over there last week."

Freeman snorted. "Bill Tracy's a gossipy old woman. Sure Jennifer took a ride over one day. Why not? As you say, we're neighbors."

"But Rosemary Sexton has never been to your place?"

"Can't say never. She may have come with Ryder one

evening. But she never came alone, if that's what you're driving at. You think I killed him to get at his wife?"

"I don't think anything right now, Jim. I'm just asking questions."

"Well, ask some others." He turned and walked from the room.

I went back downstairs and found Sheriff Lens conferring with two deputies who'd just arrived. "They're gonna take some flashbulb photographs of the lodge and then remove the body. Is that okay, Doc?"

"Sure, You're in charge."

We walked back through the woods to the hunting lodge with the deputies. The snow was starting to melt in places, but Ryder Sexton's single set of footprints was still clearly visible. "You know, Doc," Sheriff Lens began slowly, "I figure there are just three ways it coulda been done."

I was used to this by now. But Sheriff Lens was generally triumphant when he offered me a possible solution, and there was no triumph in his voice today. "What are those, Sheriff?" I asked.

"The club was thrown or catapulted across the snow somehow."

"He was inside the lodge when he was killed," I pointed out. "Even if we accept the theory that he stuck his head out at the moment the club was thrown and then fell back inside, the club still would have fallen outside in the snow. Besides, those sharks' teeth are what did the damage. A club hurled through the air wouldn't have hit him at that angle with enough force to kill him."

"You thought on that already."

"Yes," I conceded.

"Okay, possibility number two. The murderer walked across the snow in Sexton's footprints, then walked out backward the same way."

I shook my head reluctantly. "His new boots had very distinctive treads. I examined those prints and the tread-marks haven't been blurred or obscured at all. Only Sexton walked across the snow, Sheriff, and he did it only once."

Sheriff Lens took a deep breath. "Well then, Doc, that only leaves my third possibility. Sexton was killed by the first person to enter the lodge, before the rest of us reached it."

"The first person to enter was my father."

"I know," Sheriff Lens said.

We said no more about it then, but walked across the stretch of slowly melting snow to the lodge where the deputies were finishing their work. The body was removed on a suitably covered stretcher, and one deputy moved his camera out to photograph the tracks in the snow before they disappeared.

"I found this on the floor," the other one said, holding out his hand to the sheriff.

"What is it? A feather?"

"Yeah."

Sheriff Lens grunted. "Looks old. Prob'ly left over from the last duck-hunting season."

"Looks more like a chicken feather to me," the deputy remarked. "Maybe someone used it for an arrow."

"Except he wasn't killed with an arrow," the sheriff grumbled. He stuck the feather in his pocket.

When the second deputy had left and we were alone, I said, "My father didn't kill Sexton."

"I know how you feel, Doc, and I'd be the same way. I'll admit he doesn't seem to have a motive—"

"He *couldn't* have killed him. Think about it, Sheriff. How did that club, the murder weapon, get in here? It was up at the house, in Sexton's glass case, and he didn't

bring it down. We saw him enter the lodge carrying his
rifle and a sandwich and nothing else. I've already shown
that he couldn't have left again, even walking in his own
tracks, without blurring them."

"Hell, Doc, the killer brought the club with him. That
ain't hard to figure out."

"Of course the killer brought the weapon in. And that
means my father is innocent. He certainly didn't walk
through the woods with me, and enter this lodge in front
of us all, with that long shark-toothed club hidden under
his coat. There's no way we wouldn't have noticed."

Sheriff Lens relaxed visibly. "Sure, Doc, you're right.
He couldn't have done it."

"Besides, if Sexton was still alive when we approached
the cabin he wouldn't have passed up that shot at the
deer. He didn't fire at it because he was already dead."

"But where does that leave us?"

"I don't know," I admitted.

"Maybe a bird killed him! That would explain the
feather! Or maybe someone with big wings strapped to
their arms, soaring over the snow! How's that sound,
Doc?"

"Not very likely," I told him gently. We left the lodge
and started back toward the house.

"But I might have touched on something when I
mentioned concealing the weapon under a coat," I said.
"How did the killer approach with that club? Why didn't
Ryder Sexton realize what was happening to him in time
to fight back?"

"It was concealed somehow."

I snapped my fingers. "In a rifle carrier!"

"Like Bill Tracy has!"

We found Tracy just putting his rifle and case into the car.
Sheriff Lens went back for the club and we tried to fit it

into the carrier, but without success. With the rifle inside it wouldn't fit at all, and even without the rifle it made a peculiar bulge.

"I didn't even have the case out in the field!" Tracy insisted. "I just had the rifle! You guys are nuts if you think you're pinning this on me!"

"We're not trying to pin anything on you, Bill," I insisted.

He climbed into his car. "You know where to reach me if you got any more questions."

My mother came out of the house as Tracy drove away. "Sam, this whole business has upset your father terribly. I think we should leave as soon as possible."

"Of course," I agreed. "Just let me finish with the sheriff."

Sheriff Lens had gone into the house for a moment, but now he reappeared. "Except for the club none of his weapons are missing from their cases. But I have another idea, Sam. Suppose someone made one of them South American bolas with balls of ice. It coulda been hurled through the door of the lodge and wrapped itself around his neck, bashing his skull. Then the heat from the fire melted the ice balls."

"What about the cord, Sheriff? Did that melt too? And there were no puddles of melted ice on the scene. And what about the teeth marks from the club that really killed him? How do you account for them?" But the fire reminded me of the coffee, and that reminded me of something else. "The water tank!"

"Huh?"

"Come on, Sheriff! I'll explain on the way." He hurried after me as I bounded past the pump house and the barn and up the rise leading to the lodge. "Don't you see? The killer never crossed the snow because he was hidden in there all the time—since before the snow started! If that

metal tank will hold thirty gallons of water it'll hold a
small adult. He killed Sexton and then resumed his
hiding place until it was safe to escape."

We were almost to the lodge now and Sheriff Lens had
caught some of my enthusiasm. "Will he still be there?"

"Probably not, but the empty water tank is all the proof
we need. The killer would have had to empty it down the
drain in order to fit inside, and he couldn't have refilled
it later because the hose to the pump house was already
disconnected and rolled up."

I'd rarely been so certain of anything in my life.
Entering the lodge, I lifted the lid from the tank and
plunged my hand inside.

It was filled with water, almost to the brim.

Sheriff Lens tried to console me. "Look, Doc, he could
still have hidden in the tank, and just refilled it afterward."

"There was no hose."

"Maybe it's pond water."

"The snow between here and the pond was undis-
turbed," I reminded him. But just to satisfy us both, I let
some of the water run from the tank. It was crystal-clear
well water, not from any half stagnant pond.

Back at the house, I began feeling as dejected as when
Sheriff Lens had raised the possibility of my father's
involvement. There had to be an answer to the crime, but
I knew well enough that the longer it went unsolved the
less likely a solution became. One suspect, Tracy, had
already gone home.

Rosemary Sexton seemed to have recovered somewhat
and was back downstairs. She was pale and still a bit
slow of speech, perhaps because of the sedative I'd given
her. "Tell me how it happened," she said quietly.

"We don't know," I admitted. "He may have been killed by a tramp who'd been sleeping in the lodge."

She dismissed that with a wave of her hand. "Jim Freeman told me he was hit over the head with a club from his own weapons collection. That wouldn't have been a tramp."

My father came into the room in time to hear the end of this exchange. "You mean you think someone he knew killed him? I can't believe that."

"We don't know anything yet," I said wearily.

"He was my friend. I'll do anything I can to find his killer."

My mother intervened. "I think the best thing we can do is go back to town, Harry. Sam will take us."

She was right. It was time to go. But I still couldn't quite let go. "I want to see that weapons case," I said.

"I already checked it out, Doc," the sheriff said.

But I went to the den with its tall glass-doored cabinets. Jennifer followed me there and I asked, "Where did he keep the keys for these?"

"They're open. They were never locked."

I stood and stared at the empty spot in the cabinet where the shark-toothed club from the Pacific Islands had rested, remembering Ryder Sexton's words as he'd shown it to us. Someone had taken that club, crossed the unmarked snow with the wings of a bird, and slain the man.

I stared into the glass, seeing my reflection and Jennifer's next to me. "Let's walk outside," I said.

"The sun's gone in again. It's getting chilly," she said, opening the door.

I helped her down the back steps and we walked toward the outbuildings. "Maybe it'll snow again tonight."

"I feel so helpless," she said.

"We all do. It wasn't until I was looking at that glass case just now that I realized how helpless *I* was. I suddenly knew who killed Ryder Sexton, but I've got no proof that would convince a jury."

"That case told you?"

I nodded. "I remembered what Sexton said when he showed us that club. It was good for dispatching wounded deer in the field, he said. He used it for that, didn't he? And when he said this morning that he'd forgotten something, he was referring to the club. He asked someone to get it and bring it to him at the lodge."

She looked at me questioningly.

"He asked you, Jennifer. You were walking with him and I heard him mutter something to you. Then you went back to the house and got the club for him. The rest of us were off out in the fields and woods by that time, so we never saw you go back out there. The sight of you with that weapon didn't alarm Sexton because he'd asked you to bring it. He even turned his back to you and gave you a perfect target. With those sharks' teeth it didn't take too hard a blow to kill him."

"You're accusing me?"

"It could only have been you, Jennifer. I suppose you did it for the money, so your sister would inherit his fortune and it would be yours too."

"No."

"Yes, Jennifer. My mother told me you were upstairs for about ten minutes—that would have been long enough."

"How did I cross the snow? There were no tracks."

We'd reached the top of the rise and stood staring down at the hunting lodge, peaceful in the autumnal setting. There was still enough of the snow remaining to show us Ryder Sexton's footprints.

"Oh, but there were tracks," I said. "There still are

tracks, crying out at us to see them. But like Chesterton's postman they're so obvious they remain invisible. I refer, of course, to the track made by the irrigation hose that ran from the pump house to the lodge. Last night's half inch of snow fell on top of the hose, so when it was rolled up this morning the bare track of it remained across the field, running directly to the door of the lodge."

"You're mad! That hose is only about an inch and a half wide! Even walking on my toes, I couldn't follow its trail without leaving tracks!"

A cold wind was rising and I lifted the collar of my jacket. "You didn't walk on your toes, Jennifer," I said quietly. "You rode your bicycle."

If I had expected the fury of a trapped animal, there was none. She merely closed her eyes and swayed a bit. I put out a hand to steady her.

"You told me he didn't like you riding in the woods during hunting season," I continued, "so obviously it was something you'd done before. Following that narrow line left by the hose wouldn't have been difficult, and if you did edge off it once or twice, the hose itself could have made the marks when it was being dragged back. And of course you carried the bicycle from the henhouse to the pump house where the track began, so it left no new tracks in the barnyard. You probably held the club under your arm as you pedaled, and you followed the same track coming back. As long as you stayed in it there was no snow to record the tread of your bicycle tires. You left no clues, except for a single old chicken feather that must have stuck to the bicycle in the henhouse. That feather was all the confirmation I needed once I remembered you putting the bike away there yesterday."

"It wasn't the money." She spoke at last. "That had nothing to do with it. He was damned cruel to my sister.

You must have noticed how unhappy she is. Sometimes he even beat her when he was drunk. She wouldn't leave him, so I did her the biggest favor I could. I killed him."

"Will you tell the sheriff that?—If you don't, I will."

We went back to the house and I left with Mom and Dad while Jennifer spoke to Sheriff Lens. On the way to town we caught sight of that big twelve-point buck running at the edge of the woods. My father wanted me to stop so he could get a shot at it, but I kept on driving.

"That was the last time my parents visited me in Northmont," Dr. Sam Hawthorn concluded. "They said city life was a whole lot safer. Look here—the bottle's empty. But I'll have a fresh one the next time you drop by. I'll tell you about the time Sheriff Lens finally solved a mystery all by himself."

About the Contributors

ISAAC ASIMOV, widely known for his science fiction novels and stories, has also written much popular mystery fiction, including the Black Widowers series of short stories, *Murder at the A.B.A.*, *Far As the Human Eye Could See*, *The Golden Eye*, and *Azazel*. Since the publication of his first story in 1939, Mr. Asimov has published 405 books, 300 short stories, and perhaps 3,000 nonfiction essays. He currently lives in New York City.

LILIAN JACKSON BRAUN is the author of the Cat Who . . . series of mystery novels, of which *The Cat Who Saw Red* was nominated for an M.W.A. Edgar Award in 1986. She is the author of *The Cat Who Knew Shakespeare*, *The Cat Who Sniffed Glue*, and most recently, *The Cat Who Went Underground*. Mrs. Braun lives with her husband and two Siamese cats in Michigan and North Carolina.

DOROTHY SALISBURY DAVIS is a Grand Master of mystery and a past president of M.W.A. She is equally proficient in the novel and the short story form. Ms. Davis's Edgar nominations include *Where the Dark Streets Go*, *God Speed the Night*, *The Pale Betrayer*, *A Gentlemen Called*, "Old Friends," and "The Purple Is Everything." Her Julie Hayes series includes *A Death in the Life*, *Scarlet Night*, *Lullaby of Murder*, and *The Habit of Fear*.

JOYCE HARRINGTON's first short story, "The Purple Shroud," published in *Ellery Queen's Mystery Magazine*, won the M.W.A. Edgar Award in 1972. Since then, she has gone on to write many short stories and three novels including *Dreemz of the Night*, *No One Knows My Name*, and *Family Reunion*. She has received three additional short story Edgar nominations for "The Au Pair Girl," "Night Crawlers," and "The Cabin in the Hollow," and is currently working on a new novel. Ms. Harrington lives in New York City.

EDWARD D. HOCH, a past president of M.W.A., was born in Rochester, New York, in 1930 and has lived most of his life there. After service in the United States Army and a year in New York City, he returned to Rochester. Since 1968 he has been a full-time writer, publishing some 750 short stories and 30 books—novels, collections, and anthologies. He is an Edgar winner for his short story "The Oblong Room" and currently edits *The Year's Best Mystery and Suspense Stories*. Mr. Hoch's stories have appeared in every issue of *Ellery Queen's Mystery Magazine* since 1973. He is married to Patricia A. McMahon and serves as vice president of the Board of Trustees of the Rochester Public Library.

JAMES HOLDING, after graduation from Yale and a year spent traveling in Europe, joined the advertising agency BBDO, Inc., as a copywriter in its Pittsburgh office. Thirty years later, as copy chief and vice president, he retired from the advertising business to try his hand at writing fiction. Since then, he has traveled widely and has used some of the faraway places he visited as settings for many of his mystery stories and children's books. Currently, Holding lives with his wife on Siesta Key in Sarasota, Florida.

CLARK HOWARD has been writing for thirty years, full time for fifteen. He is a five-time nominee and a one-time Edgar winner for his short story "Horn Man" in 1980. Mr. Howard also won the first two *Ellery Queen's Mystery Magazine* Readers' Awards. His short stories have been selected every year since 1980 for an award or nomination for a writing honor. He is also the author of eighteen novels.

MARGARET MARON's short stories have appeared in such magazines as *Alfred Hitchcock's Mystery Magazine*, *Mike Shayne's Mystery Magazine*, *Redbook*, *McCall's*, and *Reader's Digest*, and have been reprinted in various anthologies here and abroad. The creator of the series character Lt. Sigrid Harald NYPD (*One Coffee With*, *Baby Doll Games*, *Death in Blue Folders*), she is vice president of Sisters in Crime, a member of M.W.A.'s Board of Directors, and a founding officer of the Carolina Crime Writers Association.

JOSH PACHTER's short stories have appeared in *Ellery Queen's Mystery Magazine*, and *Alfred Hitchcock's Mystery Magazine*. He is co-author of a collection of collaborative short stories entitled *Partners in Crime* and is the editor of two anthology series: Top Crime and Top Fantasy. He currently lives in West Germany and teaches at the University of Maryland in Hagenau.

SARA PARETSKY grew up in Eastern Kansas, where she attended a two-room country school. Her first published writing, which appeared in *The American Girl* magazine when she was eleven, told a story of surviving a tornado with her schoolmates. She received her BA from the University of Kansas and her PhD and MBA from the University of Chicago. Since 1986, Ms. Paretsky has worked full time as a writer. Her novels *Indemnity Only, Deadlock, Killing Orders, Bitter Medicine,* and *Blood Shot* all feature V. I. Warshawski, a woman detective living and working in Chicago. In the fall of 1986, Ms. Paretsky helped found Sisters in Crime, an organization to promote women writers, editors, reviewers and booksellers in the suspense field. She and her husband Courtenay Wright live in Chicago's southeast side with their faithful Golden Retriever Cardhu.

HOPE RAYMOND grew up in New England and the Middle West and is a graduate of the University of Chicago. She spent most of her working life in Manhattan offices. She has contributed stories in *Ellery Queen's Mystery Magazine* and *Alfred Hitchcock's Mystery Magazine* as well as several articles on gardening in the *New York Times.* Ms. Raymond has recently completed her first novel. She currently lives in New York City.

JOAN RICHTER published her first mystery fiction in the September 1962 issue of *Ellery Queen's Mystery Magazine.* She has since combined writing fiction with a successful career in other areas of publishing. As a free-lance journalist, she was a stringer for the *New York Times* for nine years. For the last ten years she has been with the magazine publishing subsidiary of American Express as director of public relations for *Travel & Leisure* and *Food & Wine* magazines. A children's mystery and a group of short stories, including "Intruder in the Maize," draw upon the two years that she and her family lived in Kenya.

JUSTIN SCOTT was born in New York City and received his BA and master's degrees from the State University of New York. He is the author of nine novels including *The Ship Killer, Normandie Triangle, Pride of Royals,* and most recently, *The Widow of Desire.* His father, A. Leslie Scott, was a famous novelist with more than 250 western novels to his credit; his mother, Lily Kay Scott, was a well-known romance writer. Justin Scott's novels *Rampage* and *The Widow of Desire* were Dual Main Selections for the Literary Guild. He lives in New York City and Connecticut with his wife Gloria Hoye and is currently at work on his next novel.

DICK STODGHILL's daily general interest column for *The Muncie Evening Press* was selected as the best in Indiana by United Press International. At various times his newspaper assignments covered the police beat, criminal courts, all levels of government, and sports. In the late 1950s and early 1960s he was an operative for the Cleveland office of Pinkerton's National Detective Agency. He is a veteran of World War II and the Korean war. Mr. Stodghill has had about fifty short stories and novelettes published in various mystery magazines and collections.

EDWARD WELLEN was born and still lives in New Rochelle, New York. During World War II he traveled to North Africa, Italy, France, Germany, Luxembourg, and England. Mr. Wellen's stories have appeared in *Alfred Hitchcock's Mystery Magazine*, *Ellery Queen's Mystery Magazine*, and *Espionage Magazine* as well as many mystery anthologies. His work also appears in men's magazines and in other publications such as *Saturday Review*, *Stamp World* and *Village Voice*. His science fiction stories appear regularly in science fiction magazines and anthologies. Mr. Wellen is a member of the Private Eye Writers of America and Science Fiction Writers of America.

DONALD E. WESTLAKE was born in Brooklyn in 1933. He was raised in Albany, New York, and attended Champlain College and Harpur College. He was in the Air Force from 1954 to 1956. Mr. Westlake has had approximately thirty novels published under his own name since 1960, in addition to twenty novels under the name of Richard Stark and five under the name of Tucker Coe. He was the winner of the 1966 Edgar for *God Save the Mark*. Films made from his Westlake novels include *The Busy Body*, *The Hot Rock*, *Bank Shot*, *Jimmy the Kid*, and *Too Much*; from Stark novels came *Point Blank*, *The Split*, *The Outfit*, *Made in USA*, *Mis En Sac*, and *Slayground*. His three original screenplays are *Cops and Robbers*, *Hot Stuff*, and *The Stepfather*; and one television movie is entitled *Father Dowling*. Mr. Westlake's latest novel is *Trust Me on This*.

GAHAN WILSON is both an author and illustrator. His work has appeared in magazines ranging from *Playboy* and *The New Yorker* to *Punch* and *Paris Match*. He is the author of *Everybody's Favorite Dog*, *Eddy Deco's Last Caper*, *Gahan Wilson's America*, and *The Man in the Cannibal Pot*. The M.W.A. cookbook published by WYNWOOD Press and entitled *Plots & Pans* is illustrated with Gahan Wilson's renditions of Edgar Allan Poe and M.W.A.'s mascot Raven. Mr. Wilson currently lives in New York City.